Widow's Peak

Widow's Peak

A Widows & Shadows Mystery

Michelle Bennington

For my friend, Bill Ekhardt

Chapter One

August 1803

Ravenna, Lady Birchfield's hands trembled as she read her niece's note.

The words blurred together, but their meaning remained clear: Georgiana was gone. Apparently, eloped with her tutor, Mr. Josiah Emmett. Upon first reading the note, Ravenna believed and set down Georgiana as the silliest, stupidest girl in England.

Her mind shifted, trying to fit the contents of this letter into reality. "This must be a joke," she said to Braedon. "A terrible, terrible joke."

William Finleigh, Earl of Braedon, read the note. "What can I do?" His blue, wolfish eyes locked on her, and the muscles in his jaws knotted.

"I-I-I don't know…." Ravenna rubbed her forehead. She reclaimed the letter and read it again.

Dear Auntie,

I'm leaving. I can no longer stay in a house where the man I love is not welcome. So he and I are eloping. By the time you read this, I will be styled...

Mrs. Josiah Emmett

It was a knife-twist in the gut. While Ravenna had noticed some fondness developing between Georgiana and her tutor, Mr. Emmett, she hadn't taken it seriously with Georgiana's exuberant, curious, and flirtatious spirit. But with the recent discovery that Emmett's brother, Robert, was working with France to foment rebellion in Ireland, it was likely Emmett was also involved. Emmett was a scoundrel of the first order and the worst possible match for Georgiana.

"There's something wrong with this note. It doesn't sound like her." The style and language seemed discordant, like a wrong note played in a song on the pianoforte. The writing, too, seemed shaky, agitated. She read it a third time.

No. This is wrong.

She turned to Sarah Keene, a maid she'd hired only a few months ago. The pretty girl with brunette hair, green eyes, and light freckles over her face was a blubbering mess.

"When did she go to bed last night?"

"It were early. About nine of the clock, milady."

A rope of guilt tightened around Ravenna. If only she'd checked on Georgiana before retiring last night, she might've prevented this.

"When did you go to bed?"

"A couple of hours later, ma'am. After I finished my sewing."

"Did you look in on her before you went to bed?"

"No, ma'am." Fresh tears sprang to her eyes, and she sobbed. "I'm so sorry, milady, I…" Emotion garbled the rest of her sentence. She sniffled and wiped her nose on her sleeve.

She handed her a handkerchief. "Keene, do show some decorum. You should wipe your nose with only a handkerchief. Did Georgiana mention anything to you about her plans to leave?"

Keene sniffled and blew her nose. "All I know, ma'am, is she mentioned her fondness for Mr. Emmett, but I thought it were only flights of fancy. Because when she first arrived at Gordon House, she claimed to love Lord Donovan. Which was a much better choice, if you ask me. Cor' who could love a lowly tutor over a Lord? And with Emmett always going on about this or that book?" She rolled her eyes and made a face. "I had no idea she were planning to run away with him."

"Did you see or hear anything unusual? Or see anyone lingering about the house who shouldn't be here?"

Keene sucked down her tears. "No, ma'am."

"Was anyone awake later than you?"

"Cook and Mr. Banks."

"Send them in here and return to your work, please."

Keene stopped at the door. "Ma'am if I'da known what notions she had in her head, I'da locked her in her bedchamber myself. I'da wrestled her to the ground. I woulda."

"Thank you, Keene. You may go." Ravenna paced while she waited for the cook and butler to arrive. She muttered to herself. "I must find her. I cannot allow this marriage to take place. Surely, they've gone to Scotland. To Gretna Green. It's the only place to marry without the banns."

Braedon touched her arm. "Correction, my dear. *We* must go. I'm going with you."

"There's no need to involve yourself in this."

"There are all manner of miscreants, bandits, and ruffians on the road to Scotland."

"Braedon—"

"Ravenna." He touched her face. "How could I live with myself if anything happened to you? I'm going home to pack, and I'll return directly. Wait for me. I shan't be long." He kissed her forehead and left the drawing room as the cook and butler entered.

"Mr. Banks, horrible news. Georgiana has eloped with Mr. Emmett."

Mr. Banks was a tall, burly man with thick gray hair and haunted gray eyes resulting from his experiences as a veteran in the American Rebellion. A cocked eyebrow indicated his alarm. "That is distressing news, indeed, milady."

"Did you notice anything unusual last night? Was Mr. Emmett here?"

"No, milady. I saw nothing when we made our rounds before bed, and I have not seen Mr. Emmett for two, maybe three days."

Ravenna focused on the cook, Mrs. Lyle, a large-boned, broad-shouldered woman with doughy jowls and gray-streaked dark hair. "Lyle? Did you notice anything?"

"Not last night, milady. However," she paused to collect her thoughts. "I did see Mr. Emmett speaking to footman Peele a couple of days ago. They seemed to be engaged in a serious conversation when I noticed Mr. Emmett handing a slip of paper to the boy. At first I thought nothing about it, and I was so distracted with the pear tarts which nearly burnt that the moment dropped from my mind entirely…until just now."

Ravenna's eyes widened. "Mr. Banks, bring Mr. Peele to me, please." Banks stepped from the room. "Lyle, you're dismissed."

Ravenna stood at the window, watching the pedestrians and carriages in the street as thoughts ran wild in her mind. How far had Georgiana traveled by now? Could Ravenna catch up to the runaways in time?

The door opened behind her, and she turned to greet the lean footman with thick red curls. His hazel eyes darted around the room as he bowed in greeting. "Good morning, milady."

"Good morning, Peele. I've heard you had a conversation with Mr. Emmett recently. What was the content of that conversation?"

He hemmed, his face flushing red. "He asked me to do him a favor."

"What was the favor?"

"He wanted me to…" He shook his head and cleared his throat. "I'm so very sorry to betray you, milady, but I needed the money desperate-like." Tears filled his eyes. "My father was injured on the farm and can no longer work, and I gave the money to him."

"Mr. Emmett gave you money?"

"Yes, milady." He sniffed and wiped his eyes.

Ravenna bit down on her anger. "For what purpose?"

"He asked me to sneak downstairs and unlock the kitchen door around midnight last night."

Now it was clear: Emmett had paid the footman to unlock the door after everyone else was in bed. But if Georgiana was going to run away with Emmett, why wouldn't she sneak *out*? Why would the door need to be unlocked?

Ravenna frowned. "Did he tell you why he wanted this done?"

Peele picked at his cuticles. "No. He paid me extra for not asking questions, milady."

"I see." Ravenna closed her eyes and pinched the tight spot forming between her brows. Peele's situation was difficult. She didn't want to fire him because he clearly needed the money, and he'd always been a good employee. However, if he could be so easily bought, she needed to reconsider his employment at Gordon House.

Irritation dripped from her words. "Thank you, Peele. Go back to work, please."

"Are you going to fire me, ma'am?"

"I shall have to discuss the matter with Mr. Banks. However, I will say, I need people around me I can trust. Surely you see that?"

His bottom lip quivered. "I do."

"And if you can be so easily bribed, then I cannot trust you, can I?"

His bottom lip quivered. "I'm very sorry, ma'am."

When he left the drawing room, Ravenna rushed to Georgiana's bedchamber in a whisper of black muslin petticoats and skirts. She threw open the door and took in the quiet, dim room, the pink walls, white bed curtains, and window treatments. The bed was rumpled as if Georgiana had been sitting in it. A book lay open near the pillow. The candle had melted completely.

She checked the vanity. Everything was still there. *Odd.* Though Georgiana had few possessions, a woman planning to leave a place to marry wouldn't leave her perfume and cosmetics behind. Unease inched across her shoulders. Moving to the writing desk, papers and pens lay scattered across the top, but nothing else was out of place. No evident struggle.

Turning to leave the room, a single dark spot by the foot of the desk chair caught her eye. Ravenna squatted to examine it. I looked like ink. She swept her finger through it. *Not* ink. Blood. Panic fluttered through her. Who had been bleeding and why? Ravenna washed her hands at the nearby washstand. Maybe there had been an accident. And it might not even be Georgiana's blood. Perhaps a maid accidentally cut herself.

Ravenna opened the wardrobe. Only a few things were missing. On the bottom shelf rested an upended bonnet. Inside was a slip of folded paper.

Ravenna pulled the paper from the bonnet and read: *Help! Edinburgh –G*

Her breath caught in her throat. One thing was evident now: Georgiana had not eloped after all. She had been kidnapped.

Chapter Two

Ravenna clapped her hand over her mouth as guilt twisted her stomach. She should've paid closer attention to Georgiana and Mr. Emmett. She should've done more to protect her niece. She studied the message. Somehow, the girl had been able to leave a note. Brave, clever girl. Clearly, marriage wasn't part of Emmett's plan. Otherwise, they'd go to Gretna Green. What was Mr. Emmett up to? Why Edinburgh?

Ravenna ran to her bedchamber.

Charlotte Hart, her ladies' maid, dressed in brown with her brown hair tucked into a neat chignon, stood at the end of the bed, packing a portmanteau. "Whatever's the matter, milady?" A hint of Scottish in her speech. "You look as though you've seen a ghost."

"Make haste in your packing. We must get on the road. Georgiana has not run away. She's been kidnapped."

"Oh, heavens! Are you certain?"

"Quite." Panicked thoughts whirled, impeding Ravenna's ability to think clearly. She closed her eyes and hid her face in her hands. She needed help. Who could help her—*Mr. Chadwick!* The Bow Street Runner. Shrewd, sharp, persistent—she feared him more than any man in London, especially in light of her past. Yet, she knew she could trust him to help.

"Bring Keene to me." Ravenna sat at her writing desk as Hart left to search for the maid. Ravenna took up a pen and dashed off a letter to Mr. Chadwick, begging for his help, telling him Georgiana had been kidnapped and that she was headed to Edinburgh. She wished she had the time to approach him in person, but this would have to suffice.

When Keene entered the room, Ravenna handed her the note. "Take this to Mr. Chadwick in Bow Street. Posthaste. If he isn't there, find out when he will be home and keep trying to deliver this letter. It must go directly into his hands. It's of the greatest urgency."

"Yes, milady." Keene curtsied and ran to fulfill her mission.

Ravenna took up her pen again and scrawled a note to her dearest friend, Lady Catherine Adair, to tell her the awful news, knowing Catherine might have connections to help find Georgiana.

> *...Worst of all, Emmett has kidnapped Georgiana. I've written to Chadwick to ask for his assistance. Braedon and I are leaving today to find her and bring her home. I hope you will have someone among your connections who may help us—discreetly. I'll write from Scotland at the first opportunity, so you may know where we are staying and to keep you abreast of our search. I hope to importune you, my dear friend, with the request of a favor. Will you please write to Harrison at Birchfield Manor to inform him of the details concerning Georgiana?*

Poor Harrison, he would be distraught when he learned of the kidnapping. He had formed a real fondness for Georgiana, perhaps even loved her, though she'd not shown much interest in him.

While she didn't want to cause him further pain, he would find out eventually, and it was best he heard it from family. She returned to the letter...

> *...Additionally, please write to Reverend Howarth at The Penitent House. Tell him a matter of business calls me away, but I will write or visit him at my first opportunity to help him plan the Christmas dinner for the women.*

Though this was hardly the time to be thinking of The Spitalfields House for Penitent Prostitutes, she didn't want the Reverend Howarth to think she had abandoned him. Commonly known as The Penitent House, the charity rescued prostitutes from the streets to give them a future. The charity was not only near and dear to her heart, but she hoped it might also help find her own sister, who had been lost to the streets for over half a decade.

Her letter written and sealed, Ravenna flew around the room like a trapped bird, gathering items to finish packing, shoving toiletries and accessories into the portmanteau. She opened her wardrobe to grab the final items when something appeared irregular—like when a vase that had always occupied the center of the table had been shifted to the side. She paused and stared at the shelves in her wardrobe. All her clothes were neatly folded, shoes lined up like little fence railings. Then she realized: The blue velvet box containing the Birchfield family jewels—*gone!*

She tried to recall the last time she'd seen the box. Unfortunately, it had been in the same location, unmoved, for years. As such, the eye and the mind had grown too accustomed to its presence and overlooked it.

Pressure mounted in her chest and rose to the top of her skull. *Josiah Emmett. Blast his eyes!* He had taken both a set of precious jewels passed down for generations in the Birchfield family and her most precious niece. He must have absconded with both before Ravenna returned to Gordon House last night. They must already be as far as Biggleswade or further by now.

Her hands clenched into tight little fists. "I'll see him hang for this."

After packing, Ravenna and Hart met downstairs in the foyer to wait for Braedon. Servants scurried to load carts and carriages and to prepare the house for the move to the country for the Glorious Twelfth. That special time in August when the social season came to an end in London, and the *ton* emptied their townhomes to return to their country estates for grouse hunting season.

Ravenna handed the letter she'd written to her butler. "Banks, please have this delivered immediately to Lady Adair, directly into her hands. It's urgent. Do not give the letter to Peele. I'm quite put out with him at the moment. We'll need to discuss his future with us later. Do keep a close eye on him and trust him with nothing discreet."

He bowed his head. "Yes, milady."

She continued, "I don't expect we'll be at Birchfield Manor for the Glorious Twelfth. Tell Lord Birchfield to continue without us. If we are lucky, we'll arrive at Birchfield Manor by the end of August."

"Yes, ma'am." He called for a footman to make the delivery to Adair House. "I have a letter to give to you as well, ma'am." Mr. Banks handed a letter to Ravenna. "This came for you earlier today."

"Thank you." Her heart stuttered. It had no address. A black seal with the imprint of a harp. The Irish Unity. She'd seen such letters far too often lately. She scratched the scar on her cheek—a little "gift" from The Unity man, Mr. Larson, when he had sliced her face in a scuffle a few months ago.

A mellow tenor laced with an Irish brogue materialized. "It seems as though you're in a rush to escape your debtors."

Ravenna looked up to see a man, tall and lean, sun-reddened face, deep lines around his smiling dark eyes. He had a long, squared-off jaw and thick black hair bundled in a ponytail.

He opened his arms. "Do you not even know your own kin?"

Niall? The very one who had slipped off in the dead of night to America these six years ago. His name caught in her throat. "Of course, I know you." She chuckled, embracing him. He smelled of saltwater and moss. "I'm only shocked. I can't believe you're here. After all this time."

"Aye. It's been too long."

Clearly, he hadn't received her letter in time. "What are you doing here? Hurry…" She scanned the street and pulled him inside as he nudged a young bronze-skinned woman forward. Ravenna shut the door behind them. "You shouldn't have come here."

"I was hoping for a kinder welcome than this after such a time and distance." He laughed.

"No. Of course, I'm happy to see you. But it isn't safe here." She showed him the black seal on the back of the letter.

The cheer dropped from his face. "The Unity. Are they threatening you?"

"Yes. They've been coming after me for some time. I suspect they think to find you through me. And here you are, serving yourself up on a platter."

"It was time to return."

"Why now?"

"Because I'm married now, as you know, and our family has started. I wanted all my family together. It's been too long." He reached for the bronze-skinned woman. "This is my wife, Aurélie."

Her black hair piled in curls on her head exposed high cheekbones, and her dark almond-shaped eyes shone with warmth and intelligence. Her thin frame carried her pregnancy unsteadily. *"Bonjour,* milady…" she curtsied. French tinted her speech. "It's a pleasure to finally meet one I've heard so much about."

Ravenna returned the curtsey. "It's a pleasure to meet you as well, and I'm looking forward to knowing you better. Niall has told me much about you. Unfortunately…" she said to Niall, "Your arrival comes at an inopportune time. Not only are The Unity a constant threat, but our niece, Georgiana, has been kidnapped. We are packing now to leave in search of her, and the rest of the house is about to depart to Birchfield Manor for hunting season."

"Kidnapped? By who?" Niall frowned.

"A scoundrel, Mr. Emmett. Whom I suspect is connected to The Unity. I think he's quite dangerous."

"You said she's run off from this house. Was she living with you?"

"She came only recently. Our Aunt Brendae abandoned her here."

His brow wrinkled with concern. "What does the letter say?"

Ravenna popped the black seal, dread crushing in around her as she unfolded the paper.

Ten thousand pounds, delivered to Battersea Fields, the grand oak by the Thames. You have three days, or the girl will die. Such pretty skin she has. How long will it remain so?

Ravenna balled the paper in her fist. "I'll not rest until Mr. Larson is jailed or dead."

"Ten thousand pounds?" Aurélie's mouth dropped open. "How could anyone supply such money? What do they want it for?"

"Munitions and soldiers, I wager," Niall said. "For their revolution."

Aurélie's dark eyes flashed with understanding. *"Mon doux.* That rebellion group you once belonged to, no?"

"Aye." He nodded, squinting one eye as their Papa used to do. "I'm sorry, Ravenna. This is all my fault. I should've been a better leader and provider for our family after Papa and Mama were killed. I wish I'd never listened to Colin and become involved with those Unity dogs."

Ravenna couldn't think of that now. She turned instead to the more critical matter. "I don't have that kind of money at my disposal. Maybe we could sell off some land with the Birchfield Estate. But it could take weeks or months to get it passed through the solicitors and banks."

"I certainly don't have even a fraction of that money. Do you have any friends who could help?"

"Perhaps, but I'd have to ask several friends to gather such an amount." She paused. "But…Georgiana had left a note stating they were taking her to Edinburgh. So, why would they want to take her so far away if they were expecting to exchange her for money?"

Aurélie said, "It must be a ruse. Perhaps they mean to keep you busy here, scrambling for money while they get further away. Or they mean to trick you into giving them the money, though they have no intention of giving her back."

Deep lines formed around Niall's downturned mouth.

"What?" Ravenna said. "Do you know something?"

"I fear Georgiana isn't simply collateral. It's likely they intend to keep her, to…"

Fear filled the pause. "What?" Ravenna's voice shook. "Keep her for what purpose?"

He hemmed. "To…use her…to make more money, if you take my meaning."

Ravenna gritted her teeth. "Not as long as I draw breath."

"That cannot be true, Niall." Aurélie touched her stomach.

"It is. I've seen it done firsthand. The rebels often lure the girls, seduce them, pass them around, and sell them to help raise money for the cause. Smuggling, theft, and all manner of things are done to raise the money needed."

"You never told me that," Aurélie frowned at Niall. "How could you have been involved with such people?"

"It's one of the reasons I left. I wanted an honorable cause. There have been honorable men and groups in Ireland's fight against England, but there were others who took advantage of the situation. Like the Unity. They're nothing more than a band of cutthroats, highwaymen, and thieves. However, though difficult to see, this can be a mixed blessing."

"What do you mean?" Ravenna studied him.

"If they plan to use her to make money, it's likely their threat to kill her is an empty one. At least for now. It's a mere pressure tactic to get more money from you. If so, this gives us time to hunt them down."

An interesting point. Ravenna's first inclination was to try to gather up the money and pay it in order to have Georgiana returned. However, could The Unity be trusted to return her? They might take the money and kill her anyway, or take the money and keep Georgiana for prostitution as well. Hunt them or pay them. Either solution incurred risk. She would rather meet the task head-on instead of sitting and waiting for The Unity to decide Georgiana's fate.

She lifted her chin. "Let's hunt."

Braedon swept into the house behind some servants.

Relief washed over Ravenna.

Tall and broad-shouldered, with dark, wavy hair cropped short, Braedon's commanding presence, when he wasn't teasing and provoking her, reassured and calmed her.

Braedon scanned the room, his focus sharp. "We should go. They get further away with each passing minute."

After introducing Braedon to her family, Ravenna said, "Unfortunately, there is more to this matter than we first realized."

"What do you mean?"

She showed him the letter and repeated what Niall had told her.

Braedon read the letter, his jaw clenched. He gave the letter back to Ravenna. "We need to go now. Make haste."

"We'll go with you," Niall said.

Ravenna searched Aurélie's face, the dark circles under her eyes. They must've been traveling for at least a month. "Should you continue to travel in your condition? You must be in need of rest and nourishment."

Aurélie offered a weak smile. "I can't imagine another week or two of travel would make much difference."

Ravenna said to Niall, "Gordon House is departing for the country today. Perhaps you two could go to Birchfield Manor instead and wait for our return there. My stepson, Harrison, would be happy to receive you."

"No," Niall said. "I think I can help find Georgiana. My foolishness is to blame for much of this mess. For the danger I've put my family in. It's my responsibility to fix this and, if I can, put what remains of my family back together."

"Very well." Ravenna sighed. "I won't argue and delay our travels any longer. Let's go find Georgiana and, with luck, forever put an end to The Unity's threat to our family."

Chapter Three

The sun had already sunk low in the sky by the time the party landed in St. Albans, some twenty miles north of London. They stopped at Ye Olde Fighting Cock tavern to rest and change out the horses. Ravenna and the other ladies left the carriage to stretch their legs. Aurélie waddled toward her husband, a hand resting against her back as Ravenna joined Braedon, who stood in the inn's courtyard, knocking the dust off his clothes with his gloves.

Braedon squinted into the waning sun, watching Charlotte, Niall, and Aurélie stroll toward the inn. "Am I wrong in wondering why he's come so suddenly into your life at this time? Especially since he was once a member of The Unity?"

"It's difficult to say. Perhaps he wishes to redeem past failures, the deep disappointments he put us through, for his disloyalty to our family, who had always been loyal to the king. He had been rebellious in his youth. Dare I hope as a man he has changed?"

They approached the water pump in the courtyard. Braedon pumped the handle so they could wet their handkerchiefs. Ravenna dabbed her hot face and neck. Braedon lifted his beaver skin hat and swiped the handkerchief over his sweaty forehead and face. "Do I overstep to say you don't seem happy to see him?"

She watched the stable boys lead the horses to water troughs. "It's complicated with Niall. He's my brother. I love him, and I want him safe and protected. But his return puts himself and his burgeoning family at risk. He was much safer in America." It was much deeper than that, of course.

But she didn't want to dive into the resentment, the heartache, the fraught family history.

"His wife seems a bright and capable sort. What do you know of her?"

She lifted a brow and smiled. "Lord Braedon, are you gossiping?"

"Merely conversation. Trying to make out the character of your brother and his wife."

She chuckled, lightly tapping his arm with her folded fan. "Careful, or you'll gain a fishwife's reputation."

He laughed, putting on his gloves. "I confess I enjoy a bit of gossip now and then." He winked at her.

How refreshing to have this lighthearted moment with him. It pulled on her affections in spite of the hesitancy she had been feeling toward him, a hesitancy born out of his past: his child with his former lover; his reputation as a rascal. Yet, in recent months, she'd seen a very different side of him, tender, generous, loving—quite unlike the reprobate the rumor mill had made him out to be.

Ravenna glanced at Auérlie, the sun marking her silhouette in her white muslin dress. "I confess, I'm curious about Auérlie, too." Ravenna dabbed the handkerchief on her face. "I'm looking forward to knowing more about her. Especially what would possess her to marry into this family." She smirked. "However, for now, we must go. We are losing precious daylight."

The party climbed into their respective carriages and headed toward Biggleswade. Charlotte took up reading while Ravenna, her mind too strained to concentrate on a book, dawdled over a bit of embroidery. She missed her fencing lessons with Mr. Norris and yearned to have an épée in her hand, lunging, parrying Mr. Norris' skilled attacks.

Braedon settled in across from Ravenna, pulling at his ascot. "I'm curious, Lady Birchfield, how is it you came to be in charge of an adolescent girl and never mentioned it in your letters to me while I was in Italy?"

"She came only recently." Ravenna pushed her thread through the muslin. "She's my sister Helen's daughter. Georgiana was a child when we came from Ireland. We had nowhere else to go when we came to London, so we stayed with our father's sister, Aunt Brendae, a bitter, vicious woman. Brendae and

Helen fought from the beginning. Though Helen and I both worked, we didn't make enough money to suit our aunt. Helen, for all her spirit, sank lower, became melancholic, and eventually fell into gin." Ravenna's thread knotted. She cut the thread and tied it off.

"That is unfortunate. Too many people have been destroyed by drink."

Annoyed with the embroidery, she cast it aside. "Helen's gin habit only exacerbated the fighting and, worse, in order to support her habit, she began selling her body for gin or money. One evening after a particularly horrible row, Helen stormed out, leaving Georgiana and me to deal with the consequences." Ravenna turned to look out the window at the pastures washed in the deep gold light of the declining sun. A hollowness entered her voice as she stepped into days she'd rather forget. "There had never been any joy in living with my aunt, but it was miserable living with her after that night. I did my best to shield Georgiana. But eventually I could take no more, so I also left. It broke my heart that I couldn't take Georgiana with me, but I was too poor to support us both."

"You can't blame yourself for your niece's situation when so many unfortunate events led to it," Braedon said.

Ravenna's eyes pooled with tears. "When I got married, I should've gone back for her, Braedon. And I didn't. I thought only of myself and of the challenges I was facing in my own life." She swallowed the lump of emotion lodged in her throat. "I *won't* fail her again." She dabbed her eyes with her damp handkerchief. "At any rate, my aunt paid a visit to Gordon House and demanded I take Georgiana in, help her debut, and get her married off now that she's of age. You were likely in the midst of your travels home when this occurred. My biggest concern is this incident will be twisted in the rumor mill and made to look like an indiscretion on Georgiana's part, ruining her reputation and any chances she might have of securing a fortunate marriage."

He gazed at her with tenderness. "She's surrounded by many great friends who will protect her and help her find a good match. Above all, she has you to guard her and protect her interests from now on."

She wanted to believe him, but young women with a past had a more difficult time navigating society. Ravenna herself had been lucky. Too many other women, the sort of women rescued by the Penitent House charity, could not overcome their mistakes or unfortunate circumstances and were cast into despair and desperate straits. She would use every resource at her disposal to prevent Georgiana's fate from following the same destructive path—if Ravenna could find her.

Upon arrival in Biggleswade, the travelers pulled into the courtyard at the Spotted Pheasant in the dead of night. The front courtyard bustled with workers assisting recent arrivals, their lantern lights bobbing like fireflies, their voices echoing in the darkness. Men removed horses from their carriages, led them to the stables for much-needed food, water, and rest.

A young man led Ravenna and her party into the inn. The place smelled of grease and onions and was likely riddled with fleas, but Ravenna was too tired to care much.

She asked the freckled lad. "Are the rooms and beds dried out?" A common problem when traveling, creating mold in the summer and colds in the winter.

"I'm not certain, ma'am. Will ye be needing any victuals before bed?"

She signed the registry. "Please bring up a few slices of bread, butter, some wine, and extra blankets for each room, if you have them. That shall suffice until morning."

"Butter is sparse just now, ma'am. But we may have beef drippings from supper."

Ravenna skimmed the other names on the registry in hopes of finding Josiah Emmett's among them. Not there. Not surprising. He'd be a fool to sign his real name.

The boy craned his thin neck, watching her read the lines. "Is there something I can help you with, ma'am?"

Ravenna closed the book and turned to him. "Yes, in fact."

His blond hair stuck out like hay all over his head, and purple circles of malnutrition and exhaustion ringed his eyes.

"Have you seen a girl pass through here, traveling with a man? The girl's name is Georgiana Connelly. She's young, pretty. Blonde ringlets, blue eyes, pointed chin, nearly your height. She also has a wounded right shoulder. She is with a man named Josiah Emmett. He's of a sturdy build with short, dark hair in the back, longer in the front. He has a long, sharp nose, dark eyes."

He thought for a moment, then shook his head. "No, ma'am, can't say as I've seen them. But I see many people in a day."

"I understand. Thank you. Perhaps you can ask around to the other workers and let me know if you discover anything before I leave in the morning?"

He nodded. "Will do. Follow me to your rooms, ma'am."

Their shoes clomped up the creaky wooden stairs. "The men are in this room…" The boy opened the door to the right. "And the ladies here…" He opened the door across the hall.

Ravenna stepped inside. The room stunk of mold and mildew, a sure sign the mattresses on the two narrow beds were damp. The boy lit the single candle on the table as Charlotte and Aurélie filed in behind him.

Ravenna cracked open the casement. Voices echoed in the courtyard below. "Charlotte, you and I shall share a bed so Aurélie may sleep in relative comfort." She pulled back the weathered blanket of thin, holey wool and felt the mattress. Damp. Ravenna sighed, removing her bonnet and gloves. "I think I shall sleep in my clothes tonight and hope for better accommodations at our next stop."

"At least we are not crammed in as tightly as the men." Charlotte wrapped her cloak tighter around her form and sat on the bed.

Within fifteen minutes, the boy delivered an extra blanket along with a tray of stale bread, cold beef drippings, and watery wine. "I found a pear, too. Thought you ladies might enjoy it."

"How kind…" Ravenna gave him another farthing. "Will there be a breakfast?"

"Yes, ma'am. Porridge, toast, and tea. Maybe some apples or pears and honey." He lowered his voice. "Don't drink the coffee if it's offered."

Ravenna smiled at the boy's kindness in warning her. Likely, the coffee would be watered down and mixed with something like sawdust to make it last longer. "Thank you. We will want to leave early. Near daybreak, so please have the carriages ready for us."

"Will do, ma'am."

Ravenna handed the extra blanket to Aurélie. "You should have this. I wouldn't want you to catch a chill from these wet mattresses."

"Thank you. You're too kind, ma'am."

"You must call me Ravenna. We're sisters now." Ravenna sliced the pear, giving the larger portion to Aurélie.

Charlotte joined the table to pour them each a glass of wine.

"Since we have no plates, we shall have to share the same drippings bowl." Ravenna stared at the brown gravy with bits of hardened fat floating on the surface.

Charlotte wrinkled her nose, plucked up a slice of bread, and turned away from the table. "More for you two, I say. I only like warm drippings." She sat on the bed, nibbling her bread.

"I'm hungry enough to eat them cold tonight." Ravenna tore her stale bread and dunked it into the gravy.

Aurélie also selected a slice of bread. "I, too, do not like the drippings."

Ravenna washed down her bread with a swig of wine, wincing at its weakness. Already she missed her rich, bold port. "Aurélie, I notice your accent is French. Are you not originally from America, then?"

Aurélie sat on her bed. "I am from America, but I am Creole."

"What is Creole?"

"It means my lineage is African, French, and Indian. Where I'm from, the Louisiana Territory, we speak a language similar to French, but it is so muddled with the other languages, it has become a language of its own." Her eyes glowed with humor. "It is unintelligible to French natives."

"I see." Ravenna finished off her bread and sat in the window casement with her glass of wine. "How did you meet my brother? And how long have you known each other?"

Aurélie removed her slippers and stretched out on the bed, propping up on the thin pillows. "About three years. We met when he delivered flour to the convent kitchen where I was working."

Ravenna tipped her head, studying her sister-in-law. "You don't strike me as a scullery, a cook, or a nun."

Aurélie chuckled. "I am none of those things. I was a teacher at the Ursuline Academy. A small convent and school for freedwomen, slaves, and Indians. But because we are so small, the teachers must help with chores when we are not teaching."

Ravenna's eyes widened. "Incredible. What do you teach?"

"Latin, French, and whatever else I'm tasked to teach." She yawned.

"Do you intend to return and teach there?"

"Perhaps. Though, Niall and I have discussed staying here and setting up a school. Once we are established, of course."

"Many a grand family would pay handsomely for a bright governess to teach their children," Charlotte bit into her pear slice.

Aurélie brightened. "Oh no! I want to teach the *poor* children. To give them more opportunities than they would otherwise have. Imagine what doors to knowledge, education, and life would open up to them if they simply knew how to read."

Interesting. Ravenna, too, believed in education. Especially for women. The Penitent House, in fact, worked to educate reformed prostitutes, to give them a chance for a better life. But was it possible to educate the masses? To go into every tiny town and village in Britain and teach all the children to read and write? "Sounds like an enormous undertaking."

Aurélie shrugged. "It takes one school in a village. We teach ten children, those children teach their children, and soon we have an entire populace who can read and write."

Now it all made sense. At first, Aurélie seemed more intellectual than Niall, and the match seemed ill-fitting. But now Ravenna understood the connection between Niall and his wife. "You're a reformer then?"

"Indeed. The French and the American Revolutions have brought great changes, and I believe we are on the brink of a new world."

"What sort of world?"

"A world without kings."

She lifted a brow and exchanged a concerned glance with Charlotte. "I don't think that's possible. A world entirely without kings."

Aurélie sat up. "Of course it's possible, though I think many countries are reluctant to topple their thrones. Instead, they will simply diminish the power of the king and give more power to their parliaments. In such a system, with their shackles removed, the poor must be able to read, write, go to school, own businesses, and such."

Ravenna considered this vision for a new society. "I don't entirely disagree. I think education is critical to shaping and molding minds and character. Especially for women."

"Then you are a student of Wollstonecraft?"

Ravenna made a face. "In a manner of speaking. Some of her ideas I do not agree with, but I do agree with her on the matter of educating our women in order to be better citizens, mothers, and wives. Women who can understand elevated topics and discuss them with ease and clarity." Ravenna paused. "However, I would offer you some sisterly advice: You'd be wise to temper your speech when discussing the toppling of kings. I have no doubt such speech is welcome in America. But you're in England now. You don't want to be mistaken for a traitor."

Chapter Four

The stuffy bedchamber, moldy air, fitful sleep, and the breakfast of watery porridge and cold tea had all combined to put Ravenna in a sour mood. She paced in the courtyard, anxious to travel. Worse, no one questioned at the inn had seen Georgiana.

A slice of the sun balanced on the horizon, opening the sky to pink and purple hues. Already, the day was moving on without them, and they still had many miles to go before their next stop. How far away was Georgiana now?

Braedon strode from the direction of the stables, flanked by two dirt-crusted, sweating young men.

"Good morning, Lady Birchfield." He bowed. "I have news." Braedon turned to the taller of the boys. "Share with Lady Birchfield what you told me."

The boy's shirt sleeves were rolled up to his bony elbows, and suspenders held up pantaloons two sizes too big for him. He removed his cap and rolled it in his grimy hands. "Milady. I saw a girl as milord described. Real pretty-like with blonde hair and blue eyes and tall as myself."

It seemed too good to be true. "Who was she traveling with?"

"Two gents."

"Two?" Ravenna frowned. "Are you sure?"

"Aye. One had dark hair and eyes, a nose sharp as a hawk's beak. There was another gent with him, pale as a ghost. Hair almost white."

Ravenna's grip tightened on her folded fan. "Did the pale gent have a limp?" The limp she'd given him after stabbing his thigh when he had attacked her.

"Aye. I believe he did."

Oh, no. Mr. Larson! That evil wretch from The Unity. Ravenna exchanged a look of concern with Braedon.

The young man continued. "The girl seemed scared of them. I offered her food, but she wouldn't eat. She seemed vexed. Like she'd been crying."

"I wager she was quite vexed. Was she in good health?"

He lifted a thin shoulder in response. "I reckon."

The shorter of the two boys with dark curly hair and a light mustache forming on his upper lip added. "She tried to give me a letter, but one of the men…" The tall boy nudged him and pointed to his head. The curly-haired boy removed his cap. "One of the men weren't happy about that. He snatched the letter from my hand and slapped the miss."

"He slapped her?" Ravenna gritted her teeth.

"Yes, milady. Then she tried to tell me something, and the man grabbed her by the neck and pulled her away. She tried to fight him, but she's just a slip of a girl, ain't she? He forced her into the carriage, and they left."

"Which man accosted her? The pale one or the dark-haired man?"

"The pale one, milady."

Ravenna muttered, "If I get my hands on that man…"

The tall boy said, "I daresay, milady, it weren't no good to the young miss even if we'd caught the note because we couldn't read it no ways."

"I understand. What else did the men say? Did they mention their travel plans…anything you can think of that could help me find her?"

They shook their heads. The curly-haired boy pointed up the road to the right. "They headed up the North Road."

The tall boy added, "The men and the Miss slept in the stables when we ran out of rooms. We sleep in the stables, too. I was preparing my bed when I heard them talking. They was talking about Edinburgh. About meeting someone there."

Braedon crossed his arms over his chest. "Did the men say who they were going to meet? Or why they were going to Edinburgh?" The boys looked at each other, then shook their heads. "How long ago were they here?"

"Only yesterday, sir. They left near dawn."

"At least we aren't too far behind," Braedon said to Ravenna, extracting his coin purse and handing coins to the boys. "Thank you, lads."

The tall boy nodded and clapped his cap on his head. "Thank'ee, sir. Milady." He rushed off to assist the driver, who whistled and called out for help.

"Come." Braedon motioned toward the carriage, taking Ravenna by the elbow.

The curly-haired boy stopped and ran back to her. "There's something else, milady."

Ravenna turned.

"When I was listening to the men talk, they was passing a bottle. One of the men asked what would happen to the miss once they got to Edinburgh." He paused, licked his lips, and shifted his weight. He glanced at Braedon. "I felt sorry for her, I did."

"What is it, boy?" Ravenna stepped closer. "What did you hear?"

"One gent asked what would happen to the miss, the other gent said he didn't care. He said, 'Put her on the street to make money. Or kill her and dump her in the river for all I care.' It made my blood turn cold, it did, the way he spoke about the miss. I hope you find her."

"Thank you. You've been very helpful." She forced herself to smile through the rage. He ran off to join the other workers as she climbed into the carriage, her temples pulsing with the fury she fought to contain. She doubled over, face to her knees, as she tried to block dark thoughts about what the men might be doing to her precious niece.

Braedon and Charlotte settled in around her as the carriage door closed and the vehicle pulled away from the inn.

"Ravenna…" Braedon whispered, placing his hand on her back. "I know you're angry. You have every right—"

She sat up, seething. "The thought of those two men, their hands on Georgiana, *slapping* her. Threatening to prostitute her. To kill her. If it kills me, they will not escape justice. I *swear* it."

Chapter Five

After traveling for most of the day, the party pulled into the Bell Inn in Stilton to rest the horses and switch carriages. They stole a couple of hours to walk around, ask workers about Georgiana, and eat a quick repast before resuming their trip northward toward Doncaster. They stopped for supper and another change of horses at Fulbeck-on-Heath as the sun sank into the horizon.

Ravenna stood in the courtyard, one hand to her stiff back and the other rubbing circles in her throbbing forehead. She noticed a man leaning against the stables across the courtyard, watching her.

Braedon approached. "I've ordered our supper. It should come soon. Rarebit, beef, and vegetables."

Ravenna nodded. "What time is it?" She continued to stare at the man.

He opened his pocket watch. "Nearly seven. We've been traveling for at least ten hours."

"Feels like forever."

"And we still have several days."

She touched Braedon's arm. "That man over there..."

He tracked the direction of her gaze.

"Do you know him?"

"No."

"He has been staring at us this entire time."

"Perhaps he's captured by your beauty."

"This is no time for your jokes."

"I'll inquire as to his interest." Braedon started toward the man, but when he arrived within a few yards, the stranger ran.

Braedon gave chase around the building and disappeared. Ravenna ran after them, her body stiff from sitting in the carriage. She gripped her fan, ready to extract the blade hidden within and use it, if necessary. Braedon stood several hundred feet away, looking around.

Ravenna caught up to him. "Where did he go?"

Braedon scanned the area. "I don't know. He slipped away."

"This cannot be good."

"Perhaps he was a bandit or pickpocket with notions of preying on us." He took her elbow and guided her back to the inn's courtyard, as he glanced over his shoulder. "Notions which he's now abandoned, I wager."

"Or perhaps he's a member of The Unity, and they're following us."

"Also a possibility. Let us see if supper is ready, shall we?"

Ravenna stopped and turned to him, her hand on his arm. "Braedon, don't you see the threat this is? What if The Unity discover Niall is returned to England?" She shook her head. "I can't protect them also. I can barely protect myself. And, apparently, I haven't been able to protect my niece at all. I wasn't able to protect my stepson, Thomas. I've failed everyone around me so far. I'm failing."

"I do understand the threat." Pity filled Braedon's frosty blue eyes. "Dearest Ravenna, you have not failed. You've been strong and fighting alone for far too long." He took her hand and kissed it. "I'm here. I will help you. I will fight alongside you, but more importantly, I will fight *for* you. You don't have to be so strong anymore."

"Once I have Georgiana again in my care, I may just let you do most of the fighting." She chuckled. She dropped her head to rest it against his chest, melting against him. He wrapped his arms around her. It had been ages since she'd felt this secure, this safe. She shifted to look up into his face. "With that man hanging about, I'm inclined to think we shouldn't stop here. Maybe we should continue on toward Doncaster."

"We'll never make it all the way to Doncaster. It's at least another fifty miles, and the horses need rest."

"Granted, but we should push through as long as we can."

"I'll speak with the driver and see how far he thinks we can make it tonight. But…" He put his hand on her chin and lifted her face. "You also need rest. I can see you are exhausted."

Her resolve solidified like a corset bone along her back. "I confess I am. But we will press through as far as the horses will carry us. We, *I*, must find Georgiana. I can't truly rest until I have her with me again. I can't bear the thought of what those animals could be doing to her."

After supper, the party decided to push through to Tuxford, stopping at the Dovecote Inn, unable to go any further. Ravenna was relieved to see the establishment was newer, the room cleaner, the beds drier, and the blankets in better condition than inns from the previous nights. Not that it mattered. She was too tired to care. She stripped down to her chemise and curled up in the bed beside Charlotte.

Just as Ravenna had drifted toward sleep, a swishing sound near the door alerted her. She sat up.

"Did you hear that?"

Charlotte shifted. "Are you unwell?"

Aurélie's voice lifted out of the darkness. "What's the matter, *mes chéris?*"

Ravenna slipped from the bed. "I heard something at the door."

Aurélie said, "Perhaps it is Niall or your Lord Braedon?"

"Maybe it's a mouse?" Charlotte said.

Ravenna bolted to the fireplace, grabbed a candle, and lit it from the low-burning embers. She scanned the room, finding there, by the door, a slip of paper. Perhaps Niall or Braedon had left a note, not wanting to wake the ladies?

She picked up the paper. A letter. She opened it and read the message within.

We've been watching you. It was a foolish choice to follow us instead of paying the money. Your niece is lost. You will never see her again.

"Blast their eyes!" Ravenna spun, grabbed her fan with its dagger hidden inside, and dashed from the room.

Behind her, Charlotte and Aurélie called out as she jogged down the steps, candle in hand, landing in the dining room below as the entrance door closed. Ravenna opened the door and ran into the courtyard in time to see a shadowy figure disappear near the stables under the light of the quarter moon. She gave chase, barefoot, holding up the skirt of her black chemise. She trailed along the side of the stables, drawing in the scent of horses and hay. The horses nickered and snorted within. Shrubbery rustled near the back of the stables.

"Stop!" She shouted. "Who goes there?" Sticks and rocks jammed into her feet, and as she pushed through the shrubbery, the limbs cut at her arms, slowing her progress. Her chemise caught in the limbs as the man dashed down the street. He was too far ahead to catch now.

Light appeared. She turned to see Braedon standing there in his pantaloons, untucked shirt, and boots. His hair was mussed and he held a pistol in one hand. Beside him stood Niall, looking much the same, and a young groom holding up the lantern.

"He escaped me." Ravenna panted, plucking herself from the shrubs. "I tried, but I couldn't catch him."

Braedon helped Ravenna extract herself from the foliage. "It's a good thing you didn't catch him. He might've killed you."

"Are you hurt?" Niall asked.

"No. Only scratched a little. I wanted to question him." She allowed Braedon to lead her to the front of the stable. "He might've known something about Georgiana." She brushed off her arms and chemise as Braedon picked leaves from her hair.

Niall continued. "What were you thinking? Chasing a man in the dead of night? And you with only a bit of clothing and no shoes?"

Braedon turned to Niall, putting his hand on his chest. "It's enough. Your point is made, Mr. Connelly."

Niall shoved away Braedon's hand. "Touch me again, and you'll regret it."

A dark glimmer entered Braedon's eye as he squared off toward Niall. "I have few regrets. I think you'll find you won't be one of them."

Ravenna pulled at Braedon. "Please, not this. Not now."

Aurélie called out. "Niall!"

"Niall," Ravenna nudged him toward the inn. "Go to your wife."

Niall glared at Braedon as he strode toward the inn.

"Please don't fight with him," Ravenna whispered to Braedon. "I can't have you two at odds when we must spend so much time together."

"I didn't like the way he was speaking to you."

"Ignore him. It's the way of siblings sometimes."

"Yet, he made an accurate assessment. What were you thinking, Ravenna?" Braedon walked her back to the inn, where Charlotte and Aurélie stood near the inn door, blankets wrapped around them.

"I had to try. Did you see the letter?"

"I did. Miss Hart showed it to me when she came running to my door to tell me what you'd done."

"It's infuriating. I can't let them—"

Braedon stopped and turned to her. "Ravenna, I understand this situation angers you. You feel powerless to help, and you want your niece back. But getting yourself hurt or killed is not going to help her. And it would devastate…" He paused as if the words were caught in his throat. "The people who love you."

Ravenna's shoulders slumped, and she rubbed her face. "You're right. I wasn't thinking. I was frightened, not only by the contents of the letter, but by the fact that whomever delivered it knows what room I'm staying in. What if he returns?"

"I'll protect you. I'll sleep on the floor by the door."

"Nonsense. You need your rest, too. We have another long day of travel tomorrow."

"I can sleep in the carriage. I'll stand watch in the hall tonight. At any rate, your brother won't want to share a room just now." His mouth formed a crooked smile.

"I can't ask you—"

"You're not. I'm insisting."

Chapter Six

Five days of travel and they still hadn't caught up with Georgina or discovered much helpful information about her, which only served to increase Ravenna's anxiety and panic. Surely the chances of finding her niece, alive or unharmed, became worse, not better, with time and distance.

When they arrived in York—a large, fashionable, tourist center in the northeast of England, they stopped at the august Guy Fawkes Inn; it was a new brown brick building with red shutters near the massive and ornate York Minster with its creamy stone, Gothic spires, and arcs. Even though Ravenna's time at the inn would be brief, she was eager to sleep in a comfortable bed, have a bath, and eat decent food.

As everyone sat down for a supper of lamb, vegetables, bread and butter, Braedon said, "A couple of days ago, when I realized we were heading toward York, I wrote to an acquaintance here to see if he might have some information to help us."

Niall sniffed. "What sort of information would a gent have about the sort of men we're following?"

A faint smile tipped a corner of Braedon's mouth. "Who said he was a gent?"

Ravenna turned to Braedon. "Who is he?"

"No one you know, but he is the sort of man every *gent* should have in his retinue for occasions such as this."

"How mysterious, Lord Braedon." Aurélie sipped her wine. "How does a gentleman like yourself come to acquaint himself with such a man?"

Braedon chuckled. "That is not a story for ladies. So, I fear your curiosity must go unsatisfied."

Aurélie lifted her brow. "I see."

"At any rate, I will meet him at the tavern across the street tonight to see if he has learned anything."

A young serving-girl brought plates of food to the table. The girl, perhaps in her early twenties and of stocky build, had brown, stringy hair. Her small, dark eyes set deep behind round cheeks bore into Ravenna.

"Is something the matter?" Ravenna asked her, touching the scar that drew the girl's focus.

"No, ma'am. Are you Lady Birchfield?"

"I am. Who would like to know?"

The serving-girl averted her gaze, flushed, then skittered away.

"That was odd." Ravenna dug into her meal. "How would a girl in Yorkshire know who I am?"

When the girl came back to refill their glasses with wine, she left a scrap of paper beside Ravenna's plate, then dashed from the table.

Glances darted between Ravenna and her companions.

Braedon scanned the room. "What does it say?" He sipped his wine.

"It says to meet her at the Minster at ten tonight."

Niall leaned on the table. "You can't go alone."

Braedon said, "She's not. I'm going with her to ensure her safety."

Niall puffed. "I can go with her. I'm her brother."

Ravenna said, "Niall, I appreciate your desire to help, but your duty is to your wife."

"What do you think she wants?" Charlotte asked, stabbing a potato.

"And why do you suppose she's so secretive?" Aurélie asked, cutting her meat.

Ravenna shook her head. She opened her fan over her chest as she slipped the paper into her bodice. "I can't imagine, but I think while we're in York, we would be wise to proceed with caution."

"Perhaps it's a trap of some sort," Niall said. "I'm not certain you should go."

Ravenna sipped her wine. "There's only one way to determine the matter."

After dinner, Ravenna and Braedon left the Guy Fawkes Inn as the rest of the party returned to their rooms upstairs. They strode down the alley between the Precentor's Court and the brick rowhouses, toward the towering Minster. The imposing structure loomed before them, washed in a whisper of moonlight and shadows, all arches, spires, and stained glass; it was like a lace Medici collar carved from stone.

Ravenna kept her fingers near the medallion at the base of her fan, ready to release her blade with a flick of the wrist. They slowed their pace and approached the front of the building.

"Psst," sounded behind them.

They turned to see a cloaked figure emerge from the door inset between the two west end towers.

"I'm here." The figure receded into the shadows.

Braedon held Ravenna back and spoke to the cloaked figure. "Are you alone?"

"Yes."

"How do we know this isn't a trap?" Ravenna said.

"I s'ppose ye don't," the girl said in her Yorkshire lilt. "But I think you'll be wanting to hear what I've got to tell ye."

Ravenna and Braedon approached with caution, glancing around to ensure they weren't about to be ambushed. Braedon drew his pistol, holding it at his side, and Ravenna released her blade, secreting it in the folds of her skirt.

"What is it you wanted to tell me?" Ravenna asked.

"First, I'm wondering what my news is worth to ye?"

Ravenna scoffed. "I don't know what the news is, so it's worth nothing."

"It has to do with a pretty girl with blue eyes and blonde hair."

"Georgiana…" Ravenna stepped forward. "What about her?" Ravenna stepped forward.

"Ah-ah…" The girl held out her thick hand. "First, I'll be needing some money."

Braedon placed himself in front of Ravenna. "Why should we pay you anything?"

"Because I've proven I know something about your niece. And since I'm putting myself at risk, I oughta make a coin or two for my trouble."

"What sort of risk are you taking?"

She crossed her arms. "Knowing what I know, I think trouble follows the likes of you. Why do ye think I asked to meet in secret? I don't want anyone seeing me talk to you."

Braedon dug his coin purse out of his pocket. "I'll give you a shilling now and a shilling after you divulge your information." He put a coin in her hand.

She dropped the money in her apron pocket. "I saw the girl near two days ago. She described you to me. The dark hair, dark eyes, scar on your face. When I saw you at supper tonight, I knew you was her aunt."

"How did you meet with her? I thought she was well-guarded. Tell me everything. I've been searching for her for days."

"When I went out near the stables to draw water one morning, she got my attention, then whispered at me through a hole in the wood of the stable wall. She said: 'Please listen. Pretend you're working. I don't have long. My name is Georgiana Connelly. My aunt, Lady Ravenna Birchfield, may be looking for me soon.' Then she described you and said, 'If you see the woman I've described, tell her those men I'm with are planning on meeting with their cohorts when we reach Edinburgh. Then we'll be sailing to France to meet with their French associates. I don't know what will become of me then. One of the men they're meeting in Edinburgh is named Muir.' I tried to ask her a question, but the men came for her, and they left."

Ravenna and Braedon caught each other's eye, communicating in silence.

"That is valuable information," Ravenna said. "Is there anything else?"

"No. I've told you everything I know, and I don't want to be here any longer. Seems you two are mixed in with a dangerous lot. There could be more of them around even now." She peeked around the corner of the building and held out her hand. "I'd thank'ee for my payment."

"Thank you." Braedon dropped a shilling in her palm.

"I never spoke to you and never saw you, if you catch my meaning." The girl flew from them, her cloak billowing behind her like crow's wings.

Braedon offered his arm to Ravenna. "Let's return to the inn before pickpockets find us."

She accepted his arm and gripped it with excitement. "We have a name. That should be quite helpful for us once we reach Edinburgh."

"Indeed."

"When are you supposed to meet your acquaintance?"

He checked his pocket watch under a gas lamp. "He should be there by now. I'll walk you to the inn."

"No, you will not. I'm going with you. Georgiana is my niece, and if he has information that could help find her, then I want to hear it."

"Very well. I'm too tired to fight you."

Braedon led her across the street to the Sheep's Fleece Tavern, a tiny, dark place full of tobacco smoke and loud conversation. Men leered and sneered and made suggestive comments about Ravenna as she passed to the back of the room on Braedon's arm. She ignored the men. Their disgusting behavior would not dissuade her from her mission.

A man stood and offered his hand to Braedon. He was a short, barrel-chested man in garments similar to a merchant, tradesman, or banker; he clearly had some money but was not of nobility. He had a square, sun-weathered face, sharp, hooded eyes, and blonde, bushy sideburns.

"Braedon, you sly-booted bastard, it's good to see ye."

As they shook hands, Braedon laughed. "You need to watch your language, Tiburn. There's a lady present."

Tiburn looked Ravenna over, taking the measure of her. He removed his hat, his stringy blonde hair falling over his face as he bowed. Then he stood and clapped his hat back on. "Good to see you're strumming with quality."

Braedon's voice deepened with warning. "I said go easy."

Tiburn held up his hands in deference. "Begging your pardon, milady." He motioned to a chair for Ravenna to sit. "And what will your ladyship have to drink?"

Ravenna had been longing for a glass of port since leaving home, but hadn't had the opportunity. It was considered a gentleman's drink, and though it would be improper to drink it in public, she didn't care. "I would like a glass of port."

Tiburn's pale eyebrows shot up. After the brief shock wore off, he burst into laughter, clapping Braedon on the back and motioning for a serving-wench.

Everyone settled in. Drink in hand, Tiburn spoke to Braedon. "It's been a long time, my friend. I trust ye've been well?"

"I have."

Tiburn looked at Ravenna. "As I can see for misself, eh?" He slapped Braedon's arm and laughed. Then he said to her, "If I had one as pretty as you on me arm, I'd give up my ways and become a right square cove like ol' Braedon here."

"Your compliment flatters me," Ravenna said with a flat voice.

After a pause to consider her, he burst into laughter. "This one has spirit."

"Indeed." Braedon smiled at her then turned the conversation to Georgiana and The Unity. "Have you heard of anything among your...cohorts?"

"Mm." Tiburn worked his beet-red lips, nodding. "I haven't heard anything of particular girls, but I know something about those Unity men." He leaned on the table. "Rough bunch. Encountered some on my last trip to France. Heard rumblings from some acquaintances there that they're planning another rebellion. Ever since the last one fell through in '98, they've been working to raise money and the like. One Unity cove offered me a pile of money to run munitions across the channel from France."

"Interesting..." Braedon downed his whisky.

"They're also running girls to France..."

Ravenna's breath caught.

"But I didn't want any part of the flesh trade. Some risks aren't worth the money." He downed his shot of whisky.

Ravenna toyed with the thick stem of her port glass. "Who's funding these men? They must be getting the money from somewhere to bring munitions from France. And I wager they must be paying men to fight for their cause."

"Aye, they are paying men. Their money is coming from various sources. Some rich sods in France are backing them, to be sure. And, of course, the French government, which has an interest in creating chaos and division in Britain."

"And through more nefarious means, I wager?" Braedon poured another shot for himself and Tiburn.

Tiburn pulled a pipe out of his pocket and packed it with tobacco. "Precisely. They sell the girls for money and kidnap children from wealthy families who will pay a mighty ransom."

"When was the last time you encountered any of these men?" Ravenna asked.

"Maybe a month ago. That was the last time I was in France. I brought some guns with me this last trip. I just dropped them off a couple of nights ago."

"Where?" Ravenna asked.

"Edinburgh."

Braedon and Ravenna caught each other's eyes.

Braedon asked, "Is anyone else running guns or girls for them?"

"I'm sure of it." Tiburn sat back in his chair and crossed his legs. "Many men in my line of work don't have the same qualms about running girls."

Ravenna watched the dance of candlelight in the prisms of her glass. "Do you know when and where they will run another group of girls to France?"

"I've heard some talk about a group of girls being sent out from Edinburgh in a few days."

"Do all the girls go to France?"

"To start. Then they're sent to other places."

"Like where?"

"All over. Brazil, Russia, India, the Levant. Wherever they can get money for them."

"Who is buying these girls?"

"Wealthy men who want wives or slaves. Soldier camps. Brothels. Ships. Princes and lords. Wherever the girls can be peddled. Biggest money is made in Barbary. But God help anyone who ends up there." He shook his head and shot his whisky.

Icy fear trickled down her spine. "Braedon, we must find Georgiana before she's sent away. Once she leaves Britain, she will be sent to God knows where and I shall never see her again."

Braedon squeezed her hand. "We will find her. Soon. I promise." He turned to Tiburn. "Is there anything else you can think of to help us find this girl?"

"From what I understand, the girls aren't sent off in shipments of just girls. They're smuggled out in shipments from other businesses, hidden in and among the goods."

"Any businesses or ships in particular we should be aware of?"

Tiburn puffed on his pipe. "As I recall, a ship called *The Milton* is one such ship. Sails out of Leith."

"That explains why Edinburgh is important." Ravenna gulped her port.

Braedon added, "Such a trip for the girls would be made more dangerous now that we're in war."

Tiburn nodded. "Indeed. French Navy. British Navy. Privateers. Bloody pirates and corsairs. Lots of danger for the girls on the sea to be captured and…" His voice trailed off. "Well, you can imagine the rest."

Unfortunately, Ravenna could imagine all too well what the rest would be.

Tiburn chewed on his pipe stem. "Sorry, Braedon. I have no other information. I wish I could help more."

"You've been a great help. Thank you."

The men stood and shook hands again.

Tiburn slapped Braedon's shoulder. "Let me know if you need more brandy. Or…" He glanced at Ravenna. "If your lady needs lace, you know I can get the best France has to offer. Got to keep the women folk happy, eh?" He winked at Ravenna and guffawed.

They bade their farewells and Braedon led Ravenna from the tavern. Once outside, Ravenna turned to him. "What are we going to do? How are we ever going to find her? What if we don't get to Edinburgh in time?"

Braedon took her in his arms. "We will. We will find her. Somehow."

Her voice broke with tears. "I can't lose anyone else, Braedon. I can't."

Chapter Seven

Ravenna dreaded another day of travel, though she was eager to get on the road since it would bring her closer to Georgiana. Ever since her meeting with Tiburn last night, she couldn't stop thinking about what he'd shared with her. She needed to find a ship called *The Milton*. She pulled up her black stocking and tied it in place with a black ribbon above the knee.

Additionally, Tiburn had revealed the girls were hidden in shipments. She drew on her other stocking. There must be some connection between the businesses and the girls being kidnapped, sold, and shipped. Perhaps The Unity was working with certain business partners, paying them to turn a blind eye to the smuggling. Or perhaps they were paying the ship owners or ship captains? How far up the line did knowledge of this sordid business go?

A panicked knock came at the door, interrupting her thoughts. "Ravenna! Ravenna!" Niall called.

"One moment!" She tied the ribbon around the top of her stocking. She shoved her feet into her boots as Charlotte opened the door.

Niall rushed into the room, the strain of fear on his face. "It's Aurélie. She's unwell."

"What's the matter with her?"

He stammered through his words. "She's vomiting and has been complaining about a headache since last night."

Ravenna grabbed her medicine chest and hurried into the room across the hall. Aurélie was on her knees on the floor in a lacy peach dressing gown, her hair tied up in a lacy bandeau with wavy, mahogany tendrils escaping around her cheeks. She hovered over a chamber pot, holding her belly. "Something is wrong."

Aurélie's face seemed larger and swollen. Ravenna remained silent, not wanting to further distress her sister-in-law.

"I think it's the baby," Aurélie whimpered. She heaved again into the chamber pot.

Ravenna swung around. "Niall out. Charlotte, go downstairs and get me the coolest water you can find and a few rags."

Niall stood in the room, staring down at his wife, frozen in fear and concern.

Ravenna touched his arm. "Niall. It will be best for you to wait outside until I get her settled. Please."

Recognition and admiration filled his eyes. "You're so much like Mama. You even look like her. I'll wait downstairs." He left the room, closing the door behind him.

Ravenna spoke in soft tones to Aurélie, her hand on her elbow. "Let's get you off the floor." She helped her stand. "When did this begin?"

"This morning I woke with a horrible headache, such that it clouded my vision. I bathed, hoping it would make me feel better, but it didn't help."

Ravenna guided her to sit on the bed, then placed her medicine chest on the small table by the window. She put a few splashes of lavender oil on a damp cloth and wiped Aurélie's face, talking to her like a mother soothing her child.

"You have a gentle touch. Reminds me of my *manman*. What I remember of her."

"How kind. We're going to get you all better." She rubbed a little peppermint oil on Aurélie's wrists and a spot on her forehead. "This should help with the nausea. And what I find helps me when I have a sour stomach…" She opened a brown piece of paper and pulled out a hard candy. "Ginger comfit. It'll help with the foul taste of the bile as well." She placed the comfit package on the bedside table. "Keep these. I can get more."

Ravenna fluffed the bed pillows and stacked them up behind her patient. "Rest here."

"But we must get dressed. We have to find your niece."

"Ah, Aurélie, I fear we're going nowhere today."

"But your niece—"

"I confess, it distresses me to get further behind in our journey, but we must ensure you and your baby are safe. Now lie back."

Aurélie adjusted herself to lie back on the pillows.

"May I see your ankles?"

"Whatever for?"

"Please."

Aurélie lifted the hem of her dressing gown to reveal puffy ankles. Ravenna pressed her thumbs into Aurélie's flesh. Ravenna had seen this only twice before. Once in Ireland, once in London. In Ireland, her mother had been the village midwife and assisted several of the village women in birthing their children. There was a woman who had been swollen beyond measure and had a habit of fainting and bleeding. *Toxemia,* her mother had called it. In the end, the woman and child both died. In London, Lady Thistlemore had a similar case. She retired to her bed for the remainder of her pregnancy, and both mother and child had lived. Rest was the only palliative Ravenna knew of.

"Your ankles appear swollen." She hoped Aurélie hadn't heard the tremble in her voice. This was the worst possible time for this to happen. Far from home, caught between London and Edinburgh, far from a settled state where the mother-to-be could get the bedrest she needed. Though Ravenna hated to be selfish at this moment, carting a sick pregnant woman to Edinburgh would slow down their search for Georgiana.

"What does this mean?"

Ravenna didn't want to scare her; yet, she needed to know the truth. "Have you been bleeding at all?"

"I had a little blood this morning. Very light."

"How long have you been with child?"

"At least twenty weeks or so."

Bleeding, headache, troubled vision, swollen ankles, and face. Ravenna sighed, pulled the covers over Aurélie. She turned from her patient, rubbed her face, and moved to the window to stare at the courtyard below, where workers bustled to serve travelers coming and going.

Charlotte entered the room with the supplies she had gathered. "Should I start a fire, milady?"

"No, that won't help us in this instance."

Braedon stood in the doorway. "How can I help? Is she unwell?"

Ravenna turned to him. "A private moment, please, Lord Braedon."

Braedon and Ravenna stepped across the hall into her room. Braedon closed the door behind them. "How serious is it?"

"Very. I think it's toxemia."

"What does that mean?"

"It means bed rest, or she could lose the child."

"Are you certain?"

"I confess, I have doubts. I've only seen this twice before. But I cannot deny there are stark similarities."

"Can you mend it?"

Ravenna shook her head. "No. As far as I know, bedrest is the best and only treatment."

"Which is the very thing she cannot have if she's traveling."

"Correct. I fear she's had too much excitement. It was wrong for Niall to bring her all this way." She flopped down on the bed with a heavy sigh. "I could beat him with a riding crop for this. Not only has he now endangered his wife and child, but my niece's situation grows grimmer." She dropped her face into her hands. "What am I going to do?" The bed shifted, and Braedon's shoulder touched hers. She lowered her hands. "I could send her and Niall back to London or to Birchfield Manor. But the long distance could prove disastrous for them."

He said, "At this point, we're closer to Edinburgh than London. It would be best to press through for now, I think."

"But we can't travel at the speed we've been traveling."

Silence opened between them.

Braedon said, "I think I have another solution."

"I hope so, because I can think of nothing."

"I could ride ahead. See what I can find."

It wasn't the worst idea. The temptation weighed on her. "But it would also put you in greater danger of being set upon by highwaymen or bandits. Your offer is a noble one, but I can't ask you to do that."

He took her hand and rubbed his thumb over her knuckle as his eyes drew her in. "*You* are my concern. Which means your family concerns me as well." Before she could say anything, he leaned in, touching his lips to hers.

Ravenna sank into his kiss. She broke away reluctantly. "I'm sorry. There is much to attend to." She stood. "I'm inclined to ask you to stay. We might need you."

"You have Niall and Charlotte. I can travel faster on my own, Ravenna."

"But you don't know what Georgiana looks like."

"I know what Emmett and Larson look like. I think I can deduce from there."

"I won't ask you to go. I will simply say: if you do go alone, please be careful. I already have too many people to worry over." A faint smile touched her lips.

He stood. "I am determined to come back to you." He touched her face and kissed her again with a deep, heated kiss that declared *goodbye.* She clung to him, to his kiss, anxious for him to stay. She didn't want to be separated from him yet again. His presence steadied her, strengthened her. He was her rock.

They parted.

"Please come back to me." She touched her forehead to his.

"I'll always return to your kisses." He smiled down at her.

He kissed her forehead and turned to leave.

"Wait!" She grabbed his arm. "How will I find you in Edinburgh?"

"You won't need to. I'll find you."

Chapter Eight

After Aurélie ate and fell asleep, Charlotte watched over her while Ravenna went downstairs to join Niall for breakfast.

Niall sat with a tankard, his face drawn.

Ravenna drew up a chair beside him. "I think you need more than small beer for breakfast. Will you join me for cold meat and scones?"

"Aye."

They ordered their food.

Niall drank from his tankard. "How's Aurélie?"

"Sleeping. She ate some breakfast and managed to keep the food down."

"Do you know what's wrong with her?"

"I think she has toxemia."

"What does that mean?" He frowned.

"It means she needs a great deal of rest until the baby comes. Ideally, she should stay in bed as much as possible."

"What about Georgiana? We can't stay here. We'll run out of money long before the baby comes."

The server placed a teapot and cups on the table. Ravenna poured her tea. "As for Georgiana, Braedon has ridden ahead of us to continue the search. We will catch up when we can."

"Why does he take this matter all on himself? And leave us to sit and not be of any assistance—"

"It was the most viable solution we could conjure at the moment." She stirred sugar and cream into her tea.

"What can this toxemia do to her?"

As the food was served, she told him everything she'd related to Aurélie and Braedon. The scent of ham and scones lit Ravenna's hunger.

"How long does Aurélie need to rest?"

She selected a warm scone and broke it open, slathering it with cream and black currant jam. "I'm hoping we can leave tomorrow, if she improves today. However, we will still need to stop often to rest, and we'll need to arrange a way for her to lie down as much as possible."

Niall selected a cut of ham. "What is your Lord Braedon going to do?"

"When he reaches Edinburgh, he's going to find a ship called *The Milton*." She told him everything she'd learned from Tiburn the night before.

"Where did you get this information?"

"Someone Braedon knows. That's all I'm at liberty to say." She sipped her tea. "At any rate, though Braedon goes before us, I want to be on his heels. Even if he manages to find Georgiana, she doesn't know him and, after her current ordeal, she may not trust him enough to accept his help. We must be there as soon as possible."

"Of course. We'll do our best."

Ravenna chewed her food in thought. She recalled the conversation she'd had with Braedon a few days ago, where he'd seemed suspicious of Niall's sudden reappearance in her life. It was a valid concern. But how to broach the topic with grace to keep him from getting upset? After all, if his motives were sound, she didn't want to ruin the chances for reuniting the family.

"Niall, I have a matter of some delicacy to discuss with you. And since this is our first opportunity for a private conversation…"

He popped a bite of food in his mouth. "What's on your mind? You're my sister. Speak plainly without all these genteel affectations."

"Very well." She sat back, leveling a steady gaze at him. "Why are you really here? At this particular time after all these years?"

"I told you. Because I wanted my family back together and I wanted you and Helen to meet my wife."

"I think there's more to it."

He drank from his tankard and worked his mouth. "Very well. In America, we Irish are treated no better than dogs. It's difficult to find work. Though I will say we fare better than the Italians. I was lucky to find any work at all. I'd be working on the docks, and new Irishmen would come off the boats every day, with high hopes and high talk about the grand new lives they'll have in America. I asked them about the circumstances in the homeland. Not one had a good story to tell. They're poor, starving, and in desperate straits. Blight. Drought. Poor crops and the English taking what they can. I came back to see what I could do."

Ravenna groaned. "Not this again. Did you come back with notions of working for The Cause?"

"Aye. But not like before when I was young and impetuous. And stupid. I won't align myself with the likes of The Unity again. There are other groups who are—"

She scoffed. "You're mad. How could you? After everything that has happened? Mama and Papa were murdered because of you and our cousin Colin's brilliant work with The Unity. We had to flee our home to live with our bitter aunt. Helen was driven to drink and to the streets. You were forced across the ocean to America. Because you could not stand with our family in our loyalty to The Crown."

His face darkened. "The same crown that holds Ireland under its thumb and is culpable for the distress of the people there? You're just as stubborn as Mama and Papa. I never could get any of you to see how you kiss the hand that beats you. *That* is madness."

"*You're* the stubborn one." She pointed her finger. "Mama and Papa could never get you to understand that it was better to be subject to a king you're familiar with than to expose your neck to one you don't know. A tyrant who could be far worse. After all, do you think The Unity men would've been any different had they come to power? You see how they operate now. Stealing girls and selling them. Smuggling and all manner of criminal activity." Her face burned with her rising irritation. "And look at the French that The Unity have been colluding with. Remember, not too long ago, the revolutionaries dragged a king and queen to the guillotine and lopped their heads off. Along with innocent shopkeepers, clergy, nuns, and merchants who dared to show sympathy for the nobility. Is that who you would side with? How is that better?"

"They lost control of themselves. It doesn't have to be that way. But anyone who must work for their dinner, which you do not, and pay the ever-increasing taxes, would think the royals and their lot are only in the way of progress."

"How dare you. I may not work now, but I *have* worked. Hard. For barely a pittance, only to give over my earnings to an ungrateful and hateful aunt. I know too well the feeling of an empty stomach and not knowing where the next meal will come from. I have not forgotten the lessons of poverty. But even at my hungriest, I couldn't imagine behaving as the French revolutionaries and Irish Unity have. Bloodthirsty and violent actions such as theirs do not belong to rational people; nor can such people truly be interested in helping the workers. They cared only about gaining power for themselves. Which is tyranny by another name, isn't it? They may not believe in kings, but they were certainly eager enough to wear the crown of tyranny just the same."

"What would you have me do, Ravenna?" His voice rose. He was getting angry now, too. "Live my life in cowardice under the thumb of a king and watch my fellow countrymen bear the burden of The Crown's yoke?"

People in the dining area looked at them.

Ravenna hissed. "Lower your voice. You know what I would have you do? I would have you be a good husband to your wife and father to your children. Kings and tyrants will always be here to oppress and lord over others. This is a broken world full of danger, war, and suffering. There is very little we can do about that. Family is all there is, Niall." Hot tears stung her eyes. "Family. That's all we have, and the only thing that matters. Raising a strong family is the best thing you can do for this world."

His face grew red. "Don't you think I know that?" He shoved his chair back with a loud scrape and stormed out of the inn.

Chapter Nine

Ravenna stomped upstairs to sit with Aurélie and Charlotte. She spent the day there, between reading, embroidery, and tending to her sister-in-law. After several hours, Ravenna tossed her embroidery aside with a huff as she stood to look out at the spires and towers of York Minster jutting against the purpling twilight sky.

Charlotte stopped reading to look up. "Shall I have some dinner brought up?"

Ravenna pressed her head against the blown glass window. "I don't want anything yet. Aurélie, are you hungry?"

Aurélie looked up from her drawing. "I am, but…" she glanced at the window, "I am more concerned about Niall. I haven't seen him since this morning. Do either of you know where he is?"

"I confess, Niall and I argued today. He stormed out."

Aurélie set her drawing aside, concerned. "What did you argue about?"

Ravenna flashed a weak smile. "Family things. Nothing you should worry about." She bit her lip. "He should've returned by now, however." Ravenna started for the door, hooking her black lace fan on her wrist for protection. "I'll have dinner sent up and then go look for him."

"Wait…" Aurélie said. "You shouldn't go out alone, Ravenna. Charlotte can go with you. I can wait for supper."

"No, you should eat. I don't know how long I'll be gone."

Ravenna sent up the food, then stepped into the bustle of York. She headed in the direction she had seen Niall go earlier. Even as darkness drifted in, the city thrummed with pedestrians, vendors, and carriages. Ladies and gentlemen in their finery descended from their carriages to disappear into theaters or assembly rooms. Small groups of officers, cutting a stark image in their red coats, white pantaloons, and shiny Hessian boots, staggered through the streets chasing their vices. Ravenna shrank from them. The sight of a Red Coat even six years later whipped up a mélange of fear, anger, bitterness, and horrid memories she'd rather forget. And the way some of them leered at her caused the bile to rise in her throat. She remembered all too well what the women of Wexford suffered that dark day.

Ravenna stopped at every shop and tavern, peering inside in search of her brother, her irritation with him increasing. A butler had just nudged her from the foyer of an exclusive gentleman's club when she saw a Red Coat fly backwards out of a door down the street. Another man jumped on him, and the two tumbled and clashed in the street as some people walked by and others began to form a raucous crowd around them.

Fools. Probably neck deep in their cups. Without stopping to regard the fighting men, with more than an eyeroll, she opened the next door—a gentleman's milliner shop. The red-cheeked elderly man behind the counter came forward, inquiring if she was purchasing for her husband, and swept her in to look at his latest creations. By the time she extracted herself from the shop, the fracas in the street had cleared. As she neared the area where the fight had broken out, someone yelled, "Ravenna!"

She turned to witness Niall, hands shackled and face bloodied, being led down the street between two Red Coats—one who was also rumpled and bloody.

"Niall!" She ran to him and said to the soldiers, "What are you doing to my brother? Why is he shackled? Let him go this instant. Please."

One of the men scoffed, pushing her to the side. "Out of the way, woman. He's wanted for felonious assault against an officer of The Crown and for treasonous speech against the king."

"Niall, is this true?"

"These curs have no conscience for what they do to men like me. They started the fight, and because I would not back down, I am now arrested."

This was not the time to argue with him or tell him his precious revolutionaries would do the same thing—or worse—to their dissenters. She hoped, instead, to get some sense from the soldiers. "Where are you taking him? Will you at least tell me that?"

"He'll be housed in the prison near York Castle, to await his trial, and eventual punishment."

She followed the men down the hill, her mind reeling. How would she ever get him free? Even if she managed it, it could take *months*. She didn't have that kind of time and she couldn't leave him here to suffer whatever fate a judge might throw at him while she traveled to Edinburgh to find Georgiana.

A man shouted behind them. "Ho, there, soldiers. Wait, wait!"

The soldiers didn't stop.

Ravenna turned to see a man jogging toward them. The man picked up his pace.

Fortunately, his height gave him a long stride. His chestnut hair was cut short in the *Coiffure à la Titus* style and mussed, which gave him the air of an adventurer. Yet, his blue worsted suit and silver striped waistcoat bespoke a man of taste, refinement, and some wealth.

He caught up to them. "Hold on now, gentlemen."

The soldiers slowed. The ruffled and beaten soldier responded. "No time for your nonsense, Muir."

Muir? Ravenna's eyes widened. The same Muir who is supposed to be meeting Mr. Larson and Emmett in Edinburgh?

Muir said, "Come now, lads. I think you're taking this a bit too seriously. We had a disagreement, that's all."

The beaten soldier stopped near The Shambles, a narrow cobbled street lined with irregular Tudor-style homes. "You started it with your outrageous talk—"

Muir, using sweet tones with a Scottish lilt. "John, my friend. We are both gentlemen. We can handle this in a civilized manner."

The scuffed-up Red Coat named John scowled. "There's nothing to discuss. This man will go to jail."

"Over a disagreement? Why? Because he said something you didn't like?

And didn't he speak the truth, by the way?"

The soldier hemmed.

Muir clapped his arm around the soldier's shoulders. "Just one moment of your time. Come now. We've had worse disagreements than this."

The soldier glanced at his colleague. "One moment. Nothing more." He stepped several feet away to have a private conversation with the Scotsman.

Ravenna spoke to the other soldier. "What will become of my brother if he's put in jail?"

The soldier shrugged. "That's the judge's concern. Could be transportation. Could be a hanging."

Ravenna squeezed her eyes shut. This could not be happening.

She clasped her hands. "You can't, please. You can't jail him. He's newly married with a child on the way. He's lived in America these five years, and he's only here for a visit. I'm certain he has family and friends back in America who are relying on his return."

"I suppose he should've considered those things before attacking my friend."

Her attention turned to the stranger, Muir. He and John were in a deep conversation.

Muir handed a pouch and a paper to John, who, glancing around, slipped the pouch into his coat pocket. He then read the paper, issued a sharp nod, then handed the paper back to Muir. The men returned to where Ravenna stood with Niall and the attending soldier.

John said, "Set him free, Isaac."

"What? Set him free?" Isaac scowled. "He committed a crime."

"Against me. And I'm not going to press the issue. I've been…convinced otherwise." He removed a key from his pocket and unlocked Niall.

Thank heavens! Ravenna hugged her brother. He stank of liquor.

Isaac said, "I'd recommend staying out of trouble while you're in York, sir."

Niall let out a sigh of relief. "With luck, I won't be in York this time tomorrow. Or ever again."

The soldiers sneered at them and walked away.

Niall said, "Let's return to the inn."

"We should probably thank the man who intervened on your behalf." She turned to express her gratitude to the beneficent stranger, but he was gone.

"Where did he go?"

"I don't know. But I don't want to linger in case those officers decide to return." He pulled her to walk with him. They cut down an alley, and when they came out the other side, he asked a salep vendor for directions back to the inn.

They followed the curve of the street in the direction of York Minster, pushing through the pedestrians, blending into the shadows.

Ravenna asked, "Do you realize that the man who helped you was Mr. Muir?"

"Who's that?"

"The man that Larson and Emmett are supposed to meet in Edinburgh."

He stopped. "Truly?"

"Truly." She couldn't hide her disdain. "Were you drinking and gambling with him all evening? Does he know that you were once with The Unity?"

"Yes, I was drinking with him. He doesn't know about my former connections."

"Why did he help you?"

His voice rose, sounding pinched. "I don't know, Ravenna. I was half-sprung. I only knew him as Marcus. He never told me his last name."

She planted her hand on her hip. "What's more, why were you fighting? Your wife is lying sick in a bed, and you're out drinking and fighting like a common lout."

He ran his hands through his hair. "The fight started because I was talking to that man, Marcus, Muir, or whatever. We had been playing Hazard for some time when those officers came along. They were fairly flush in the pockets, so I didn't mind. I was happy to take the Red Coats' money. Marcus mentioned something about Ireland and how he's heard rumblings of rebellion there again."

"How did Ireland come up?"

"My blasted accent." He pointed to his mouth. "At any rate, I told him I hadn't heard anything about it, but it was a good thing for Ireland to shake off the chains of England once and for all. That we should've never united under The Crown a couple of years ago. The officer took offense and said bad things about the Irish, and I said something back. The one slapped me and called me out. So, I did him the honor of whipping him in the street."

"And nearly landed us all in a devil of a scrape."

"I stood for my honor and the honor of my country."

"What about your *family*? You put *everything* at risk!" She whacked him with her closed fan twice. "Think about that."

They strode toward the inn in tormented silence. When they arrived, they climbed the stairs in a huff. Ravenna threw open the door to Auérlie's room, where Charlotte and Auérlie sat in quiet conversation over their embroidery.

"I found him." Ravenna snapped open her fan to cool herself after the exercise of walking, climbing hills, and fighting with Niall. She pushed tendrils of hair from her sweaty forehead.

Auérlie's glittering dark eyes widened with concern as she lowered her embroidery. "Where were you? I've been worried."

"No need to worry, love." He bent to kiss her forehead.

She put her hand under her nose. "You reek of liquor. Please don't tell me you've been drinking again. You know I don't like it when you drink."

"A little, but a drink was spilled on me."

"That's not entirely true." Ravenna put her hands on her hips. "He has been drinking, gambling, and fighting. He was arrested and nearly thrown into jail, saved only by the kindness of a stranger he'd been gambling with. And guess who the stranger was?" She paused. "Mr. Muir. The very man who is supposed to meet up with Larson and Emmett in Edinburgh."

Auérlie and Charlotte's mouths dropped open.

"Ravenna, stop," Niall warned.

"I'm not afraid of you. Your wife deserves to know the truth."

Auérlie frowned. "Gambling? Niall, you know we don't have the money to waste on gambling. How much did you lose?"

"Not much, love, truly." He sat on the bed beside her and held her hand. "Only a few dollars."

"A few dollars? We needed that money."

"Don't worry. All will be well. Trust me. I will provide for us. You needn't worry about anything." He smoothed a hand over her cheek.

"See what you have done?" Ravenna said to him. "Had you stayed here and put your family first, none of this would have happened."

He glared at her. "I—" He stopped and seemed to roll something over in his mind. He deflated. "You're right. I made a horrible mistake. My ire gets up when I'm dealing with Red Coats. I hope you will all forgive me."

Ravenna blinked. She had been steeled for a fight. Ready for him to argue. She studied him with suspicion. "You can't mean that."

"I do."

"What are you up to, Niall?"

A smile crept over his mouth.

Chapter Ten

Over the course of the next two days, Ravenna and her party passed through Durham and Newcastle, along the eastern coastline, through Haddington, and finally, in the wee hours of the night, landed on the fringe of Edinburgh at the end of the Royal Mile near Holyrood Palace. They turned into Boyd's Inn, a white stone structure with a tiled roof and a cobblestone courtyard in the center, lit up by torches.

The courtyard buzzed with activity, the sounds of horses and their tack, carriage wheels and voices, as people loaded and unloaded carriages, and climbed the stairs to the inn entrance. With stiff back and legs, Ravenna dragged herself up the stairs to a room with two narrow, straw-stuffed mattresses and sparse furnishings.

Ravenna collapsed onto the bed fully clothed but for her shoes, spencer, and bonnet. Thankfully, the bed was dry, with only the faintest scent of straw and mildew.

Charlotte shimmied out of her dress and climbed under her blanket, her long braid trailing over her shoulder. "My cousin says we can stay here as long as we need to. He'll reduce the price for us."

"You must thank him for me. But I couldn't bear to pay less than the room is worth."

"You're getting Scottish hospitality, now, ma'am. You'll find he won't be gainsaid in the matter. There's nothing to do but accept it."

Ravenna chuckled and cocooned herself into the thin wool blanket. "We can discuss it in the morning." Relief washed over her in knowing she had finally reached her destination. Aurélie and her child were safe, and

Georgiana was here somewhere. She would find her. Surely, it would be only a short time now. She closed her eyes and drifted into sleep with Braedon on her mind. Had he made it safely to Edinburgh? Had he discovered anything yet? Would they meet again soon? She would try to find him first thing in the morning.

Ravenna woke early, eager to get started in her hunt. She bathed, dressed, and ate a large breakfast before the clock downstairs struck eight. After her breakfast, she carried a tray of food upstairs to Aurélie, who was sitting in bed, dabbing her eyes and sniffling.

"Whatever is the matter?" Ravenna placed the tray on a table. "Are you unwell? Has your condition worsened?" She examined Aurélie's face and hands. In fact, the swelling seemed reduced, which was a most welcome relief.

Aurélie gently pushed Ravenna's hands from her face. "I'm well. I'm still weak, and I have another headache, but I'm not worse." She blew her nose into her handkerchief. "It's Niall. He's gone. Left early this morning. Wouldn't tell me where. When I insisted he tell me, he maintained he couldn't. For the safety of all concerned."

Ravenna blew out a breath and pushed a tendril of hair out of her face. "What does that mean?"

Aurélie shrugged. "I don't know."

"I'm sorry, Aurélie. I've tried to get through to him. But, to be honest, my brother has always been difficult and determined to have his own way."

"Do you think he's back with The Unity?"

"It isn't likely. I'll see if I can find out what he's up to."

Aurélie's voice cracked and grew watery. "I'm sorry. For everything. That I'm stuck in this bed, that I'm a burden to you right now. That—"

"No, please." Ravenna held her hand. "Don't say such things. It will all be well. I'm glad you're here, though I wished you were in better health." She stood and brought the table and tray closer to Aurélie. "I have to go search for my niece and Braedon right now. Please eat, and I'll have Charlotte check on you and give you some treatments."

"I wish I could help you. I feel so powerless sitting in bed all day." Aurélie gasped and put her hand to her belly. Her face brightened. "The baby's kicking something fierce today!" She grabbed Ravenna's hand and put it to her belly. "Do you feel it?"

After a moment, the baby kicked. Joy sparked in Ravenna. The joy of new life and another branch expanding her family. A light tickle of jealousy brushed like a feather around her heart. To be a mother. To know the powerful love of bringing a baby into the world. She had wanted that at one time, but Philip already had children when she married him. Further, he had been too dedicated to his work to build a new family. Now in her early thirties, she worried she was too old to have children. Perhaps she would have to be satisfied with being an aunt.

Ravenna bit down on her growing sorrow and withdrew her hand. "Just get better. You have plenty of time to rest now. It'll be a long trip back home, and rest is the best thing you can do to regain your strength."

Ravenna returned to her room. As she dressed to go out, she left instructions with Charlotte. "I'm going to try to find Braedon and Georgiana." She tugged on her black kid gloves.

"I wish I could come with you." Charlotte coiled her hair into a chignon.

"I know. I won't keep you here watching over Aurélie the whole time." She hooked her black lace fan on her wrist and donned her black bonnet, tying the silk ribbons. "I imagine you must be eager, at least in part, to explore your old home?"

"In part." Charlotte's face brightened some. "My memories here are not wholly unhappy."

Ravenna adjusted her bonnet ribbons. "Now, perhaps you can tell me: if I were Lord Braedon, where in Edinburgh would I be?"

Charlotte's brown eyes filled with warmth and amusement. "I think if I were Lord Braedon, I would be up the High Street just past St. Giles' Cathedral where Lawnmarket meets Bank Street. There, on the right corner, will be Brodie's Docket. If I were Braedon, I would be there."

Ravenna laughed. "Knowing Lord Braedon, I'm intrigued as to what I might find at Brodie's Docket."

Though a much smaller city than London, Edinburgh pulsed, full of the life associated with a quickly growing town. Ravenna stepped onto the Royal Mile, hopping with a throng of people, carts, carriages, and livestock. Thick coal smoke from the various homes and businesses hung in the warm air. However, the wind kept the smoke moving to allow for spare moments of sunlight. Though there were many similarities to London in terms of the smoke, smells, noise, and crowds, Edinburgh was distinctly different. In some ways, it reminded her of London town center rather than Mayfair, where the streets were narrower, houses closer and pushed together in an uneven, ramshackle manner. Many of them were wood, blended with sandstone and limestone structures, all of which were dingy with coal smoke—a blemish shared among many large cities.

The greatest difference between Edinburgh and London became evident as her whalebone stays crushed against her ribcage: the hills. Edinburgh seemed to be made of continuous hills in all directions. Up ahead, a grand castle crowned the top of a massive hill, towering over the city. Edinburgh Castle. Many fireplaces and turrets shot up against the clouds gathering around the sun. The angled wall zigged and zagged up the rocky hillside and around the castle, both of which were fashioned from expensive gray-brown Craigleith sandstone. Like something from a fairy tale, it was a majestic and awe-inspiring sight, indeed.

Soon, on her left emerged the spiky roofline of St. Giles' Cathedral with its one grand spire surrounded by shorter spires at the corners. It was a short, unimposing structure compared to Westminster or York Minster, but no less beautiful or grand with its brilliant stained-glass windows all around. While she respected the architecture, skill, and artistry of the larger churches, Ravenna rather liked this smaller, less ostentatious church with its simpler lines and ornamentation.

She walked on, happy the ground was leveling out more so she could catch her breath as she watched the crowd for any sign of Georgiana, her captors, or Braedon. Soon, a building emerged on the corner of Lawnmarket and Banks streets just as Charlotte had described. It was a white Tudor-style structure with black-trimmed windows and door frames. A black sign with gold lettering hung above the door: The Deacon's Docket.

Ravenna entered the building, boisterous with men discussing every matter from politics to prices of wool and harvest yields. It was highly improper for a woman to enter a public house like this alone. Thankfully, as a widow, she enjoyed some protection against such judgments. Also, while in Edinburgh, far from nosy gossips and backbiters, she cared little for what might be said of her. A few men leered, some called out to her as their companions sniggered in their cups and tankards. She ignored them all.

The low ceilings were of dark wood like the tables, floor, and bar. The dim light in the room filtered through a few small windows. She searched the faces among the light and shadows to pick out one recognizable to her. It was only when he stood and sauntered in her direction that she recognized Braedon.

He bowed. "Ravenna. How fortuitous. I was going to come in search of you once I finished my coffee. A little bird told me you had landed last night."

"A little bird?"

"Yes." He guided her to sit at the table by the window. "The street urchins are quite useful for a few coins." He held a chair for her as she sat. "I've had them posted at the watch on the edge of town since I arrived a couple of days ago."

She smiled. "Quite resourceful. Have you been to the Port in Leith in search of *The Milton* yet?"

"Yes." He requested a server to bring Ravenna some tea as they took their seats by a window. "Unfortunately, the ship has not yet returned. It's expected back to shore today."

The server gave Ravenna a cup of tea. She stirred in some cream and sugar. "I would like to go with you."

"I suspect you wouldn't allow me to say no, so I must say yes."

She sipped her tea. "You would be correct."

"How is Mrs. Connelly?"

"She is well. Resting. We had a bit of a scare with Niall the other day, so I am happy we are here."

"What happened?"

She told him of her argument with Niall and his near-imprisonment. "The strangest part was the man who helped secure Niall's release was none other than Mr. Muir."

Braedon frowned. "The man Emmett and Larson are supposed to meet?"

"Precisely."

"Are you certain your brother can be trusted?"

Snakes of fear, suspicion, doubt, and betrayal twisted in her gut. She didn't know what to feel. She didn't want to doubt or mistrust her brother. But he had proven himself disloyal before. She didn't want to suspect her own kin of colluding with the enemy who kidnapped their niece.

"I'm sorry," Braedon said. "I didn't mean to—"

"I understand. Your doubt is legitimate."

"I had to ask. After all, what interest could Muir have in seeing Niall set free?"

Her heart sank. "I only wish I could say with certainty. I want so much to trust him."

Braedon thought. "However, don't try to draw a confession from him. Just watch and wait for now."

She nodded. It would be difficult to be in a room with her brother, knowing he could be, once again, betraying her family.

He relaxed against the back of his chair, the light from the window washing his face in a silvery light. "My most significant question, my dear, is how you located me."

"I confess, I had some help. Charlotte, if you recall, is from Edinburgh. She seemed to think this place best suited you."

He laughed.

She looked around. "This looks like any other inn. Why would she think this is the place you'd land?"

"Likely because of the history of this place. This used to be the house of a man named William Brodie. He was once a reputable man in the light of day, but by night he turned to criminal pursuits." He sipped his tea. "Though I'm concerned about how your ladies' maid perceives me. Is my reputation so disgraceful?"

She flashed a coy smile over the rim of her teacup. "I used to think so, but I think you've improved upon acquaintance."

"As long as you think so, then I am happy, indeed." He refilled their tea cups.

"Have you discovered anything regarding Georgiana?"

"I spoke to a man in the street last night who claimed he saw a girl of her description with two men in Cowgate. When I asked him if he knew which direction they traveled, he said he thought they might've been going toward South Bridge. I searched the area for a few hours, but couldn't find her."

Ravenna downed her now lukewarm tea. "They can't stay indoors forever. And I'm going to find them."

He stood and offered his arm. "Yes. Shall we start with the Port in Leith and the ship *The Milton*?"

Chapter Eleven

They caught a hackney coach outside the inn and rode to the Port of Leith, where they trod the boardwalk and docks among the workers scurrying with nets, barrels, and crates, loading and unloading the ships of various sizes. The wind full of the scent of the ocean fluttered the flags on the masts, and the water lapped the sides of the ships.

"I don't see *The Milton* anywhere," Ravenna said.

"Let's inquire at the customs office there."

They entered the small building near the docks where an old man bent over a ledger. He looked up with large jowls and thin, grizzled hair sticking up erratically. He studied them with rheumy eyes. "What're ye needing?"

"We're looking for *The Milton*," Braedon asked.

He screwed up his stubbled face. "What are ye needing that ship for? It ain't a passenger ship."

"I'm aware, sir. I'm simply curious."

"Well, she ain't here yet."

"When do you expect her?"

"Any day now. She shoulda been here a few days ago. I wager she's caught in storms. The weather's been fouler than usual. Even for Scotland."

Ravenna and Braedon stepped outside. In the distance, dark clouds hovered over the water, and the wind had picked up.

"I suppose we can come back tomorrow or the next day." Ravenna sighed, holding her bonnet against the wind.

"We could…" Braedon nodded, his keen eyes watching the activity on the docks.

"In the meantime, we can ask questions of some people here. Maybe they've seen something suspicious related to what Tiburn had told us."

"I was thinking the same thing. I say we begin with them." He nodded in the direction of a few ragged men sitting on crates, smoking pipes and passing a bottle.

They approached the men, weathered skin, longish, greasy hair, their clothes dirty.

"Good day," Braedon said with a dash of cheer.

The men raked their bloodshot eyes over him with suspicion.

The skinnier one lifted his chin. "Sire…"

The man with a scruffy beard didn't say anything. He leaned his elbows on his knees, puffing on his pipe and whittling a chunk of wood.

Braedon continued. "I have a few questions, if you don't mind."

The man with the long nose said, "Depends what yer asking about…" He laughed with a snort.

Skinny Man cleared his throat and spat a wad of phlegm on the dock near Braedon's boot. "I s'ppose it also depends what it's worth to you."

A young lad pushed between them with a load of rope

Braedon ignored the spit. "I'm looking for a girl and I've heard girls can be found here sometimes."

They squinted with confusion. "What d'ye need a strumpet for when you have a lady right there." Big Nose motioned with his chin.

"Not that kind of girl. Her niece is missing. And we've heard sometimes girls are brought here, and shipped to France."

Big Nose and Skinny's gazes shifted, as if they knew something. They both pushed out their bottom lips and shook their heads. "Nope."

The third man stood up and walked away.

"Wait…" Braedon tried to grab his arm.

He slipped out of Braedon's reach. "I've got work to do." He slumped away.

Ravenna crossed her arms and directed her question to the remaining men. "Are you certain you haven't seen or heard anything about those girls? We've heard they are brought here at night and hidden among the shipments."

Skinny glared at her, malice sparking in his dark eyes. "Are ye calling us liars? We told ye we dinnae know what yer talking about."

"Even for a price?" Braedon pulled his money pouch from his pocket.

Humor lit their eyes and Big Nose scoffed. "Even for a price, dandy man. Go away now. Leave us be."

"Very well." Braedon offered his arm to Ravenna. "Shall we go? We can look elsewhere."

She accepted his arm with reluctance, but it had become clear that the men weren't going to say more. "I think they know something."

"I do, too, but if my money won't move them, I'd wager someone else is paying them a great deal more for their silence. I think we should try again when *The Milton* comes to port. Then we'll try to talk to someone who works on the ship."

As they stepped off the docks, someone whistled.

Ravenna and Braedon looked around to see Scruffy Beard. He stood against the side of the customs building, out of sight of his friends. He jerked his head, motioning for them to come to him.

Braedon and Ravenna approached.

Scruffy Beard's brown beard waggled as he talked. "Them coves back there was lying."

"I suspected as much," Ravenna said.

"Yer right about the girls. They are brought here at night. Not every night and only five or six at a time as to not draw much attention."

She drew closer to Braedon. "How many ships are carrying them?"

"I only know of *The Milton* doing that job."

"How long has this been going on?" Braedon asked.

"At least a few years, about four times a year."

Ravenna frowned at him. He seemed to be offering up the information too easily. "Why are you telling us this so freely?"

"I used to work on *The Milton.* The captain was a crooked cove and didn't pay me my cut on the last brandy run. And it wasn't the first time. So's I punched him and he kicked me off his ship. I'm settling my score."

"Why not tell a magistrate or—"

He scoffed, a dark humor in his eyes. "You mean the magistrates that are probably getting a cut of the money?"

Revenge rather than decency or integrity was this man's motive. He seemed entirely disinterested in saving or protecting the girls. "How do we know we can trust you?"

He spit on the ground and sniffed. "Trust me or not. I'm not caring either way. I heard you asking those coves about the girls, and I had the information you was looking for, and I'm sure it's worth something to you."

Braedon said, "But you haven't told us anything we didn't already know."

"And ye haven't produced any coin, have ye, dandy man?" He smiled, revealing a mouth of rotten teeth.

"Very well." Braedon removed his coin purse from his coat and shook it, the money jingling like horse tack. "What information do you have?"

"*The Milton* is due back within the next few days. When it comes back to dock they're going to pick up more girls. They're being held here in Edinburgh, waiting for shipment."

"Where are they being held?" Ravenna asked.

"That I don't know. Only the cove who made the arrangement with the captain knows that. But they'll be brought in soon."

"Who's the captain?" Braedon asked.

"Captain Henry Gilroy."

"Do you know who any of the girls are?" Ravenna watched his face for signs of lying.

"Nah. None of us knew that. Nor does the captain. The men in charge of the girls keep quiet about their business."

She asked, "What time do they bring them?"

"In the wee hours. Around two or three in the morning." He scratched his beard.

"What's the name of the men transporting the girls?" Braedon asked.

"Don't know. Not always the same man. One of them is an Irishman, Emmerson or Emmett or something..."

Ravenna pressed her fingertips to her lips. Emmett. The scoundrel. *So foolish, Ravenna, to let that man into your home.*

He continued. "He's the one I dealt with the most, but I get the notion they ain't working alone. I think there's gents involved too."

Braedon squinted. "A gent? Like a nobleman?"

"Nah, a self-made one. A merchant or something. But I don't know his name."

Braedon worked his mouth in thought. "Would you know what he looks like? Have you ever seen him?"

"Saw the gent once at night. He was about your height and bony-like, but I didn't get a good look at him."

"Did you see his carriage? Anything at all to help us identify him?"

"Nah." He glanced around, nervous. He sniffed and held out his grimy hand. "I told you everything I know."

Braedon placed a quid in his hand. "Thank you."

Ravenna leaned against the building, watching the man walk away. "I wonder if Georgiana will be among those girls?"

Braedon leaned on the wall beside her. "It's possible. Unless we find her first."

"How are we going to search for her and watch the docks?"

He checked his watch. "Let's search the town. We'll come back here tonight."

Chapter Twelve

Ravenna and Braedon caught a hackney coach back to Lawnmarket. They stood on the street, taking in the buildings around them stretching several stories high.

"Where should we begin?" Ravenna watched the dark skies which seemed to have followed them from Leith. "And will we have time to search before the rain sets in?"

"We shall do our best."

Pushing through the crush of people as they progressed, they stopped at every building to ask about Georgiana and her captors until they reached the end of Cowgate, where it opened into a wider strip of road.

At the last house, a dumpy woman and her friend, surrounded by children, sat on the stoop sewing and talking.

Ravenna approached them. "Pardon me. Sorry to interrupt."

The women eyed her suspiciously, much the same look she had received at every location. One of the women spoke in Gaelic, which sounded both familiar and strange to Ravenna's Irish ears. Then they smiled and chuckled.

Ravenna was losing her patience. "You may say whatever unkind things about me and laugh about it all you wish."

The women exchanged an amused glance.

"I'm trying to find my niece, who was kidnapped, and brought to Edinburgh. I believe she may be in Cowgate." She described the girl and her captors. As she spoke, the women's brows crinkled with concern and pity. "Have you seen anyone fitting that description?"

"Oh, you poor dear," the dumpy one said. She stood and dropped her sewing in the basket by her short stool. "Please, come in. I'll give you a scone and some tea. Truly, you seem reedy to boak."

Ravenna had no idea what *boak* meant, but assumed from the context it meant to be sick. She couldn't help but smile at the thick rolling Rs on the woman's tongue. The delightful sound like a babbling brook lifted her. "Thank you. I won't keep you long."

As she stepped into the dim rowhouse, she glanced over her shoulder as Braedon watched her from across the street. She held up a finger, indicating to him she needed only a moment. He touched the brim of his hat. The sister shuffled away.

The woman pulled out a chair at a small table. "Please, sit, my dear. My name's Aven Brown."

Ravenna nearly introduced herself as Lady Birchfield out of the habit of living in her own circle. Yet, it didn't seem appropriate here. "I'm Ravenna."

"Oh, what a lovely name. And unusual." Aven bustled around the tiny space, gathering scones and jam and putting a kettle on the fire.

"Thank you. My mother was Italian. It's the name of her home town in Italy."

"How lovely."

"Your name is very pretty too."

"Aye, my mum named me after the tiny yellow wood aven because I was born a wee bebe." She stopped, planted her hands on her broad hips, and boasted. "No' that I have that problem now, eh?" She laughed a deep, jolly cackle that drew laughter from Ravenna as well. "And as she was rumored a witch, she believed the wood aven kept away evil spirits. Imagine thinking a wee bebe could take on the demons. And I know it's not true because of how she ended."

"What do you mean?"

"Because they burned her at the stake for a witch, a stretch up the hill when I was but a wee lass. If she was truly a witch, she might've been able to escape, don't ye think?"

Ravenna's eyes widened. "I-I-I...." Her voice trailed off, unsure how to respond.

"Ah, but my mum was a good 'un, strange and wild in her way. I miss her every day, I do." She turned back to her work. "She liked a good fight. That's why she never cowered under the false accusations. Not even when they tormented her. I reckon I like a good fight, too."

Only feet away in the corner of the room lay a man propped against a pile of pillows in a bed. A sparse auburn brown beard covered his face and a bulbous nose and sunken eyes sat under a jutting brow. His head lolled to one side as he snored, and one of his arms was wrapped in gauze. "Don't mind my Samuel there."

"Your husband?" Ravenna couldn't help staring at the thin man.

"Aye."

"Is he very sick?"

"He was injured at the weaver's mill. Got his arm caught in one of the gears. Ripped up the skin and tore into his arm a bit. He lost some blood, but I think he's healing proper now."

"Oh, dear. How tragic."

"Aye. Almost as tragic as the pay he received for his labor and half his arm, eh?" She placed tea and scones on the small rickety table. "But since my Samuel's injury, there's been talk of the workers striking for higher wages. They work hard, long hours, and many have been injured of late. They deserve better pay. And it's not like the rich mill owners can't afford it. They sit in their fancy homes, eating their fine foods and wine while we…" She stopped short, raking her eyes over Ravenna. "Well, at any rate, they'll get what's coming to them soon enough."

Aven wiped her hands on her apron and sat across from Ravenna. They each dug into their scone with eagerness. Ravenna resisted using the cream or jam for her scone or the sugar and cream for her tea. Aven and her husband needed it more than she did.

"Thank you for the scone and tea. They are most welcome. It's been a long day."

Aven selected another scone and split it. "Now tell me more about your missing lass."

"I'm desperate to find her." Ravenna described Georgiana. "Her tutor, a

Mr. Josiah Emmett, absconded with her and—"

"Mr. *Josiah* Emmett, you say?" Aven lowered her teacup, eyes wide. "Are you sure?"

"Yes. Of course. Do you know him?"

"Aye. I don't know him well, but several months ago he was here in Edinburgh. He was at my husband's mill, passing out tracts about fair wages, the rights of the working man, and the wrongs of the king. And flirting with the girls who work there." Aven studied Ravenna with keen interest as if trying to read her.

Aven continued. "At any rate, I didn't like him from the start. He killed old Tom Tabor at the tavern one night. They got in an argument, and he stabbed him. He must've run to London, and that's when you met him, because I didn't see him no more after that."

The more Ravenna learned of Mr. Emmett, the more she feared for Georgiana.

Aven drank her tea. "You know, now that I think of it, I believe I have seen your lass. Yesterday. In Candlemaker's Row. She was running down the street. Her face bruised. A man was chasing her."

Ravenna's insides twisted as she listened to Aven.

"She was fast as a colt. I thought surely she'd get away from him, but, in the end, he caught her. She screamed for help, but no one dared. I thought it was a lover's quarrel. I'm sure everyone else thought the same. He carried her off down Candlemaker's Row toward Bristo Street."

Ravenna closed her eyes. "And you're sure they matched the description I gave you."

"I cannae make ye promises, Ravenna. But I believe in my heart she was the lass yer seeking."

"Where is Candlemaker's Row?"

"Outside my door and to the left. And if ye keep straight, you'll find Bristo Street."

Ravenna stood, feeling the weight of the work ahead. "Thank you, Aven, for your kindness and the refreshment." She stopped at the door. "If you should find my Georgiana or see her, I'm staying at Boyd Inn in Canongate."

Aven nodded.

Ravenna stepped outside the door where Braedon waited for her.

"Did you discover anything?" he asked.

She shared what Aven had told her.

"Then we shall look there." He offered his arm.

They turned down the cobblestone street. The scent of burning animal fat filled the air around the stone buildings. Some of the wooden shop faces were colored green, blue, brown, or black. But others had no face at all. The street was typical of the rest of the city with crowds of people, animals, carts, and carriages. They searched all along Candlemaker's Row and Bristo Street until the sun began to sink low in the sky.

Ravenna stopped on the corner of Bristo Street. Aching as though she'd been beaten all over, she leaned against the iron gate of the kirkyard. Hunger raked her ribs.

Braedon scanned the street. "I'm certain you're tired and hungry. As am I. And the sun is getting low. Should we stop for the evening?"

She rubbed her face. "I can't bear the thought of quitting, but I don't know if I can go on tonight." She watched the swirl of colors spinning from the setting sun. "It crushes me to know we're so close. She's here, somewhere, and I can't…" Emotion knotted her words. She cleared her throat and spoke, her voice quavering. "I can't reach her."

"All will be well," Braedon touched her cheek. "We will try again in the morning. Perhaps we should return to our respective inns to rest before we visit the docks tonight."

Ravenna walked beside him toward her inn on Canongate.

A high whining sound floated toward them. Ravenna stopped, transfixed on finding the source of the haunting music.

"*Píob mhór,*" she whispered. Her spirit unfolded its wings within her, the pipes of her homeland calling to her, tugging at her to lift her up out of the mire of grief, worry, and fear that had weighed on her for years. Tears sprang to her eyes. "I haven't heard the pipes in ages." The last time she heard such music was at her sister Helen's wedding, before their lives were forever changed; a time where pipes and fiddles filled the air as the family danced, sang, and enjoyed fellowship over a wedding feast brought together by the village women. All turned to ashes now.

"Bagpipes," Braedon said. "It's a shrill, frightening sound."

"Not to me. It's the music of my blood, my family and my home. I confess, these sound a little different, though. In Ireland, the tones were lighter, sweeter. There's a fierceness to these, I think."

The music grew closer as the piper marched in front of a unit of red coats. Ravenna's shoulders tightened upon seeing the bright red uniforms. The same uniforms that had once flooded her village and wreaked havoc, burning homes and brutalizing people. The same uniforms that had prompted Niall and her cousin, Colin, to join The Unity. Though she and her parents had remained loyal to The Crown, she would never trust a Red Coat again and hated the sight of them. Her family had been loyal, yet the commanding officer had painted all the Irish with a broad stroke. She took a deep, steadying breath. It was a strange juxtaposition to see a piper leading a band of soldiers; at one time, they would've killed him for playing the pipes that The Crown had declared an instrument of war after the Jacobite Rising in 1745.

As they neared their destination, Ravenna paused and pointed at a grand house, painted in the deep amber of the sunset, sitting on a large hill behind the inn. "Look. I didn't notice that when I left the inn this morning. It's practically a palace." Ravenna's gaze trailed along the sturdy limestone structure. Simple in its design, it consisted of a large rectangle with a flat roof set between two pyramidal towers. From the right tower extended a squarish building with a peaked tiled roof. A shudder passed over her. "It's a cold building. I wonder who lives there?"

"I don't know," Braedon said. "But whomever the owner is, he is quite wealthy, judging by the great number of windows."

"He must pay a fortune in window taxes alone." They turned down the lane toward Boyd's Inn. Ravenna paused. "I just realized this isn't your inn."

"I couldn't let you journey alone." He smiled. "I shall eat a hearty supper here to carry me back up the hill to Brodie's Docket. " He smiled and opened the door for her. "Shall we see what's on the menu this evening?"

"Strong wine, hot food. I can't imagine a better ending to this unfruitful day."

They sat down to a delicious dinner of a hot fish chowder called cullen skink, buttered bannock bread, and a bottle of wine.

Braedon dunked his bread in the stew. "You've been in your widow's weeds for some time. Do you think you would want to marry again?"

Ravenna washed down her surprise with a gulp of wine. "What a strange question. Why do you ask?"

"Mere curiosity."

He had said it with an affectation of nonchalance, yet she detected a certain reticence and sincerity. She broke into laughter. "Are *you* thinking of marriage?"

He toyed with the stem of his wine glass, his ruby pinky ring glinting in the candlelight. "I confess, I toy with the idea on occasion. I wonder at your laughter. Is the notion of me as a husband and father so absurd?"

She buttered her bread. "Well…" She fought the smile still tugging at her lips. "Surely, you're not ignorant of your reputation."

"I am aware."

Did she detect pain flashing over his features? Braedon had always had a rogue's reputation, running through society women like a fire. And for that reason, she'd been hesitant to open her heart or to get close to him. However, in recent months, he seemed to have grown sober, thoughtful, respectable, even—dare she think it—*gentlemanly*. In the past few months, he had even claimed to have feelings for her, swearing he wanted only her. Yet, she had regarded his proclamations with skepticism, never allowing herself to succumb to his many charms. Was this just part of his seduction game? She stared at the creamy pale stew in her bowl. How open should she be with him? Was he toying with her?

"I'm sorry. My question is inappropriate."

She searched his eyes. The sincerity there lured the truth from her. "I don't know. I haven't thought much about it. I've been in mourning. This month marks a year already." The words stunned her. Where had the time gone? "And this incident with Georgiana…I can't think about it now with much seriousness or clarity." She scratched the scar on her cheek, wishing she had some chamomile ointment.

"Of course. I suppose I shouldn't have asked."

"I suppose from time to time I've wondered if I might marry again. I don't want to be alone. A generous, intelligent, refined, and patient man might catch my interest. But I would want a man who wanted to be with me, a true partner. Someone who enjoys a bit of adventure, someone brave."

"So, the late Lord Birchfield wasn't adventurous or brave?" He lifted his wine glass to his lips.

She recoiled. It was her duty to protect her late husband's memory and legacy—even his worst characteristics. Just as he had always protected her reputation among his friends and family who had looked down on her because she was Irish and had once worked as an orange girl and an actress. She was a commoner, and Philip had shielded her from the ugliness of those who thought being born in a low station was in itself a crime.

"Perhaps I pry too much," Braedon said. "My apologies."

"No, it's not that." She dithered, searching for the appropriate words. Blast "polite" society for all their dancing with language. She deflected the focus from Philip. "I will simply say, my next husband, should I have one, will leave no doubt of his adventurous and brave spirit."

He scoffed. "Adventurous, brave, generous, intelligent, patient. The perfect man. Is it possible you know any men by that measure? Plus he must be an excellent dancer, sit a horse exquisitely, and be excessively wealthy. Perhaps you ask for too much."

She batted her eyes. He seemed almost offended. Was he right? Did she expect too much? "Well...I-I-I..."

"Excuse me." He jumped from his seat. "I should be going. I need to get some rest before going to the docks tonight."

"Should I meet you somewhere?"

"You shouldn't be wandering the streets at night. I can go alone."

"No..." She began her protest. "I—"

"Good evening." He offered a perfunctory bow and left the inn.

Chapter Thirteen

Ravenna rose in the dead of night. Braedon might've had notions of going to the docks by himself, but if Georgiana was among the girls on the ship, Ravenna wanted to be there so Georgiana could see a familiar face and so Ravenna could hug her and comfort her. Yet, it was dangerous wandering around at night alone. It was a risk she was willing to take.

Charlotte woke. "Milady? What's the matter?"

Ravenna slipped her feet into her boots. "Nothing is wrong. Go back to sleep."

Charlotte sat up. "Are you going out now? In the wee hours?"

"Only for a bit. I'm going to the Port of Leith docks. Braedon and I found some information that might involve Georgiana."

Charlotte threw off her covers. "You must be mad to think of going alone." She drew on her dress. "I am going with you."

Ravenna didn't bother to argue. They slipped out of the inn, borrowed a lantern from a servant in the courtyard, and traced the shadows from Canongate, passing in front of Holyrood Palace, and headed toward Leith. The air was thick and warm, heavy with the scent of heather and moss, with a faint wind rippling their skirts.

They made it to the docks. The water lapped against the wharves, and the boats rocked gently in their berths. The scent of the ocean rose up to greet them.

Ravenna extracted her dagger from her fan in a preemptive protective measure as they checked each ship to find *The Milton*.

However, as they approached the last ship in its berth, they heard the voices of men. Then, when they passed a stack of crates, they witnessed figures unloading items from a ship. Ravenna and Charlotte dropped back behind the crates to watch.

"Do you suppose that's the ship we're looking for?" Charlotte said.

"It must be." Ravenna craned her neck. "I wish I could better make out the men, though. The lanterns are too dim."

Behind them, the scuff of boots and a male whisper emerged. "What are you two doing?"

Ravenna and Charlotte both gasped and flipped around to see Braedon.

"Shhh!" Braedon warned with a finger to his lips as he squatted. He was without a hat and ascot. His shirt neck was open, and his hair mussed.

Ravenna slapped his arm. "You scared me near to death!"

He chuckled. "You must have both lost your senses to come out here by yourselves." Then he said to Charlotte, "Miss Hart, I expect this behavior from Lady Birchfield, but I thought I could rely on you to be her voice of reason."

Charlotte hid her smile behind her hand.

Ravenna said, "I'm here to find Georgiana."

"There are many men near the ship. Do you think two slips of women like yourselves can prevent being captured and carried off to France? What exactly was your plan?"

"I'm not certain," Ravenna said. "I thought if I could see the boat, see if Georgiana is there, then I could decide how to proceed."

He shook his head. "And?"

"I don't know. Perhaps I can sneak aboard and look for her."

"A horrible idea."

"What do you propose?"

"I propose we check again tomorrow night."

"Why? We could miss everything."

"No, we won't. I've been here for two hours, watching. They just arrived, and I've spoken with a contact. Right now, they are unloading the illegal items they've smuggled from France into that cart over there." He pointed to a cart parked several feet away. "Tomorrow, by light of day, they will unload the legal products they're carrying. Then they'll work on loading the ship with legal products. So, they will load the girls tomorrow night or the next night. Depends how long it takes to load everything else. I was on my way back to the inn when I saw you two sneaking about."

Ravenna peeked over the crates. "I think we should get closer. Try to see if we can identify any of the men. It might be helpful."

He said, "I know how we can get close."

"How?" Ravenna said.

He smiled. "A bit of acting. I can be a drunken gent with a lady on his arm, looking for a quiet place." He winked at her.

Ravenna rolled her eyes and shook her head. Charlotte giggled quietly. "It's not the worst idea. Charlotte, you wait here, in case something happens, you can tell someone."

Braedon stood and offered his arm. Ravenna pulled the top of her dress off one shoulder, pulled strands of hair out of its chignon, and accepted his arm. They staggered together as if they were drunk. As they neared the docks, he broke out in a drinking song, and she giggled.

They stopped near the cart of smuggled goods. The men loading the cart froze.

"Essuse me," Braedon said in his best drunken imitation. "My woman and I are looking for a comfortable place. Do ye know of any rooms to rent nearby?"

Ravenna giggled and rubbed her hand over his chest. Though she pretended to be drunk, she marked the description of every man present.

"I don't know of any rooms." One giant bald man said. "Take her into an alley." He motioned toward the buildings across the street.

"Oh, I can't do that. I'd like to get more gin too." He asked one of the other men. "Do you know of a place?"

"Go two streets down…" The man said.

Ravenna didn't listen. Instead, she watched the three men coming toward them off the wharf. One of the men was tall and wiry, but a complete stranger. The middle man was Mr. Muir, the very man who had talked the officer out of arresting Niall in York. The third man was none other than her own brother. *Niall.* Why was Niall here? She clamped down on her desire to fly at Niall in a rage.

She turned on her giggle and, walking backward, pulled on Braedon, though she communicated her distress with her eyes. She put on a thick Irish accent. "Come wi'me ye drunken addle-pate. I'll shew ye a night ye'll ne'er ferget."

He followed her, playing along. When they reached a safe distance, he said, "What are you doing? Why did you pull us away from them?"

They turned down the cobbled street to the left, making their way back to Charlotte.

Ravenna pulled up her dress to cover her bare shoulder, checking behind them to ensure they weren't being followed. All clear. "Niall was there. He was with Mr. Muir. I'd like to beat him with a riding crop. What is he doing?"

"I don't want to get between you and your brother, but you need to find out why he was there with those men."

"I know that. But I'm afraid of what I might learn."

When Ravenna and Charlotte returned to the inn, Charlotte went upstairs to bed while Ravenna stayed in the courtyard, waiting for Niall.

He strolled into the courtyard an hour later, whistling.

Ravenna stepped from under the tree. "What are you doing, brother?"

Niall stopped, hand to his heart. "Ye scared the soul out of me. Why the devil are you down here?"

"Where have you been?" She crossed her arms.

A slow smile of disbelief spread over his face. "Who do you think you are? Mama or Papa? I don't need to explain myself to my sister. Even if she is a noble now."

"I saw you tonight. Down by the docks."

"Then why are you asking me, if you know where I was? And what were you doing by the docks at night? Are you mad?"

"Why were you down at the docks with Mr. Muir?" Then it occurred to her. "Were you trying to find Georgiana? Does he know where she is?"

The smile died on Niall's face. "Why were you on the docks?" He stepped closer. "Were you following me?"

"No. I was down there looking for Georgiana. What were you doing?"

He paused. "Looking for Georgiana."

Her intuition prickled the roots of her hair. "You're lying."

"I'm not. I was looking for her."

She narrowed her eyes. "How did you know to look for her there?"

"How did *you* know?"

"Braedon and I questioned someone who gave us information."

"So did I."

She shook her head. "I don't believe you."

"Well, if you're determined to not believe anything I say, then I don't know why we're talking." He tried to step around her.

She stepped to block him. "I want the truth, Niall. Why are you hanging about with that man? What does he want with you?"

He nudged her out of the way. "I don't have to tell you anything. I'm going to bed."

"Niall…"

He turned on her, pointing at her. "Enough!" His voice echoed in the courtyard. "Leave it alone, Ravenna."

She watched him disappear into the inn. One way or another, she was going to find out what her brother was up to.

Chapter Fourteen

The next morning's breakfast delivered a most pleasant surprise to Ravenna in the form of her best friend, Lady Catherine Adair. Catherine sat by the window, reading a newspaper and drinking tea. She looked like a peony in her pink traveling kit and a pink bonnet sitting askew atop her pale blonde curls. In her mourning weeds, Ravenna looked like a crow in comparison. She recalled her conversation with Braedon about marrying again. Perhaps it was time to shed her widow's weeds, and start bringing more color into her life.

Ravenna rushed toward her. "Catherine?"

Catherine beamed and stood to receive Ravenna's tight embrace. "Oh." She chuckled. "You act as though we haven't seen each other in years."

"It feels like years."

They sat down at the table and ordered breakfast as Ravenna gazed at Catherine as though she were a miracle dropped from the sky. "How...why... I-I-I'm utterly baffled."

Catherine laughed. "Oh, my darling. You didn't think I would leave you to deal with this tragedy on your own, did you? Upon receiving your letter, I followed all your directions: wrote to both Harrison and Reverend Haworth, then I packed my things. And..." She dropped some sugar into her tea with a smile. "*Me voilà!*"

"I am so thankful you're here. Is Yarford with you?" Yarford was Catherine's cohabitant lover for these last seven years at least.

"He is. He and Donovan are at Iverloch Hall. They're attending to some business."

"Where is Iverloch Hall?"

"On the hill above Holyrood Palace, just as you enter town. We arrived in the wee hours last night."

"Do you mean that large, unwelcoming structure on the hill? Aren't you afraid to stay there? It seems so cold and uninviting."

"The exterior, I confess, is not very pretty, but the interior is quite comfortable with ancient tapestries, lush furnishings, and such. I think, were you to see it, you would approve."

"Who owns the house? And how do you know him?" Ravenna's food was delivered. She cut her ham.

Catherine folded her newspaper. "Lord Iverloch is Lord Advocate for Scotland, the highest-ranking official in the kingdom, second only to King George himself. He's Yarford's second cousin. I met him and Lady Iverloch at the King's birthday celebration last year and we've summered here in Scotland with them a couple of times before I met you."

"It's good you can visit with family while you're here." Ravenna stuffed a large bite of ham into her mouth.

"I didn't come all this way to talk about me. How are *you*? How do you fare in your hunt for Georgiana?"

Ravenna washed down her food with tea. "Things do not go well, unfortunately. I still haven't found her. We have discovered some information, but so far it hasn't led anywhere. The more I find out about Emmett, the more I'm convinced Georgiana is in a desperate and dangerous situation." The food turned to a rock in her stomach. "Furthermore, Aurélie is ill and currently resting in bed. I fear her pregnancy may be in danger. We were delayed an entire day because of her illness. And, my brother is behaving…strangely." She lowered her voice to a whisper. "He's been hanging about with a man named Mr. Muir, who is the very man Emmett and Larson were supposed to meet here in Edinburgh."

Catherine blinked. "You jest."

Ravenna shook her head. "I can't figure out what he's up to."

"He isn't still working with rebels, is he?"

"I want to say 'no,' but, I confess, I can't be sure."

"When did he get into town?" Catherine split her scone and slathered it with cream and black currant jam.

"He and Aurélie arrived just as I was preparing to leave for Scotland. He insisted on coming along to help, but he has been more of a hindrance." She told Catherine of all that had happened with Niall.

Catherine tsked and shook her head. "I hate to hear it. You don't need to be worried about Niall when you're trying to find Georgiana." She bit into her scone. "It's a shame he learned nothing from his last venture into rebellion. Maybe he's been working for Ireland while in America?"

"That's what I'm afraid of." Ravenna sipped her tea.

Catherine cocked her brow and flashed a playful side glance. "At least Braedon was here to assist you." A sly smile spread over her face behind her teacup.

"Yes…" Ravenna blushed. "There is that. He happened to be at Gordon House when I discovered Georgiana missing. He insisted on coming with me. As did Charlotte."

"Quite a coterie." She perked and lifted her hands. "And here I am with a coterie of my own!"

"And most welcome, I assure you. I am so happy you're here. You're the only one I can talk to about all of this."

Catherine placed her cup in the saucer. "Better yet, I come with news which, I hope, will be welcome to you and your party." She grabbed Ravenna's hand. "Lord and Lady Iverloch have generously invited you all to stay in Iverloch Hall."

Ravenna tensed. "I don't know, Catherine. I would hate to be an imposition. Does he realize how many of us there are?"

"Nonsense! You wouldn't be an imposition. Iverloch is family, and you've seen the size of the house, which is sitting practically empty. It's only the lord and lady. They have more than enough rooms for us all. We have no idea how long we will be here looking for Georgiana. We might as well be comfortable." She wrinkled her nose as she studied the room. "The food is far better than this inn serves, there's privacy, clean environs, no fleas, and, if none of that convinces you, there's an enormous library, the finest wine, and hot baths. And wouldn't it be grand for us all to be under one roof?"

Hot baths. Good food and wine. Privacy. A library. A good opportunity for extended bed rest for Aurélie. Even though most of Ravenna's time would be spent searching for Georgiana, having such niceties would be a great blessing. "I confess, that all sounds heavenly. I'll speak with the others. I'm sure we will all be most grateful to accept the offer."

Catherine glanced out the window. "There's Braedon now." She knocked on the glass and waved at him.

Braedon swept into the room and pulled Catherine into an embrace, kissing her cheek. "I'm so happy to see you. Why are you here?"

After a few moments of catching up, Catherine said, "Ravenna and I were just discussing lodging. You are also invited to stay at Iverloch with us."

"Gladly." He removed his hat and sat down. "I grow weary of the noisy Deacon's Docket Inn." Braedon said to Ravenna, "I've spoken to my contact. He thinks the girls will be moved onto the ship tonight."

"Can this contact be trusted?" Ravenna bit the inside of her lip.

"I can only hope. We shall know by tonight."

"Did he say what time?"

"The same as last night."

Charlotte jogged down the stairs and approached the table. "I'm ready to go—" She paused to bob a curtsey and greet Catherine and Braedon.

Ravenna stood and said to Charlotte, "I fear I must give you another task. We are moving to Iverloch Hall. But first, I need to speak with my brother and Aurélie. Come with me." She excused herself from Braedon and Catherine before she and Charlotte climbed the stairs.

Charlotte said, "Are we not going to hunt for Miss Sullivan today?"

"I am, but I fear I must ask you to stay behind to ensure our things get packed and moved to Iverloch Hall. Aurélie and Niall may need help with their things, too."

"I see." Charlotte's voice betrayed her disappointment.

Ravenna turned to her in the dim, narrow hallway. "I'm sorry, Charlotte. I know you want to help search for Georgiana, and you could be of enormous use to us out in the town. But for the moment, I need your help with this.

Once we're settled at Iverloch Hall, there will be staff to assist Aurélie, which will give you freedom to help me in the search."

Charlotte lifted her chin and stood proud. "I understand. Of course, I'll do whatever you ask."

"You're very good. However, I would like to utilize your expertise on one matter."

Charlotte perked.

"Where might I look for the sort of men who would take Georgiana? Or where might I look for Georgiana herself? Are there any particular areas of town or hideaways?"

Charlotte thought for a moment. "It's difficult to say. Mr. Emmett may have wealthy friends helping him, and they could be hiding in New Town. But there are slums near Grassmarket, Cowgate, and South Bridge. It would be easy for them to hide out in any of those areas."

"We were there yesterday. I suppose we will go back today. Are there any taverns or public houses in particular we should try?"

"You might try the Blue Boar in Cowgate. It's always been a seedy place where all manner of thieves, swindlers, and rogues gather. Do be sure Lord Braedon goes with you and that you both have weapons."

"Thank you. Now let's tell the others about the move to Iverloch Hall."

Niall jerked open the door. "What are you two out here clucking about like two hens?"

Ravenna said, "We've been invited to stay at Iverloch Hall."

"Never heard of it." He left the door open and turned away. He flopped down in the wooden chair by Aurélie's bed and stretched out his legs, resting his linked hands on his flat belly. His dark hair was out of its ponytail and fell over his shoulders.

Ravenna asked Charlotte to begin packing, then entered the room.

Aurélie pushed herself to sit up, and pink bloomed into her pale bronze cheeks. "What is Iverloch Hall?"

"My friend, Lady Catherine Adair, has arrived with Lords Yarford and Donovon. They are all staying at Iverloch Hall, that large house on the hill above Holyrood Palace. We are invited to stay there. Not only will it be far more comfortable, but they will have plenty of servants to look after you as you recover."

Niall winced. "We are not going. Iverloch Hall sits further away and up a great hill. We'd be better off staying here."

Ravenna sighed and rubbed the tight spot forming in her forehead. Why was her brother so stubborn? "Niall, be logical. If we stay here, we have to pay for our room and food. The lodgings are noisy, uncomfortable, and not as clean as Iverloch Hall is likely to be. Since we don't know how long we'll be in town, it's best to conserve our money by taking advantage of the free lodgings. Unless you have some great fortune I'm unaware of."

"Very well." He stood. "We'll go to the blasted Iverloch house."

"Be ready within the hour. I'm sending Charlotte and Lady Catherine with our things while Braedon and I go hunting for Georgiana."

"I want to come with you."

"Then you'd best make haste."

Chapter Fifteen

When Ravenna, Niall, and Braedon stepped into the street, Niall announced, "I'll explore New Town, and you two can hunt wherever you'd like."

Before Ravenna or Braedon could say anything, he strode across the mucky cobblestone street.

Ravenna glared at her brother's back as he wove through the carts and carriages. Why did he ask to come with them only to go off on his own? What was he up to? Ravenna sighed and rolled her eyes. "I apologize for my brother. He's always been difficult and stubborn."

"A family trait, I presume?" Humor lit his demeanor.

Her chuckle broke through her annoyance. She nudged him. "Must you always try to provoke me?" She looped her arm with his, and they began their trek up the Royal Mile toward Grassmarket.

"Oh, yes. Because I like watching your fire, the way it makes your eyes gleam like polished jet. It's quite entertaining…and alluring."

"Then I shall stop letting you provoke me."

"I doubt you are capable of controlling your emotions so well."

A man exited the Black Horse Inn to their left. They stopped short to prevent running into him.

"Pardon me." The man touched the brim of his hat and bowed his head.

When he looked up, Ravenna gasped. "Mr. Chadwick? When did you get here?" Her feelings were mixed. Though she had written to him in hopes that he would help search for Georgiana, he intimidated her and left her nerves in a jumble.

The Bow Street Runner wore a red waistcoat with a navy suit and black cravat. His dark, stony eyes studied her and Braedon. His brows puckered in confusion.

"My apologies, Lady Birchfield. Lord Braedon. You catch me quite… astonished. I hadn't expected to see you here, though you seem to have expected to see me."

Ravenna squinted at him. "Didn't you receive my letter?"

"No." He tucked his thumbs in his fob pockets. "I'm here on an errand. Magistrate Sir Fordham sent me to find the rebels who escaped us after we arrested Mr. McKirk and some of his associates. McKirk has informed us that his cohorts have come as far as Edinburgh." A twinkle rose in his eye. "My question, milady and milord, is why you two are here. I find it interesting that everywhere I'm searching for crimes and criminals, you are near."

"Those men you seek kidnapped my niece and stole my family's jewels. We have followed them here."

He winced. "I'm sorry to hear about your niece."

"I had written to you before leaving London with the hope that you would help us locate her. Mr. Josiah Emmett, the man who took her, is a scoundrel of the first order. I've learned he has killed at least one man prior to coming to London to create chaos in my family."

Braedon added, "We have also learned that Emmett and his cohorts are involved in the flesh trade, kidnapping girls and selling them in other countries for money to support their rebellion."

He clasped his hands behind his back and rocked back on his heels. "I see. How did you learn of this?"

"We've talked to a few people around the docks who have informed us of this."

"What are their names?"

Braedon's lip twitched. "Irrelevant. The name of the ship involved is *The Milton.*"

"Irrelevant?" Chadwick's left brow crept upward. "I need to know names so I can question these men."

"If I tell you who they are, they will stop talking to me. I need these connections. Can you not simply take our word for it?"

"For now, I suppose..." Chadwick sighed. "What else do you know about this ship and how they move the girls?"

Braedon and Ravenna told him everything they had learned so far.

Braedon crossed his arms. "I suspect they'll load the girls tonight. We're hoping to find

Lady Birchfield's niece among them."

"Perhaps we can all work together to find my niece?" Ravenna toyed with the ribbon on her fan.

Chadwick said, "I understand your impatience, Lady Birchfield, but my current mission is a delicate one. I can't risk exposure."

She suppressed a smile. If only he knew how discreet she could be.

"Further..." Chadwick continued. "You should not attempt it. This would be best left to me and my men. There are several here with me."

Ravenna looked through him. She would not stand down while those animals had her niece, but it was foolish to argue with Chadwick.

Braedon said, "We wouldn't dream of getting in your way. If we have your assurance that you will help us find her."

"Of course, of course." Chadwick squinted. "What does this girl look like?"

Ravenna said, "Her name is Georgiana. She is pretty, blonde ringlets, blue eyes, lithe figure, nearly my height."

"Any distinguishing features? You just described half the girls in Britain."

"She has a dimple here in her chin." She touched the center of her chin. "And she has a scar on her right shoulder where a bullet grazed her."

A bark of laughter escaped him. "Pardon me, but it seems your family leads quite the adventurous life, Lady Birchfield."

"It was an accident."

He lifted his chin, disbelief marking his features. "I'll keep an eye out for her as I'm going about my other business. It's very likely the people you seek are the people I'm seeking." He removed his watch from the pocket in his waistcoat. "I do need to be on my way. I do hope you can stay out of trouble, milady. Though, I daresay, I'm certain we'll meet again. And probably too soon." He dipped his head, touching the brim of his hat. "Good day."

Ravenna watched Mr. Chadwick zigzag through the crowd as she spoke to Braedon,

"We're still going to the docks tonight to search for Georgiana, aren't we?"

He looked down at her, his blue eyes shadowed under the brim of his hat. "Only death itself could stop us."

Ravenna and Braedon split up to visit homes and businesses to ask if anyone had seen Georgiana or Emmett. They planned to meet at the base of Edinburgh Castle, where it connected with Grassmarket. After Ravenna had exhausted her search, bearing no fruit, she crossed the street to Grassmarket where cheap tenements and lodging houses wrapped the base of the castle. In the open-air market vendors had gathered and farmers and merchants bartered over corn and other goods. Many of the pedestrians around her spoke with Irish accents or in Irish Gaelic, calling her heart and thoughts toward her homeland.

Her skirts whipped around her legs when the wind picked up and darker clouds rolled in. The black ribbons of her bonnet fluttered around her neck and face as she searched the area for Braedon. He crossed the street, his long black coat billowing behind him. Her heart leapt. For a moment, he looked like a great adventurer stepping from the pages of a novel.

"Do you have news?" His spicy musk cologne wrapped around her.

She breathed him deep into her lungs, looking up into his eyes like pools of blue water luring her into their depths. Depths which could prove to be dangerous, but she couldn't resist. She could spend a lifetime exploring those eyes and the mysteries they contained. Her gaze fell to his lips, the memory of his last kiss rolling back to her. The feel of his mouth on hers hovered over her lips like a ghostly imprint. She grew warm, pushing the memory away. For now.

He touched her elbow. "Ravenna? Are you unwell?"

She shook off her reverie. "Uh…I learned nothing new."

"I spoke to a woman across the street who thinks she noticed Georgiana in Blair Street. I think if we continue in this direction, we'll reach Cowgate, which we can follow down to Blair. However…" He glanced at the sky. "We might not get far. Looks like rain."

"We'll do what we can," she said.

They charged down the hill, crossing onto Cowgate, the stench of burning fat and fish filling the air from nearby Candlemaker's Row. The first sprinkles of rain began to fall, but they pushed forward through the coal smoke, through the crush of poor and working people.

The rain fell heavily, the stones growing slicker along the narrow Cowgate street, which seemed all the more closed in by the tall buildings and tenements. Though it was August, a chill from the rain and wind soaked close to her skin. Water dripped from the brim of her bonnet, and the wind blew rain into her eyes and down the neck of her spencer.

To the left, a blue pig-shaped sign hung from the side of a smoke-stained building. "Braedon. The Blue Boar. This is the place Charlotte told me about."

She scrutinized Braedon's face as she blinked against the rain. "Let's go inside." He opened the door and nudged her in.

Everyone in the dimly-lit room stopped to look at them. The conversation paused, then resumed its low grumble. Wooden beams crossed the ceiling, the walls had yellowed with age, and grime coated the windows. They took a table and chair near a low-burning fire.

A woman with tousled brown hair and a bruised face approached. She said in her thick Scottish brogue, "I think ye stumbled into the wrong place."

"Do you have ale?" Braedon asked.

"Aye."

Braedon slapped some coins on the table. "Then we're in the right place. We'll each have one. And if you have a bit of bannock bread and butter, we'll have that too."

She sneered and strolled away to get the food and drink.

Ravenna pulled her chair closer to the fire, placing her feet on the hearth to dry out her damp shoes.

The rain splashed against the window, coming down in thick sheets. "I hope this rain doesn't last long." She slouched in her chair, soggy and limp as a leaf in a puddle. "I don't know if my nerves can take much more of this searching. Truly, my patience grows thinner by the day…"

Braedon filled in the words she left off. "And your brother certainly hasn't improved your situation, if you'll forgive me for saying so."

"What's to forgive when you speak the truth? I wonder if he's made any progress at all? Or if he's even truly here for our niece?"

The serving wench delivered the ale and bread. They ate and drank, their eyes roving the room.

Ravenna whispered, "I don't like this place."

He glanced over his shoulder. "Your intuition is correct. When the rain stops, we'll leave."

The door opened, and a few men entered, removing their caps and hitting them against their thighs, beads of water flying. One of them signaled to the serving wench and shouted out an order for ales all around as they took a seat at a table in the corner. One man had a bandaged arm, a sparse auburn brown beard, a bulbous nose, and sunken eyes under a jutting brow.

"I've seen that man." She motioned with her chin. "The one with the bandaged arm."

"Where?"

"When I was searching for Georgiana. At Aven Brown's house. The house I went inside yesterday while you waited in the street. His name is Samuel. He hurt his arm working in a mill."

Moments later, another man walked into the tavern. Tall with an athletic build under his blue worsted suit, he seemed as out of place in this public house as Braedon and Ravenna. He wasn't nobility, but his clothes and manner marked him as a man of taste, refinement, and some wealth. His chestnut hair was cut short, *a la Titus*, and mussed.

Ravenna gasped, grabbing Braedon's hand. "That man!"

"What's the matter?"

"That's the man who helped Niall in York. The one who is supposed to meet Larson and Emmett. *Mr. Muir.*"

Muir lifted a hand to the serving wench. "Murdie, *feasgar math.* Bring me an ale, will ye?"

The woman laughed and said something in Scots Gaelic, making him laugh.

"What are they saying?" Braedon asked.

Ravenna shook her head. "I don't know. Their Gaelic is different from the Irish. The meaning is clear enough, I think. He appears to be from a different class, but he's quite at home here."

The men greeted Muir, then they all huddled and whispered over their ale tankards.

Ravenna wanted to approach the table, say something to Muir. She moved to stand, but Braedon stayed her. "Not yet. Not the right time."

She sat and watched them as she sipped her ale and nibbled at her bread.

One of the men was Samuel Brown. The man across from him was, like Samuel, from the working class. But the other man at the table—the one with the boyish face, thick brows, and mussed hair—was at odds with the others. Though his appearance was scruffy and rumpled, it gave the impression of a mask. Something in his demeanor and behavior—a sort of refinement— seemed discordant with his clothing.

As they talked, their manner, the angry set of their jaws, the high tension in their shoulders raised the hairs on Ravenna's neck. "These men are up to no good," she whispered. To think that Niall had been in the company of Muir and may still be dealing with him! It was intolerable.

"I wish I could see them, too." Braedon thought for a moment, then stood, moving to the window on the pretence of looking out. He wandered back to stand beside Ravenna, one foot planted on the hearth as he leaned against the fireplace mantle. In this way, he could talk to her, yet see the men.

A young woman in a striped cotton dress entered the tavern with a basket of flowers on her arm. She sat with a loud sigh by the window as she and Murdie greeted each other with familiarity. The woman pulled off her straw bonnet and fanned herself with it, sitting with her legs spread wide under her dress. Murdie put an ale, bread, and an apple in front of the woman. They both had dark feline eyes and the same pert nose. Ravenna guessed they must be sisters.

The boyish-looking man pulled a scroll out of his coat arm and opened it on the table. He poked at the paper and trailed a finger over its surface. Ravenna craned her neck. "I can't see. Maybe I should go over and say something to him, so I can see—"

"No, Ravenna. If those men are involved in something nefarious and they perceive you've witnessed something, you'd be in grave danger."

"Can you see?"

He stretched his chin. "Not well enough. Seems to be a map of some sort." He scanned the room. "Could be a mine map or a map for a journey. Might be entirely innocent."

She tipped her head and regarded him with disbelief. "You don't believe that any more than I do."

"Granted." He sipped his ale. "But I have an idea." He turned to the flower woman behind him. "Miss…" He waved her over. "Bring your basket, please."

She pushed herself to stand and approached with her basket of flowers. "Yessir."

"What's your name?"

"Esther."

He reached in his pocket and showed her a quid. "I was hoping you might do us a favor. It seems a strange one, but I'll pay you handsomely."

The smile faded from her face, and she glanced at Ravenna. "Depends on what yer askin.'" She planted a hand on her hip.

"See those men over there?" He motioned toward the table with his head. "Yeah."

"Will you offer to sell them flowers and tell me what's on the paper in front of them? However, I need your utmost discretion. Be subtle. Understand?"

"Why should I do that? And why do ye want tae know?"

"Ah, but I don't answer questions."

Esther's feline eyes flinched a little wider. She licked her lips and ran her hands over her apron. "I'm nae sure…" She turned back to Braedon. "I'm only asking them to purchase flowers and look at that paper? For an entire quid?"

"That's it. And then tell me anything you see or hear."

"Very well…" She held out her hand. "But I want my money first."

"Certainly…" Braedon handed her the coin. "May I have a nosegay for my lady?"

"That'll cost ye two pennies more."

He shook his head, amused, and handed her two more pennies, knowing he was paying at least double their worth.

Braedon handed a small bouquet of flowers to Ravenna. "For you, my darling."

Ravenna accepted the white rose surrounded by sprigs of heather and greenery. "Thank you." She tucked her nose into the flowers, taking in their scent.

Esther dropped the money in her apron pocket and meandered around the room with her basket. She stopped at a couple of other tables first, then made her way to the men in the corner. They declined. She lingered for a moment, making small talk, then returned to Braedon. She said, "Perhaps you'd like another bundle of flowers, sir. You look like you can afford it." She fixed a determined gaze on him.

"Yes, please," Ravenna said, smiling. "I can take one to my sister."

Braedon gave Esther two more pennies, selected another nosegay, and handed it off to Ravenna. He whispered, "We will meet you outside so as not to stir up suspicion."

Esther returned to her table as light poured through the window. The rain had stopped.

At the corner table, Samuel Brown used his good arm to hand a stack of papers to Muir and the poor man, who each tucked the sheets inside their coats. The boyish-faced man rolled up the paper and dropped it into a bag he carried. Finishing their drinks, they stood with a loud scrape of their chairs against the wood floor. They all chattered and shook hands. All but Samuel, who strode from the tavern as if on an important mission. Muir lingered.

Ravenna wanted to speak to him, but wasn't sure what to say or if it was safe to let him know she recognized him.

Muir checked his watch and sauntered toward the door, whistling. He stopped to chat with Murdie. She laughed and pushed his shoulder. He turned again to leave.

The words were out of Ravenna's mouth before she could stop them. "Excuse me, sir."

He stopped and frowned at her breach of etiquette. It was improper for women to approach strange men when they hadn't been formally introduced. "Yes, madame? Do I know you?"

"Not really. But you may know my brother, Niall Connelly. You kept him from getting arrested in York."

The frown lines etched deeper. Yet, was that a flash of recognition in his eyes?

"I'm sorry, madame. You must have me confused with someone else."

"No. I do not. Your name is Muir, is it not?"

"It is, but I do not recall you or your brother." His face softened with humor. "You must forgive me. I had perhaps imbibed too much to recall many particulars of my time in York."

She pretended to believe him. "I understand. At any rate, my family is thankful for your intervention on my brother's behalf."

He flashed a brief smile. "Good. Very good. Well…I'm sorry to rush off, but I have a matter of business to attend to." He touched the brim of his hat. "Good day." He strode out of the tavern.

A bit of white caught the corner of Ravenna's vision. There, at the table where the four men had been sitting, a paper lay crumpled on the floor. Ravenna crossed the floor and grabbed up the paper. A pamphlet.

Ravenna and Braedon stepped outside, the world slick and fresh with the recent rain. Water trickled from the gutters and dripped from the trees and rooftops.

"What's the paper you picked up?" Braedon asked.

They stood against the wall, their heads lowered together as Ravenna read in a quiet voice:

The madness of King George can no longer be denied. He is a danger to his subjects and his nation. He must be forced to abdicate by any means necessary. His first duty is to his kingdom and his people, not his pride and vanity. In fact, perhaps it is time for Great Britain to go the way of France and America. To cast off the crown! To at last be done with the antiquated and voracious monarchy that drains the blood from the populous like a surgeon's leech! Perhaps it is time for us to replace the Mad King George and his corrupt parliament with a Republic, placing the power of government in the hands of the rightful owners, The People. We are working for a free and independent Republic of Great Britain. Will you join us?

Ravenna and Braedon looked at each other, shocked.

"This is unconscionable," Ravenna hissed.

"It's worse than that, my darling. It's high treason."

The door opened, and Ravenna spun to hide the pamphlet behind her as Esther joined them.

"Thank you for helping us, Esther," Braedon said. "What did you see on the paper?"

"It were a map. I think a house. The word 'gardens' was written on it. But if it were a house, it were a grand one. Like a palace."

"Did you hear them say anything?" Braedon asked.

"Something like '...regimented schedule. He walks the gardens every afternoon,' and another said, 'my man says this is where he sleeps' as he tapped the paper. They locked up their mouths as soon as I appeared."

Ravenna and Braedon raised their brows at each other.

Braedon put on his charming smile, the same smile that had captivated Ravenna months ago. Or, if she were being honest, six years ago, when they first met at Lady Catherine's, right before Ravenna had married Philip. All those years ago, when Ravenna believed Braedon didn't even know she had existed because he was too busy chasing more acceptable women in the *ton*. He said to Esther, "Thank you, my dear, for your assistance. You have been most valuable to us."

"I have one question," Ravenna said to Esther. "Do you know any of the men's names? I only recognized a couple of them."

Esther shook her head. "No. Edinburgh is a big city, and I cannae be knowing every soul walking around."

Braedon added, "Understood. We would appreciate, of course, your well-paid discretion."

Her dark brown eyes flashed "Do ye think I'm a dolt? Do ye think I'd say a word and risk my neck or my family? I don't know what yer up tae, but I know I don't want any part of it." She shifted her basket to the other arm. "Now, the sun's come out an' I'd thank ye tae be on yer way afore ye bring the devil to the doorstep of my sister's 'stablishment. She dinnae need any more problems."

"Yes. We won't trouble either of you again," Braedon liked arms with Ravenna, and they walked down the street, pressed close together so they could talk.

"There were four men there. One of them dropped it," Ravenna said. "And there's little chance that even one of them is ignorant of the contents of this pamphlet."

She didn't want to acknowledge what this meant for her brother. Niall had been in the company of Muir when they were in York. And they had been at the docks together. Questions flooded her mind. How long had they been together? What had they discussed? Niall had a bad habit of drinking too much and barking about Ireland's freedom. Did Muir see a brother-in-arms for his own fight? Did Muir work with The Unity? Truth be told, Niall had been acting strange ever since York. Had he known Muir prior to their arrival in York? Or was their meeting and sympathies pure coincidence? Were they colluding now? And worse, how deeply was Niall involved in Muir's schemes?

As if reading her mind, Braedon said, "This doesn't bode well for your brother, does it? I'm sure many people have witnessed him in Muir's company. Or, if Muir is caught, he might implicate your brother in order to save himself."

"Hell's fire!" She shook her head. "Worse, Muir could threaten Niall with implication in order to blackmail more money from us. Or get Niall executed. There are a number of horrible ways this could be used against us." She rubbed the center of her forehead in an attempt to calm the dull ache pulsing there. "What am I going to do?" She tried to push through the flurry of thoughts to grab hold of one coherent idea.

Braedon took the pamphlet from her and tucked it inside an interior pocket of his great coat. "You will do nothing."

Ravenna stopped walking to gape at him. "Nothing? He's my brother."

"Yes, my little raven, but he is not a child. He's a grown man who fully understands the consequences of his actions. If he is determined to destroy himself, there is nothing you can do about it."

"But his family—"

"Will be cared for regardless. Either he will live to care for them, or he will continue along his foolish path and leave you to care for them. Or his wife's family will care for them. Surely, Mrs. Connelly isn't entirely friendless in the world. People make choices, Ravenna. And choices have consequences, my darling. You know that. Try as you might, you can't control what other people do."

He was right, of course. She couldn't decide what was more irritating: her powerlessness or Braedon being right.

Braedon touched her cheek. "My love…"

She looked up at him.

"Your only responsibility is to find Georgiana and protect her until she marries one day. She is under your guardianship. Niall is not."

She softened and leaned into him. "You're right…again."

A faint smile touched his lips. "I grow weary of this burden."

"I know. I'm sorry. I don't want you to shoulder my problems—"

"No. I mean, I grow weary of bearing the burden of being right." He broke into a smile.

She couldn't help but chuckle as she pinched his arm. "Let's continue our hunt."

He motioned down the street. "Let's. I believe we still need to explore Blair Street."

They resumed their trek, weaving through the workers carrying their pails, bags, and tools; the gentlemen and ladies in their fine clothes; the businessmen rushing toward their offices.

The wind pushed against them as they neared Blair Street, and clouds gathered to shield the sun. Ravenna admired the flowers Braedon had given her. She drew in their perfume. "You know something troubles me about this matter with Muir and his cohorts."

"What concerns you?"

"When I consider the verbiage in the pamphlet and the things Esther said…" She bit the inside corner of her mouth and looked at her flowers. "She mentioned they were talking about regimented schedules. A man who walks in a garden every afternoon, and where that man sleeps."

"Indeed…" Braedon fell into thought. "Why would they care about where a man sleeps or his schedule? Unless…"

Ravenna halted and turned to Braedon. "It's a plot against a man," she said. "They're targeting someone."

"My thoughts precisely. But who?"

They batted ideas back and forth like a badminton match.

"Someone important," she said.

"The regimented schedule and the garden."

"Esther said the map on the table seemed to be of a large, important house." Ravenna's eyes widened.

They spoke in unison. "Like a *palace*."

Ravenna recalled the pamphlet found under the table where the men had been sitting and the things in the pamphlet. She clutched Braedon's arm. "The king! "They're planning to kill King George!"

Braedon scanned the streets and the skies, his jaw set like stone as he turned something over in his mind. "We need to postpone the search for your niece, only temporarily, and write a letter to London. Catherine is intimate friends with one of Queen Charlotte's ladies' maids."

"I can't stop looking for Georgiana. I'm so close now. I feel it."

"We must warn the king."

"Braedon, if you do that, it could lead back to my brother. And while I accept I cannot be his keeper, I cannot be party to implicating him in a plot to assassinate the king. My entire family will be brought to ruin as a result. Can you at least give me time to talk to him first?"

"Would you sacrifice our nation and our king to save your family's reputation? Perhaps you have more of the Irish rebel in you than you realize."

Rage flashed like lightning. Without thinking, she slapped him. "How dare you." Her chest heaved, and her body shook with rising emotion. "You who knows what I've given to this country." Her voice cracked, and hot tears stung her eyes. "You who knows what The Crown did to my village. My family and friends. I daresay I've sacrificed more than *you* ever have."

He looked down at the ground, an imprint of her hand blooming on his pale cheek. "I suppose I deserved that." He sniffed, refusing to look at her. "I will do everything in my power to ensure your family isn't implicated or discovered." His frosty eyes, electric with fervor, held her. "But I will not allow the king to be ambushed and murdered." He took a couple of steps, then turned to her. "Are you coming?"

"It seems we're at an impasse. I have to find Georgiana. I won't quit my search."

He nodded. "It seems we each have our duty." He turned to walk away.

She stamped her foot. "Where are you going?"

"To try to save the life of the king."

Chapter Sixteen

Ravenna watched him stride down the hill, glaring at his back, yet wishing he'd return. But he didn't. He continued walking, with no sign of weakening resolve. And to involve Mr. Chadwick! She slammed the flowers on the ground, leaving their broken blooms in a puddle as she stormed down the hill to Blair Street. Chadwick was the last person she wanted involved in this aspect. He already believed she was corrupt. It was one thing to involve him in the hunt for Georgiana, an innocent girl set upon by wolves. It was another thing to involve Chadwick in something that could implicate Niall and open herself to scrutiny. If Chadwick discovered Niall's connection to The Unity, he might also discover her own treasonous past.

She turned left down Blair, a narrow street between two tall tenements. The stench of urine and refuse filled the air, and coal smoke veiled the sky above. Water trickled down the gutters, pooling alongside the walls where rats scurried on the hunt for food.

She entered one tenement and visited each door, speaking to whomever would answer, describing her niece and her captors. Whenever someone claimed they hadn't seen Georgiana, she begged them to contact her at Iverloch Hall should they come across her. Some chased her away from their doors, while others didn't answer. She slogged down the stairs, defeated and tired, desperation tearing her apart. She wanted to scream at the top of her lungs, *Where is Georgiana?*

Pushing open the door to the tenement, she stepped into the road and headed toward the next building, where a group of adolescent girls sat, singing and peeling potatoes.

She stopped, on the chance one of them might've seen her niece. Though, at this point, her spirits sank as low and limp as the potato peels lying on the stones. "Pardon me."

The girls cast their attention on her, their eyes filled with wisdom and confidence beyond their years. One of them greeted her. "Good day to ye. Ye look *dreich* as the weather, ma'am."

"I'm looking for my niece. She's been kidnapped." For what seemed the hundredth time that day, she described Georgiana and her captors.

One girl with a dusting of freckles across her nose and strawberry blonde hair peeking from under her mob cap said, "I'm not certain, but maybe I saw her."

Hope lifted Ravenna. "Truly? Are you sure? Was she close by? Where was she?"

"Yes'm. I remember her because I remarked tae Suzie here that she looked like a lady fallen from her horse. A nice dress, but torn a bit, and all dirty and bruised. She carried herself different-like. Like you. She were over near Adams Square."

"Where is that?"

"Just across the way…" she pointed with her knife, "on th'other side of Cowgate."

Excitement cut through Ravenna. Could Georgiana be so close? Could this nightmare be so near its end? "How long ago was this?"

The girl wiped her nose on the back of her wrist, blew a hair out of her face, and shrugged. "It were during the rain."

That was a couple of hours ago. So close. Georgiana might still be nearby. "Thank you! Thank you!"

The girl shouted, "Ye can cut through Adams Alley tae take ye faster!"

Ravenna waved in acknowledgement and ran toward the end of Blair Street, where it opened onto Cowgate.

She turned down Adams Alley, dim, narrow, and dirty as most other alleys. Just ahead was a turn to the left that might lead to her niece. *So close. Georgiana, I'm coming!*

A rustle and the presence of another person rose behind her. Just as she stopped to turn, someone grabbed her and slammed her against the wall. Her head smacked the stones, jarring her vision and knocking her bonnet askew. Thankfully, her bonnet cushioned some of the blow. She scrambled to pull herself together, but before she could, a gloved fist cracked her across the face. She slid down the wall, holding her face, stunned, blinking, trying to see her attacker.

"I owe you that one for my leg, *cailín*." Her attacker's pale blonde hair hung around his red face.

Larson. The Irish Unity man who had been hounding her for months. The devil who had cut her face and whom she had barely escaped once before. The root of all the evil in her life.

Because of her connections to the English government, The Unity had threatened what remained of her family to force her into stealing secrets. When her friend, the foreign secretary, had caught her, he then blackmailed her into double-crossing The Unity on the threat of treason charges. The foreign secretary then used the information to crush the rebel forces in Wexford. Several of the rebels had been caught and executed. Larson and a few others had escaped. Ever since, Larson had been seeking revenge.

"Aye. And now you get your comeuppance. First, I'll take care of you. Then I'm going after your brother. Then that pretty little niece of yours. Oh…" He released a dry chuckle. "I've been waiting a long time for this." Kicked her. "This is for Wexford." Kicked again. "This is for betraying us." Kicked again. "This is for my men who died because of your betrayal." Kicked again. "This is because your brother betrayed us." He kicked again.

With each kick, pain shot through her body. She caught gasps of breath as she coughed and rolled into a fetal position, covering her head with her arms, trying to protect herself from his boot. Her fingers touched the medallion on her fan. She worked the blade out of its holder. But she was growing weak. Tired.

A woman's voice rang out. "Stop that! Stop this instant, ye beast! Help!"

The sound of scuffling feet and men's voices surrounded her, along with the sounds of fighting, before she slipped into darkness.

A voice drew her back to the light. "Wake up now, love. Open yer pretty peepers, milady."

Ravenna's eyes fluttered. The voice and taps on her face insisted until she forced open her eyes to view the face of Aven Brown. "Mrs. Brown. I'm so thankful…" Ravenna's words pushed through her puffy lips, and pain shot through her jaw. She clutched Aven's arm.

"Oh, milady, let's get you up out of this muck." She reached down and helped Ravenna to stand. "What happened to ye? Did'ee get crossways o' that man?"

Ravenna felt along the wall and inched her way over to a wooden stool near a step. She eased down on the stool, pain fired in her head and burned through her body. Planting her elbows on her knees, she put her face in her hands, groaning, "I was so close." *Damn that devil Larson.*

"My boys and I chased him off. He won't be botherin' ye now."

"Your boys?"

"Ehrm, good friends of Mr. Brown. We was visiting a friend. Yer lucky I happened upon ye. You poor dear."

Ravenna pushed herself to stand, lightening bolts of pain shooting through her back and limbs. "I need to get back to Iverloch Hall."

"Come now, let's get ye cleaned up first." Aven looped her arm around Ravenna's waist and supported her, helping her walk a few doors down. Aven knocked on a blue door until a handsome man with reddish hair and warm chocolate eyes opened the door.

"Can ye help us, Callum? A man skelped her in the alley."

"Aye, come in." He stepped back and rushed to pull up a chair for Ravenna.

Aven helped Ravenna into the seat while the man rushed to pour her a drink. He handed her a cup; black stains marred his fingers. "Here, lassie. Take it all at once. This'll give ye strength." Ravenna liked the music of his soft tenor.

A narrow, bony woman poured water into a bowl. She eyed Ravenna with suspicion and spoke to Aven in Scots Gaelic.

Ravenna threw back the drink, which burned like fire down her throat and spread fingers of heat through her chest and around her ribs. Whisky.

"Thank you. May I have another?"

The man released a soft chuckle and spoke to the women in Gaelic. Ravenna tried, but couldn't grab any of the words, slippery as fish.

Callum handed her another drink, which she swallowed in a single gulp. Ravenna pressed the back of her wrist to her swollen mouth, and soon, the pain grew dull. Her eyes darted around the room, landing on the large piece of furniture covered with a sheet. She blinked, her head swimming in the liquor. A piece of paper peeked from under the sheet. The man traced the line of her attention. He stepped over to the sheet and kicked the paper beneath it.

The stranger woman, with her sharp features, approached with a bowl of vinegar water. Slumped, and wrapping her arms around her midsection, Ravenna didn't want to answer any questions, so she was thankful for Aven's incessant chatter while she cleaned Ravenna's injuries. The bitterness of the vinegar cut through Ravenna's senses and stung the wounds. The woman and the man stood in the corner, whispering. Even in Ravenna's hurt and addled condition, she felt the tension and suspicion.

A knock sounded on the door. Everyone in the room grew rigid. The woman flew to answer it, wiping her hands on her apron. She whispered in sharp tones in Scots Gaelic to whomever was on the other side.

Ravenna cut her eyes between the man and woman.

A smile faltered on Aven's mouth. "Well, there, dear. All is well. You won't be needing any stitches, thank heavens. And I see ye've had some recently." She touched the scar on Ravenna's cheek.

Ravenna flinched and turned her face. "A previous gift from the man who just attacked me."

Aven's eyes grew round. "Truly? What bad luck ye have." She turned to the woman. "Mable, do ye have any borage ointment?"

Mable pulled her lips into tight little lines. She drew a jar from her shelf, dumped some of the contents into a bowl, and set about mixing and slamming jars and bowls.

Aven reached into her apron pocket and pulled out a small brown stone, placing it in Ravenna's hand. "This here is toad stone. It'll protect ye in battle."

Ravenna sniffed, amused. "I could've used this a few moments ago."

Aven chuckled. "Aye. But since yer attacker ran off and is on the loose, I've no doubt he'll be returning to finish what he started."

"I can't take this from you." She held it toward Aven.

Aven put her meaty hands over Ravenna's and pushed them toward her. "Aye, ye can and ye will. I have another at home. You need this far more than I do."

Mable handed a small bowl to Aven, then spun away and stood by the window, peeking out of the curtain.

"I think I'm not wanted here," Ravenna whispered.

"Don't worry yer head about it." She slathered the oily mixture on Ravenna's face. "This is borage oil. Made with borage, a few other herbs, and pork fat."

The concoction smelled of cucumber and pork, but soothed her bruised face. A palpable tension filled the room, pressing against Ravenna like bodies in a crowded street.

When Aven had finished, Ravenna stood, swaying a little from the previous scuffle and the whisky. "Thank you all for your help and attention. I'm indebted to you and grateful."

The man nodded, his demeanor calm and sweet. "Yer very welcome, miss."

Mable's demeanor, anxious and gloomy, stood in stark contrast to the man. She gave a sharp nod. "Yer welcome."

Aven smiled. "I'll walk ye to the street and get ye a carriage to Iverloch Hall. Ye shouldnae be walking, especially that ruffian fool running about."

Chapter Seventeen

Ravenna hired a hackney coach to take her to Iverloch Hall. The rain had begun again by the time she descended from the carriage and crossed the stones to the large oak door. She knocked and looked around, taking in the stark environs. The house loomed cold and uninviting, purely utilitarian—all sharp angles without ornament or beauty—more prison or fortress than a home. Ravens along the flat roof cried out and jockeyed for position as the wind and rain increased.

The door opened to reveal a lanky, large-boned gray man with a bumpy nose and long face. "Good day, ma'am." His gray rheumy eyes raked over her torn dress and bruised face. His bushy brows drifted upward.

"I'm Lady Birchfield. My friend, Lady Catherine—"

He interrupted, animated. "Oh, yes, yes." He stepped aside. "Do come in, milady. We've been expecting you. It looks as though you've run into some trouble."

"Yes, I have, unfortunately." She stepped into the foyer and was transported back hundreds of years. The buttressed ceiling stretched about four stories high, rimmed with a gallery at each level, accessed by a large stone staircase. The walls, too, were stone covered with gilt-framed portraits, deer heads, tapestries, shields from various ally clans, and weapons.

Catherine came from a hallway behind the stairs. "Ravenna!" She gasped. "What has happened to you?" Before Ravenna could say anything, Catherine turned to the butler. "Grissom, please send Elsie to Lady Birchfield's room with bath water and some refreshment."

"Yes, ma'am." Though he appeared brittle as dried leaves, he moved with agility and vigor. He rang the bellpull as Catherine linked her arm with Ravenna's.

"Come, my friend, I'll show you to your bedchamber."

They climbed the green carpet rolled over the stone stairs, Ravenna's back and hips aching with the movement. On one side of the staircase loomed a life-sized portrait of Lord Iverloch in his hunting kit, a blue plaid kilt, and a blue velvet coat. He held a rifle, standing among his horse and hounds. Over his horse's saddle hung a dead deer, and at his feet lay a covey of dead grouse on craggy ground. The landscape behind him was moody, filled with mists and hills. He wasn't an ugly man, nor an attractive one, but interesting to look at with eyes too small and nose too large for his narrow face. His dark hair reached his shoulders and bushy sideburns trailed along the sides of his jaw.

Across from this portrait hung another of equal height, but far more dazzling. A dark-haired woman with sapphire eyes and pale skin. Hair braided with pearls crowned her head, and long dark ringlets trailed over her décolleté. The train of her crimson velvet dress pooled around her feet, where one slippered foot peeked out. She leaned on a stone balustrade, a shy smile on her face, staring out at onlookers from under her dark lashes, lending her a quiet allure. Lady Iverloch, no doubt.

"Who did this to you?" Catherine asked.

Ravenna pulled her gaze away from the portraits to look at the rain splattering the large arched window at the top of the stairs. The whisky was wearing off, and the pain splintered across her body. "Larson."

"The man who attacked you before? The one from The Unity?"

"Yes." She shuddered against the memory of his recent violence against her. She could still feel his hands around her throat, the jab of his kicks against her ribs and back, the sound of his raspy laughter.

"Oh, dear."

"I fear for Niall. I suspect he's unaware of Larson's presence. Have you seen him yet? I need to warn him."

"No, I haven't seen him."

They turned down the hall, lit by the windows on the left. Ancient portraits and a few ornamental tables topped with vases or statues lined the right side.

Catherine opened a door on the left. "This is your room. Beside mine." She pointed across the hall. "The room in the corner is Niall and Aurélie's. Your Miss Hart has been housed upstairs with the other servants. Across from you is Braedon." She waggled her brows.

Between her argument with Braedon, Mr. Larson's attack, and missing her chance to possibly save Georgiana, Ravenna wasn't in the mood to think about Braedon or any matters of the heart.

"At the moment, I'm more concerned about my family."

Catherine grew serious. "Of course.I apologize. Your tub and repast will be here soon. Supper will be at eight, I'm told." She patted Ravenna's arm. "Get some rest." She disappeared down the hall.

Ravenna knocked and entered Aurélie's bedchamber first. "Good afternoon."

Aurélie stood at the window, watching the rain. She gaped at Ravenna's face when she turned. "What happened to you? Have you found Georgiana?"

"I have not." Ravenna sighed, already tired of telling the story. She related a condensed and diluted version designed to mitigate Aurélie's worries. "I know, I appear frightening. I'm stiff and in a little pain, but I'm well. More importantly, how are you?"

Aurélie scratched her head. "Bored. I'm doing my best to get as much rest as possible, based on the orders of the last surgeon who saw me. However, I'm not accustomed to sitting in bed all day. I'm sick of sewing and reading. I want to be out in the fresh air. My baby is kicking my stomach to bits any time I try to sleep." She chuckled, touching her stomach. "And Niall…" She heaved a sigh and motioned at the window. "He's out there somewhere. I haven't seen him since he left with you and Braedon this morning. Do you know where he is?"

"No. I'm sorry. Did he tell you anything?"

"He said he was going out to meet someone, but he would not tell me who. Claimed it was better for me if I didn't know." Aurélie sat in the window and poked at the floor with the toe of her slipper. "I'd go look for him myself, if I could."

If Niall wouldn't tell his wife who he was meeting, it couldn't be a good thing—especially since the only person he knew outside of family and friends in Edinburgh was Mr. Muir.

Aurélie sat on the window seat. "You never answered my first question. What happened to you?"

Ravenna didn't want to induce worry and fear in her sister-in-law. She looked down at the floor to gather her thoughts.

"Your hesitation speaks volumes. It's The Unity, isn't it?"

Ravenna sighed. "Yes. Mr. Larson is here in Edinburgh, and he's hunting Niall and he's the man who attacked me."

Aurélie cradled her belly. "Are my child and I in danger, too?"

"I don't know, but it would be nearly impossible for anyone to breach Iverloch Hall." Honestly, Ravenna didn't know if that was true or not. She could only hope. "I believe you're safe."

They made arrangements for Aurélie to dine downstairs with everyone else, then Ravenna stepped into the hall, her heart heavy with suspicion over her brother.

Braedon was knocking at her bedchamber door.

"Braedon?"

He turned and wrapped her in an embrace as Ravenna grunted and winced in pain.

"I'm sorry." He pulled away. "Catherine told me you were injured. What happened to you?" He looked her over. "I'm so sorry I left you. I'll never forgive myself." He touched her face, tenderly, kissed her forehead, and stroked her hair. "Where are you hurt?" He held her hand and kissed her fingers, one by one.

"I hurt all over it seems, but I'm well. Only bruised and cut some." She told him what had happened.

His eyes flashing, he practically snarled. "I'll kill him for touching you. I will track him down and make him beg for death."

She caught his arm. "Braedon, there are more important matters." She told him about Niall. "Aurélie and I need to know he is safe."

He rubbed his chin. "Very well. I'll bring your brother back to you first."

Chapter Eighteen

s Braedon strode down the hall, apprehension tugged at Ravenna. All of her previous annoyance with him vanished into concern. Further, his search could take the rest of the night, and she couldn't afford that time. She needed to get to the docks by midnight at least to see if the women were going to be boarded on the ship tonight. Maybe he would return in time. But, if he didn't, she'd go without him.

Ravenna entered her bedchamber, where a small tub and a couple of buckets filled with water had been placed behind a screen near the fireplace. Gingerbread and tea sat on the table by the window.

A maid kneeling in front of the fireplace popped to her feet and curtsied, staring at Ravenna's face.

"I'm aware I look like a bog witch."

The maid bit down on her smile. "I've lit a low fire for ye, so ye don't catch a draft."

"Thank you. Will you undo my buttons, please?" The maid worked the buttons as Ravenna examined her surroundings. A thick wood bed frame with blue velvet drapes jutted from the left wall. A matching counterpane covered the fluffy mattresses. The space held sparse furnishings for its size, but had all the essentials: a washstand with a mirror, table, and chairs by the widow, a bedside table, and two chairs near the fireplace. The room might've been cozy but for the bare stone walls. Ravenna's portmanteau rested at the end of the bed, and her medicine chest sat on top. A nice enough room. Certainly better than the inns she'd been forced to occupy of late.

When the maid finished, Ravenna thanked her and stepped into the basin as the maid left the room. It hurt to squat to bathe, so she bathed quickly, splashed rose water on her skin, and dabbed chamomile ointment on her wounds. Wrapping herself in a lilac dressing gown, she sat to enjoy some gingerbread and tea.

A knock sounded on the door, and Catherine peeked into the room. "May I come in?"

"Please do. Join me for tea and gingerbread."

Catherine sat across from her, the stormy day casting her delicate features in a silvery light. "Before your arrival today, I spoke with Braedon." She folded her hands on the table. "He seemed quite agitated, but he wouldn't talk about it. Which surprised me greatly. I've always been his greatest confidante."

Ravenna nodded, swallowing her gingerbread. She related the story of her argument with Braedon.

"That explains why he wanted Lady Bess's address."

"Yes. He said you knew someone close to the queen. He didn't tell you any of this?"

"No. He said he didn't have time. It seemed quite an urgent matter, so I didn't press him. What danger threatens the king?"

"A potential assassination plot."

Catherine put her hand to her chest. "No, it can't be true!'

"I assure you, it is. We found a seditious pamphlet." She recounted everything she and Braedon had seen and what the pamphlet contained. "There is certainly a sense of unrest among the citizens."

"I have heard grumblings along those lines, too. I was speaking earlier to the maid assigned to me, and she said there are some weavers who are quite upset. They're threatening a strike."

Ravenna had heard from Aven about the weavers' discontent, but it was best to keep the information to herself for now. "Why?"

"As I understand it, their wages have been cut by twenty-five percent in the last several months."

"Which might explain the action against the king as well." Ravenna sipped her tea. "Perhaps the two groups think striking together will improve their chances of getting The Crown's attention."

"Do you think they're actually working together, though? Or is it coincidence?"

"It's difficult to say with any certainty."

Silence opened between them as Ravenna stared at the steam rolling off her tea. Her thoughts turned through the events of the day. She sighed and propped her head against her hand.

Sympathy notched a line between Catherine's brows. "Do you think you're getting closer to finding Georgiana?"

"I've run out of options so far. I've had only a few witnesses and little information. Without new and substantial information, I'm at a loss." She sat back in her chair and crossed her arms, staring out the window at the gray clouds and rain. "I hate to think of my failure, how I've let Georgiana down." Her throat tightened with emotion. "I was so close, Catherine. And then…" She snapped her fingers. "Gone."

"Oh, darling. Mr. Emmett and Mr. Larson are to blame. Not you."

Ravenna nodded. "I know, but it's hard to accept. Perhaps I might've prevented this somehow."

Catherine stood and came alongside Ravenna to place a hand on her shoulder. "You need rest. I should go. I only wanted to ensure all was well with you. And Braedon. You're the closest to family I have."

Ravenna put her hand over Catherine's. "I'm grateful for your friendship, and you are as much my sister as any born to me." She stood, her body protesting in pain. They hugged. "I think I'll take a nap before dinner."

"Of course. Come to my room when you're dressed, and we'll go down together."

When Catherine left, Ravenna crawled onto the bed, cocooning in the counterpane. Over and over her mind raced around Larson, the attack, Georgiana, Niall, and Braedon—his recent kindnesses, so different from what she had believed of him—and their argument this afternoon. Surely, if he had entertained any thoughts of marrying her, he'd probably given them up now. Braedon was everything Philip had never been, and he seemed fond of her. Though he provoked her mercilessly, and they didn't agree about everything, she couldn't imagine wanting any other man in her life. Was this love? How could she even entertain such thoughts? Even if she did love him, she wasn't sure she was ready to marry again. It was pointless and silly to think of marriage at any rate—especially in light of what was happening with Georgiana and Niall. She rolled her eyes at her own foolishness.

She stared at the wall, turning her mind back to business and mentally picked over what she'd seen at the home of Aven Brown's friends, their nervousness and agitation. The covered structure with paper sticking out from under the cover. It must've been a printing press. Were they working with the men at the Blue Boar? Were Callum and Mable the ones who printed the seditious pamphlet Samuel Brown and his friends possessed?

Then there was Niall. Hanging about with Mr. Muir. Was Niall involved with Muir's cause? Or was he somehow trying to find Georgiana through Muir? If only he would talk to her instead of being so secretive. In retrospect, his current behavior was quite similar to when he worked with The Unity. He had told Ravenna he wanted to heal the past and put the family back together. Had he lied to her?

And Aurélie. What would become of her and the baby if something happened to Niall? Would she return home, and Ravenna would never know her niece or nephew? Pregnant, far from home, ill, and in danger of losing her baby and her own life. She was fighting a long, silent battle against an invisible enemy.

Then there was Georgiana. Poor Georgiana. What must she be enduring? Where was she?

Ravenna closed her eyes and tried to stop the barrage of thoughts. But every time she closed her eyes, she saw Larson, the hatred in his eyes, felt his hot breath on her face, and heard his raspy laugh. This would not do. She threw off the cover and rolled out of bed. A touch of laudanum would help with both the pain and her sleep.

The wind whistled outside her window, and rain flew like spears against the glass. She looked out the window, shocked by what she saw—or didn't see. There were no city streets or gardens. Only rocks and crags and a steep drop. Apparently, the house was built on the edge of the hill. She stepped away and turned to her medicine chest, removing the chamomile liniment and a vial of laudanum. She smeared the liniment over her face, then, wincing, imbibed a few bitter reddish-brown drops straight from the laudanum bottle. Ravenna returned to the bed, listening to the whistling wind until the laudanum carried her away.

Ravenna woke from her nap, her head heavy and dull as though filled with mud. She slid from the bed to dress for dinner, tripping over the dress she'd left on the floor earlier. Picking it up, she examined it, noting the tears in the skirt, in the shoulder hems. Maybe the dress could be saved. Hart was an artist with the needle. If anyone could save it, she could.

She sat on the bed, the dress in her lap, running her hands over the soft muslin. Ravenna turned her mind again to Braedon, the night they dined together when he had asked her if she'd thought about marrying again and what sort of man she would marry. Maybe it was time to let the dress go—let all her widow's weeds go—to make changes. At least in that, he was likely right. It had been a year of mourning, after all.

But she'd grown accustomed to her weeds. In many ways, they were like armor, a defense. Her widowhood allowed her to move with the freedom through society she'd never known before. Many times, it was as though she were invisible. She could enjoy her eccentricities, like her fencing lessons. She didn't have to simper and play the coquette with men. She didn't have to attend functions she had no interest in. Best of all, she could own her possessions and have her own money. There were many benefits to being a widow.

Yet, she was lonely. Many times, she *wanted* to be *seen*, not ignored and rendered invisible. Was it possible she could be herself and enjoy the things that made her happy, with a man who appreciated her for *all* her little quirks, eccentricities, habits, abilities, and imperfections?

Her late husband, Philip, hadn't been the right one. He had loved her and she had loved him. But he had wanted to perfect her, wanted to educate and train away her imperfections and quirks. Ultimately, one of them would be miserable. But Braedon…The image of his bright blue eyes settled on her. Nearly every time she'd met with him, his eyes were filled not only with desire, but admiration and amusement. She charmed him. She entertained him. He *liked* her quirks and imperfections. He accepted her eccentricities. Philip would've never allowed her to dress in fencing kit, complete with pantaloons, and spar with a fencing master. But Braedon delighted in her unusual hobby.

Perhaps it was time to come out of mourning, to once again open herself to…possibilities.

Charlotte entered the room. "Are you ready to dress for dinner, milady?"

"Yes, of course." Ravenna stood, holding the dress. Her heart dipped into disappointment. She had packed only mourning dresses. Shedding her widowhood completely would have to wait until her return to Birchfield Manor. Yet, she could begin with a small change. She held out the dress to Charlotte. "This dress was ripped today in the attack. Do you think you could make some adjustments? It can't be patched, but perhaps it can be reconfigured. Maybe with the addition of another color?" She wanted red, bright, bold, passionate, adventurous red. But she erred on the side of caution and decorum, settling for a sober hue more in line with her situation. "Lilac, perhaps? Or puce?"

"Oh, yes!" Charlotte's face lit up. "First thing in the morning, I'll set out to the linen-drapers and find a suitable fabric. I'll have this dress refashioned for you in no time. Though it won't be elegant."

"It doesn't need to be. A day dress would be perfect." Ravenna stood at the washstand, examining her bruised face and swollen, cut lip in the mirror. "Now what do I do about this?"

Charlotte winced. "Perhaps you shouldn't go down to dinner tonight. Beg off with a headache."

"I hate to do that when I haven't even met our host and hostess yet. I don't want to seem ungrateful for their hospitality." She sighed. "I suppose I'll have to look frightful." She shrugged, dabbed powder on her face and applied a little rouge to her lips. Though it was frowned upon for a respectable woman to apply eye blacking, Ravenna hoped the accentuation of her eyes would detract from her bruises. She plucked a coal from the fireplace, crushed it up into an empty jar from her medicine chest, added a little almond oil, and gently applied the paste to her eyelashes and under her eyes, smudging the black lines to make them less stark

She showed the results to Charlotte, who wrinkled her nose. "I suppose it'll do, milady. The house is pretty dimly lit."

Ravenna laughed. "It's much lighter than when I wore it for the stage." She finished her outfit with a pearl necklace and earrings. She would have to make the best of her situation and hopefully tell the story only one last time at dinner.

"Have Braedon or Niall returned yet?"

"I'm sorry, milady. Neither have returned."

Chapter Nineteen

Ravenna, Catherine, and Aurélie descended the stairs together. Donovan, Yarford, and two gentlemen Ravenna had never seen stood at the bottom of the stairs. One of the men bore a striking resemblance to the giant portrait of Lord Iverloch on the wall. When they reached the bottom of the stairs, the men all bowed.

Yarford, Catherine's cohabitant lover, stepped forward and offered his hand to Ravenna. "My dear, Lady Ravenna…" The rules of politeness prevented him from bringing up her attack in front of strangers, though the marks were evident. "Please allow me to introduce you to my cousin, Lord Oscar Iverloch."

Lord Iverloch wasn't as handsome as his portrait, with pox-scarred, oily skin, and long, thinning hair with gray streaks pulled into a ponytail. Yet, there was a charisma and charm about him. He was the sort of man that men would follow into battle. He wore a blue tartan kilt and a matching sash across his navy-blue suit jacket. He bowed and spoke with an English accent, "Lady Birchfield. What a pleasure to finally meet you."

She blinked.

"I have surprised you somehow?"

"I was expecting a Scottish accent."

The skin crinkled around his eyes. "Ah, yes. I'm only part Scottish with ties to a laird's estate, which is why I have a position here. But I was raised and schooled in England."

"I see. Though I'm surprised, it's not for lack of pleasure in meeting you." She curtsied.

His eyes caught on her bruises. "I, too, find myself…surprised. Did you fall from a horse?"

She blushed. "I'll have to tell you the story at dinner, perhaps."

"A story?" Deep laughter bloomed from his broad chest. "I only wish I'd been told we have an adventuress in our midst."

Ravenna smiled. "I'm no adventuress, sir. I am, however, deeply grateful that you have provided us with lodging until I find my niece."

"It's my pleasure to do so. And how goes your search?"

"Not as well as I would hope."

He frowned. "That is unfortunate. If there is anything I may do to assist, you will let me know. Perhaps I have some connections who can help."

"You've done so much already just in providing us all a place to stay, and I would appreciate any and all help in finding my niece. Thank you."

He looked around at the group. "Please allow me to introduce Mr. Alistair Sinclair. He's a good friend and an important businessman here in Edinburgh. He owns a mill near Calton Hill.""

Mr. Sinclair was a lanky man with an angular face, a broad mouth full of large teeth, and a head topped with a mop of frizzy blond hair. His dark eyes displayed a sharp intelligence. He bowed, speaking with a nasally voice. "Lady Birchfield. A pleasure."

Iverloch clapped his hands together. "Since we are still waiting on Lady Iverloch, let's step into the drawing room for an *aperitif*, shall we?"

Ravenna glanced at the front door as they stepped into the stone room on the right. Paintings, sconces, mirrors, and tapestries covered the walls. Thick cream curtains hugged the windows, plush blue rugs blanketed the stone floor, and a low fire burned in the fireplace at one end of the room. In the center, under a crystal chandelier, several chairs and two sofas formed a conversation circle where Aurélie, Catherine, Donovan, and Yarford gathered. Though the walls and floor were stone, there was a cozy, home-like feeling about the space. The wind wailed outside, and rain pelted the windows.

Ravenna's mind turned toward the maelstrom and the descending darkness outside. Where were Braedon and Niall? Were they safe?

Lord Iverloch hovered near Ravenna as she walked the perimeter of the room, taking in her surroundings.

"It's a lovely room. Is this a family home?"

"Yes. It's been in my family since at least a hundred years before the Jacobite Risings."

Ravenna lifted her brows, interested. It now made sense why this house seemed like a medieval relic.

He pointed to a man in a black velvet suit with puffy pants and a large white ruff. "That is Lord Montrose. He was an uncle from many generations back. He once served the unfortunate Charles I, who was defeated by the English, the Scottish Loyalists, and a constitutional monarchy. When he was captured and sent back to London, Lord Montrose here helped him escape in 1647. They made it as far as the Isle of Wight and sought refuge with Colonel Robert Hammond, who they believed to be sympathetic to their cause. But Hammond was more interested in saving his own head. He gave Charles and Montrose refuge…then reported them to parliament."

They stepped to the next painting, which was an image of Iverloch Hall on a stormy day. Lord Iverloch said, "The king and Montrose, which is my mother's side of the family, were captured and taken back to London, where they stood trial—and were executed. The king, as a royal, was given the luxury of a beheading, whereas my uncle was drawn and quartered. A most horrible way to die. He left behind a wife and her five children."

The Iverloch Hall painting displayed the back of the house, where it rose up out of the side of the rock. Apparently, at the time of the painting, there had been a body of water at the base of the hill. Iverloch said, "According to legend, Lady Montrose waited for her husband to return, falling deeper into grief every day he remained absent. And, every day, she stood at the top of this tower, waiting and watching for him…" He pointed at the tall tower at the back of the house.

Ravenna tried to imagine where her room was in relation to the tower. It seemed to be at the other end of the hall. Rather than beginning at the ground floor, the tower began at the first floor and extended upward a couple of stories.

"Months later, when Lady Montrose heard the news of what had happened to her husband, she threw herself from this tower."

"Horrible. What happened to the children?"

"Family took them in until the eldest came of age to take over the lands and titles. The house passed through many hands until it eventually passed into the Iverloch line through marriage." He fixed his gaze on Ravenna. "Here's the interesting bit. Around a hundred years after the death of Lady Montrose, another widow, the first Lady Iverloch, whose family was Jacobite, lost all hope after their defeat at Culloden. When her husband died in the rebellion, she, too, threw herself off the tower rather than suffer capture or punishment."

"What a dark history," Ravenna said.

"Indeed. But it doesn't end there. Not fifty years ago, a young Lady Mary Iverloch lived here. She had secretly married her lover in a handfasting ceremony against her family's wishes. When her father, the third Lord Iverloch, discovered the secret and killed the young man in a duel, his distraught daughter threw herself from the tower out of grief and revenge."

He continued, "Ever since, the tower has been known as The Widow's Peak and has struck fear into the townsfolk and the staff. The staff refuse to enter the tower because, apparently, the ghosts of the widows roam the tower. Many years ago, one of my maids, who had been brave enough to explore the tower, swore that one of the ghosts attempted to shove her off the tower. She quit her job and never returned."

A chill passed over Ravenna. His small, hard eyes glinted with something like animus or malice before they slid under a veil of hospitable host. "Obviously, that's all silly rumor. I've never encountered any spirits. But, as you can see"—he pointed to the tower above the jagged hill—"it's quite a fatal drop to the ground below."

The door opened, drawing the attention of everyone in the room. A woman appeared in a thin gold dress with a low-cut bodice, long, dark ringlets falling over her ample bosom, and a mass of curls twined with pearls piled high on her head. She cast a timid smile.

"There's my angel now. Darling, you've met everyone except Lady

Birchfield. Come, let me introduce you."

Iverloch left Ravenna's side to offer his arm to his lady and escort her to where Ravenna stood. "Lady Ravenna Birchfield. This is my cherished Lady Fiona Iverloch. Lady Ravenna comes to us from London, my dear. In search of her niece, who has been kidnapped."

Lady Fiona curtsied. Her Scottish accent lilted, dipping deep into round O's and rolling over R's. "Oh, dear! I'm very sorry about your niece, and I hope you find her soon. It is a great pleasure to meet you, Lady Birchfield. A friend of Yarford's and Lady Adair's cannot be a stranger in this house. I hope you find our home comfortable." She batted her dark blue eyes.

Ravenna curtsied. "I do, thank you."

"Excellent. Should you need anything at all, please do not hesitate to ask. I'm sure we shall be great friends."

Ravenna smiled. Surely, she'd never seen a noblewoman, a woman of the world, educated and refined, so shy, inward, and ill-equipped for her role in society. Yet, there was a feline light in her eyes, sharp and cunning. Though she presented herself as soft and willowy, Ravenna suspected this lady was bolder and smarter than she seemed. Ravenna put on a gracious smile. "I'm sure we shall."

A man entered the room. He had short brown hair and long sideburns that marked his boyish face. "My apologies, I'd hoped to be here sooner."

Ravenna's breath caught as she stepped back. She had seen this man before. He was one of the men who had been with Muir at the Blue Boar.

Chapter Twenty

"Rotherden," Iverloch said. "So glad you came." He clapped him on the back and shook his hand.

"I wouldn't miss it, milord. I know there was a matter you wanted me to discuss with Lords Donovan and Yarford. I do apologize for my lateness. I had a matter of business to attend to."

Iverloch turned to the group. "Please allow me to introduce Lord Malcolm Rotherden. He's a clerk at my office with grand potential."

Formal introductions were made all around.

The dinner bell rang, and the guests paired off to file out the door. Lady Iverloch glanced back at Rotherden as she moved to mingle with the remaining guests.

Ravenna wrung her hands. *Where is Braedon?*

Catherine and Yarford sidled up to her. Catherine linked her arm with Ravenna's. "Darling, you look as though you've seen a ghost. Are you unwell?"

"I'm well." The wind howled outside. "I just wish I knew where Braedon and Niall are. The weather is getting worse." Which was only half of the truth. She also wanted Braedon to see that Lord Rotherden was the same man who sat with the conspirators at the Blue Boar; that a potential assassin was about to join them at dinner.

Pity traced lines around Catherine's cornflower blue eyes. "Oh, darling. They'll be back soon. All will be well. Come, eat dinner."

Ravenna trailed behind the other guests. As she crossed the foyer, the front door opened, and Braedon blew into the house.

"Braedon!" Hope skipped and fell flat when she realized he was alone. She ran to him. Water dripped from the brim of his hat and beaded his skin. The butler collected his drenched hat and great coat.

"Did you see Niall at all?" She pulled her handkerchief from her bodice and wiped his face with it.

"No, I'm sorry. I searched every tavern and inn I could find. I even asked around for gaming halls and checked those too. The darkness and weather made it impossible to look further. I'm sorry, Ravenna."

"You tried. Thank you. Surely, he's inside somewhere out of the elements. We'll just have to keep hoping he'll return to us."

He nodded. "If he doesn't come back tonight, then we'll try again tomorrow as we continue our search for Georgiana."

"We have to go back out tonight. Remember *The Milton*? Your contact said they might move the women to the ship tonight."

He rolled his eyes back. "Yes. You're right. You can't go. I won't have you out in that weather. Let me go. I'll take Donovan and Yarford."

She shook her head. "Maybe the weather will settle soon."

He grabbed her upper arms, his blue eyes fastened on her. "Ravenna. Listen to me. It's too dangerous, and the weather only makes it worse. After your attack today, I cannot take the risk of you going tonight."

He would brook no argument. Truth be told, she still ached down to her bones after the attack. Though she would much rather rest in front of a fire with a book and a glass of wine, she was determined to find Georgiana. She would contend with this issue later. There was still time to decide her course of action. She stepped closer and whispered. "I have other news."

"Oh?" He used her handkerchief to wipe his neck and under his shirt collar.

"There's a man here, a Lord Rotherden. He was at the Blue Boar. He's one of the conspirators."

He lifted a brow. "Are you certain?"

"Yes."

He tucked the handkerchief in his coat pocket. "Did he recognize you?"

"I don't think so."

"Let's hope not." He sighed. "We'll decide what to do about that soon. But for now, we must dine. And if we delay here any longer, we're likely to start a scandal." Amusement filled his eyes. "A lonely widow alone for an extended time with a wild buck of a lord. What things will they say about us?"

She tapped his arm with her fan. "Do be serious."

He checked himself in the hall mirror, arranging his clothes and running his hands through his damp hair. "I don't have time to change for dinner, so I suppose I must go in a bit soggy." He offered his arm. "Shall we dine, my little raven?"

The guests all sat around the table in the center of the dim stone room lit with candles. The dining room reminded her of a medieval banquet hall with deer heads, tapestries, coats of arms, weapons, and sconces hanging on the walls.

The conversation began with horses and sport, then Lady Iverloch said to Aurélie, "I understand, Mrs. Connelly, you are from America."

"Yes." Aurélie stirred her soup. "I am."

"I've always admired the Americans." Lady Iverloch took a bite of her soup. "For a small set of colonies to rise up and succeed in releasing itself from the British Empire is remarkable."

A cautious smile played on Aurélie's lips. "Perhaps. But there are still many problems to overcome in our country."

"No doubt." Lady Iverloch's jewels twinkled in the candlelight. "But you have independence, freedom. And *that* is a precious gift, indeed."

Lord Iverloch cleared his throat. "Well, I—"

Lady Iverloch cut him off. "So what province do you come from?"

"From the Louisiana Territory. We feared what would become of us with Napoleon, but right before sailing, we learned that our leaders had purchased the land from France. I'm not certain what will happen. I suppose it will become a state. Or several states since the territory is quite large."

"Napoleon…" Iverloch scoffed. "Damnable fellow."

With that, the conversation turned to Napoleon, England's second engagement with him, and how the war affected life at home.

"I hear talk of unrest here in Scotland," Lady Iverloch said.

"Indeed," said Sinclair. "Another group of workers walked out of my mill this evening. A full two hours before they were due to quit working."

Rotherden and Lady Iverloch locked eyes across the table. She smiled, sipping her wine. Rotherden's attention lingered on Lady Iverloch, almost like…a lover.

"Why would they leave? " Aurélie asked. "What is their reason?"

"It's my understanding they have just cause." Ravenna lowered her spoon. "I've heard their wages have been reduced as much as twenty-five percent in the last several months."

Sinclair cut his meat. "I'm sure the workers believe they have reason to complain, but they would be wise to remember a reduced salary is better than none at all. With so few factories, the influx of the Irish and the tenant farmers clearing out of the Highlands, the striking workers can be quickly replaced. Further, with the prices of cotton and the tariffs placed on our exports by the American colonies, we have little choice. We must save money where we can, or we all will be out of wages. It's best to keep some sort of job. Don't you agree, Rotherden?"

Rotherden paused to swallow his food. "I think you're correct. While many of the Scottish and Irish are immigrating elsewhere, thousands have remained here, desperate for employment."

"But a twenty-five percent reduction in pay? Surely that is too severe. What of their families?" Ravenna tasted her lobster bisque.

Iverloch wiped his mouth on his napkin. "But if the mills go out of business completely, there will be no jobs at all, which will guarantee the starvation and despair of the workers and their families."

"You aren't wrong, sir." Ravenna sipped her wine. "But shouldn't there be some wage protections for the workers?"

Sinclair smirked. "Such as, milady? Your compassion is admirable, but I think your lack of experience in running a business must interfere with your understanding of the matter. If we mill owners allow the workers to have everything they desire, they will run roughshod over us, and we will lose complete control."

Ravenna bit into her bread with herbed butter. "I suppose you aren't wrong on that point, either. Though I think protecting only business interests over the survival of workers is worse than unkind. It's wicked. After all, how can a business stay in operation without its workers?"

Sinclair snickered. "What should I do? Allow the workers to have their way in everything? Should I give them brandy and pineapple ice cream for their tea and allow midday naps? Respectfully, if you knew anything of business, milady, you would know that handling workers like kittens only spoils them, and they begin to behave as though they should be treated like royalty."

Ravenna glared at Mr. Sinclair through the flickering candles, fighting her desire to throw a chunk of her bread at him.

"Have the men become violent?" Braedon asked.

"Not yet, milord." Sinclair pushed back his empty soup bowl.

Rotherden added, "I wager, if the workers become too raucous, they will be swiftly managed."

"Indeed." Sinclair looked down his nose. "We will not tolerate insubordination."

"How will they be dealt with?" Lady Iverloch lowered her soup spoon.

"Our king's soldiers will put the rebels in proper order, and production will continue. We can't allow complete anarchy." Sinclair sipped his wine.

Ravenna blinked. She knew all too well what 'soldiers' and 'proper order' meant. The protestors would be rounded up, put in prison, and possibly hanged. Or, in some cases, shot on site. "You would call in troops to suppress workers who are rightfully angry?"

Humor entered Lady Iverloch's voice, "You sound like a Jacobin, Lady Birchfield. Would you prefer chaos? Would you prefer the workers burn down mills and have their way in everything?"

Ravenna frowned at her. Only a moment ago, she was singing the praises of the American rebellion. Yet now she dared accuse Ravenna of Jacobinism? "I am no Jacobin. Further, I've been a commoner for most of my life until these last five years…" Under the table, she balled her hand into a fist. "I understand the grievances of commoners in a way few at this table can possibly comprehend, and I will not be called a Jacobin. Whatever their complaints, however valid they may have been, their behavior in France—the murder of innocent people, the violence—is insupportable. Regardless, it's outrageous to turn troops on subjects who simply want to feed their families. Do you not think that is cruel and wicked?"

Something dark and angry slithered over the sweet mask on Lady Iverloch's demeanor. "I wonder what you would have our government do? Let the workers burn down mills and riot in the streets? Our business owners and other subjects deserve protections, too, do they not?"

Catherine, ever the proficient hostess, turned the conversation to lighter topics. "You know, I believe Scotland is one of the prettiest places I've ever seen. Lord Iverloch, do you have good sea-bathing here? Where is the best place? I do love a bit of sea-bathing in the summer and would like to partake before summer ends."

Lady Iverloch brightened, the dark thing in her demeanor dissipating. "Scotland has some of the loveliest beaches for bathing you'll ever see! Not long ago bathing machines were brought in to help us ladies maintain our modesty. I don't go to the beach often, for I prefer the wilds of the Highlands myself. Now, *there* are the most magical, majestic, sublime landscapes you'll ever lay eyes on."

Ravenna gazed at her in wonder. Lady Iverloch had transformed into something near angelic. She softened toward her hostess. "You are from the Highlands then, I gather?"

"Oh, yes. My homeland was the most beautiful of all: mountains and glens, moors, and lochs surrounded by giant ancient trees. Most of my childhood was spent playing along Loch Ness, climbing trees, and playing in the water with my siblings and cousins. My family lived not a mile from Urquhart Castle, until the tenant clearances. A dark glitter entered her eyes. That was a bitter time in our family's history. We had lived on and worked the land for many generations. Then, all of a sudden, we were forced off the land into the lowlands. Scotland is in my bones and blood, my flesh is fashioned from this land."

When dinner was finished, and after the men enjoyed their brandy and cigars, everyone gathered together in the formal drawing room.

Ravenna, Braedon, and Donovan gathered in a corner with sherry cordials.

"Conversation at dinner was interesting, was it not?" Donovan said.

Braedon sipped his sherry. "Indeed. Sinclair strikes me as something of a despot."

Donovan nodded. "It's worse than Iverloch and his friends imagine. This goes beyond some disgruntled millworkers."

Ravenna's brows shot up. "Oh? What makes you say so?"

He lowered his voice. "My concern for Georgiana is only part of the reason I'm here. I was sent here for an official purpose. I've been asked to confirm that a different sort of rebellion is fomenting in the streets of Edinburgh and perhaps over all of Scotland."

Ravenna and Braedon exchanged a look of concern.

Donovan caught the silent communication. "What? What do you know? What have you two heard?"

Ravenna stepped closer and whispered behind her open fan. "I think there is a rebel faction developing plans to assassinate the king. They may be colluding with others who seek to invade England while the nation is in turmoil."

"What makes you say so?" Donovan leaned closer.

Braedon reached into his coat pocket and withdrew the folded pamphlet they picked up at the Blue Boar. "We found this today."

Setting his sherry glass on the window casement, Donovan accepted the pamphlet and skimmed it. "My God," he whispered.

Ravenna said, "I saw a man named Muir with three other men. I didn't recognize one of them, but I believe the other man was none other than Lord Rotherden."

Donovan frowned and glanced over his shoulder at Rotherden. "Who is this Muir you mentioned?"

Before Ravenna could tell him what she knew, Lady Iverloch approached their group. "The gossip in this corner must be incredible, the way you're all huddled together. I confess, I do like a bit of gossip."

Donovan whipped around, hiding the pamphlet behind his back.

Ravenna put on a smile. "Yes, but I'm sure our gossip would bore you since it involves my family."

When Lord Rotherden walked up, distracting Lady Iverloch, Donovan folded the pamphlet and slipped it into his coat pocket.

Rotherden said, "Lord Braedon, Lord Donovan, I almost forgot to tell you: I'm having a special dinner tomorrow night for some businessmen in town. I'm looking for investors for a new mill I'd like to open. Since you care about workers finding employment, you might want to join us."

Donovan said, "It sounds fascinating, but I'm otherwise engaged."

Braedon smiled. "I'd be happy to attend. What time should I be there?"

"Dinner is at eight, but please do come early. We'll play billiards or shoot targets to pass the time."

"I look forward to it." Braedon sipped his drink.

Rotherden emptied his sherry glass. "Lady Iverloch, I have good news for you. I've heard talk of King George visiting Scotland within the next couple of months."

"I'm very glad to hear it!" She beamed. "It's time he comes to visit his Scottish subjects. We love our king and have been loyal to him. We'd welcome a visit from him so he can see for himself not only our loyalty, but how quickly we're growing here. I'm sure he'd consider us his crown jewel."

Donovan frowned. "I'm curious, Lord Rotherden, where did you hear this news?"

Rotherden thought. "I can't quite remember. These things get passed around so quickly and from so many corners. Perhaps as England's envoy, you can confirm the report, Donovan?"

Donovan shrugged a shoulder. "I'm sorry to disappoint you, Rotherden. I'm not privy to the king's itinerary."

Rotherden handed off his glass to a footman circulating with a tray, "I wonder if he comes in hopes of appeasing the people and suppressing the outrage brewing in the mills and among the workers?"

Donovan swirled the sherry in his glass. "I think the unrest brewing in Edinburgh goes deeper than angry workers."

"What makes you say so?" Rotherden smirked.

"The Irish, among others, have come here in droves to find work. In order to secure employment, they accept a cheaper wage, which undercuts the Scottish weavers and puts them out of work. Naturally, this agitates the Scottish. I don't necessarily fault the starving workers who come here looking for work, but it's hurting the Scots who already live here. Of course, the mill owners care little who's doing the work as long as it gets done. And they're happy enough to pay these people far less than they pay the Scottish to get the same amount of product."

"A harsh view of the mill owners, don't you think?" Rotherden said. "After all, they, too, are Scottish. Usually. I'm sure they want the best for their people."

"I don't think it's a harsh view at all. Hear me out." Donovan accepted a full glass of sherry from a footman's tray. "The mill owners' greed is driving the workers toward radicalized groups that have become a hiding place for political dissidents."

Lady Iverloch and Rotherden glanced at each other.

Ravenna studied them. They seemed concerned, but not as though they were concerned about the workers. Unless she misread their demeanors, their concern seemed more… self-interested.

"Have you heard anything definitive about such dissidents?" Rotherden's hazel eyes darted.

"Not yet," Donovan said. "But I expect I might hear something soon."

A nervous laugh escaped Lady Iverloch. "I'm being a horrible hostess. I need to attend to the other guests. Please excuse me."

Lord Rotherden hesitated. "I, uh…" He bowed. "Excuse me. There is something I would discuss with Mr. Sinclair."

When Lady Iverloch and Rotherden were out of earshot, Donovan turned to Ravenna and Braedon. "Thank you both for the information. Since the king is planning a trip here, I've been asked to report my findings to the prime minister to ensure the trip will be a safe one. Reports I've heard indicate he may be in great danger. I will certainly make sure the prime minister sees the pamphlet." He patted his pocket. "If either of you hear of anything else, do not hesitate to let me know."

Ravenna did know more, and she wished she could tell him everything she knew. Donovan was a friend, and she hated lying to him, but she couldn't tell him the whole truth. Not yet. First, she didn't want to implicate that poor, injured man, Samuel Brown. Granted, he might be involved in a plot against the king, and that was unjustifiable, but her sympathies for the workers tore at her loyalties. She liked Aven Brown. She didn't want to get them into trouble—even if they had made their choices and the subsequent consequences. Also, she was afraid of saying much more for fear of implicating Niall or herself.

She hadn't heard of potential worker uprisings, but something was clearly bubbling under the surface of the city. She'd encountered Larson, which meant the Irish Unity was in Scotland, but to what degree did they influence the local political climate? Were they working to unify with Scottish dissidents and disgruntled workers? Possibly.

Best to keep quiet for now.

Chapter Twenty-One

When the clock rang midnight in the foyer below, Ravenna stood, already dressed in her weeds and a black cape, her hair pinned into a tight chignon. She opened the casement to check the weather. The storms had passed. The night smelled fresh and clean as sun-dried laundry.

She hooked her fan on her wrist and, quiet as a whisper, carrying her boots in one hand and a rushlight in the other, she slipped out of her bedchamber and down the stairs. A lantern sat on the table by the front door. She lit the lantern, put on her boots, and left the house.

As she passed through the courtyard, she heard whispering and soft laughter. She followed the sound to the side of the house. Pressing against the wall, she peeked around the corner to find Lady Iverloch entwined with a man who was not her husband. *Lord Rotherden.*

She bit down on her lip. *Oh heavens!*

Lady Iverloch pulled Rotherden against her. "I have an important letter hidden somewhere on my body. It contains critical information I've received from our friends in London."

"Do tell."

"They've settled on a date. I wanted to give it to you earlier, but couldn't find a good time. Too many people milling about. When our guests are gone, it'll be easier to proceed." They kissed hungrily. "Can you find where I've hidden it?"

He laughed, his hand roving her body in search of the letter as she giggled. He pulled it out of the top of her stocking as he kissed her.

"You found the letter much too quickly." She pouted. "I'd hoped this game would last longer."

"My dear, this game has just begun." He kissed her again, his mouth trailing down her neck.

Ravenna backed away. She didn't want to see more, though she wished she knew what the letter contained. She lowered the light on her lantern and shielded it with her cape as she followed the path down the craggy hill, traveled past Holyrood Palace, and took the Easter road, along the stone fences lining the pastures on either side, until she reached the Port of Leith.

A breeze rolled off the water, carrying the scent of fish and mud. Ships lined the wharves, bobbing gently in the water. She passed up the street and around the buildings to come down the row of buildings nearest *The Milton* without attracting any attention. She lowered the light on her lantern and passed down the alley closest to the ship. She stood in the alley and put the lantern behind her as she peeked around the corner at the ship.

Several men stood on the dock in front of *The Milton*, talking and laughing. Had she missed the girls?

"When will the shipment be here?" One man asked.

"Any moment now," another answered.

Soon, the sound of carts and horse tack sounded nearby, and the noise grew ever closer until a cart passed where she stood, followed closely by a few men on horses. She drew back, moving deeper into the alley.

When the men jumped down from their horses, she returned to her spot, pressed flat against the wall, peeking around the corner. The men on the dock carried lanterns. One of them called out, "We've been waiting all night. We need to hurry and get the chits aboard. Where're they at?"

A few men surrounded a farmer's cart loaded with about ten girls, all bound, gagged, and ragged. Some cried and whimpered. Others sat stoic and still. Pity and anger twisted together and knotted her throat. She wanted to rush from hiding and do something to save the girls, but she couldn't. It was impossible to fight against so many men with her little dagger. She squinted her eyes to see better, but the darkness hindered her ability to make out anyone's features at this distance. Except for one man. His pale hair and skin practically glowed in the dim lantern light. *Mr. Larson.*

Images of his attack flooded her, and her body shook in response. She shut her eyes and swallowed, struggling to still her breath. At least she knew Braedon's contact was telling the truth. The Unity was working in Edinburgh, and they were involved in the flesh trade.

She opened her eyes to examine the men again. None of them seemed to be Mr. Emmett. *If only I could get closer to see if one of those girls is Georgiana.* She bit down on her lip and dug her fingers into the stone wall.

One of the men spoke, a tight, nasally voice. "When will you sail?"

"Tomorrow at dawn."

Panic rose in Ravenna. Dawn was only a few hours away. Once those girls were on board and hidden away, the chances of rescue were nil. There was nothing she could do. She leaned limp, powerless against the wall. Those girls were going to be loaded up like livestock and shipped away from their homeland, never to be seen again, and there was nothing she could do about it.

Chadwick! She grabbed her lantern and picked her way down the alley on tiptoes. She traced the way she came, the long way around the buildings to avoid the men near the ships.

Once Ravenna made it to the edge of the docks, she glanced behind her to ensure she wasn't being followed when someone said, "Have you lost your senses to be wandering around the docks at night?"

She gasped and spun around to face an irritated Braedon and an amused Donovan and Yarford, all dressed down without hats or ascots. And all carrying pistols.

"Perhaps in your attack this afternoon, your brain became addled, and that's why you're putting yourself in this extreme danger. Are you and your family not in enough peril, so you decided to come out here and tempt fate? I cannot believe your temerity, Ravenna—"

"I don't have time for this. I have to find Mr. Chadwick." She pushed through them and ran in the direction of Holyrood Palace.

Braedon followed her, grabbed her, and turned her around.

"Let me go!" She slapped at him with her folded fan. "I don't have time!"

CHAPTER TWENTY-ONE

"What are you doing?"

"The girls are at the docks. The men are preparing to load them on *The Milton* now, and they're sailing at dawn. We need to get Chadwick. Maybe he can gather some men to help and put a stop to this. We have to rescue those girls before the ship sails. I could lose Georgiana forever!" She jerked her arm away and ran.

Braedon called out to Donovan and Yarford. "Stay here and watch them. Ravenna and I will fetch Chadwick."

Mr. Chadwick descended the stairs at the Black Horse Inn in a rumpled shirt and pantaloons, his hair mussed. The innkeeper followed him, apologizing. "I'm sorry, sir. They made me wake you."

"It's all right, all right, McGriner. Don't fret. What time is it?"

"Two in the morning, sir."

He reached the foyer and stared, bleary-eyed, at Ravenna and Braedon. "I might've known you two would be involved." He ran his hands through his hair and huffed. "What is this about?"

Ravenna wrung her hands. "Remember when we told you about girls who are being kidnapped and sold abroad?"

"Yes." He put his hands on his hips.

"I was down at the docks tonight, looking for my niece, and I saw a cartload of girls. They're boarding them now and plan to sail at dawn. I couldn't tell if my niece was among them. But you have to help us, please. If that ship sails, I may lose my niece forever. And even if Georgiana isn't there, those girls will certainly be lost forever. I can't live with that on my heart. Please. Help us."

He nodded and looked down, his eyes darting across the floor. "How many men?"

"Maybe a dozen. Maybe more," she said.

"I have four men with me."

Braedon said, "Donovan, Yarford, and I will help you."

"That evens up the numbers some. Good. I'll rouse my men. We're right behind you." He spun and ran up the stairs as Braedon and Ravenna left the inn to return to the docks.

Upon returning to the docks, Ravenna and Braedon knelt beside Donovan and Yarford, who hid behind some crates several yards from *The Milton.*

Donovan whispered, "They loaded the girls onto the ship soon after you left."

"Chadwick is on the way with about four other men. When they get here, we'll help them." Braedon peeked over the crates, watching the men.

Yarford said, "They'd better get here soon. It's very near dawn."

As several men came off the boat, talking, men on horses rode by the spot where Ravenna, Braedon, and Donovan were hiding.

"That's Mr. Chadwick," Ravenna said. They all ran after the men on horses.

The men slid off their horses to confront the shipmen. The shipmen scattered in all directions. A melee ensued. Braedon, Donovan, and Yarford all jumped into the scramble of punching and shouting.

Three of the flesh traders ran away from the fight and jumped on their horses. Ravenna shouted, "They're running! They're running!" She pointed in the direction of the men.

Donovan gave chase, but couldn't match the speed of the horses. He jogged back to the fight, stopping to retrieve something from the ground before hopping back into the scuffle.

Chadwick landed a punch to one man, sending him reeling. Then he held him down while Braedon rushed to help tie the man's hands.

Ravenna stood on the fringe, wanting to both help and not get hurt or get in the way. How could she help? Then it hit her…She grabbed a lantern, skirted the perimeter of the fight, and ran toward the ship. She skittered up the gangway, across the deck, and opened the hatch. She climbed down into the hold. The girls had to be below deck, where the shipments were stored. She walked through the crates, all marked Gutherie & Sons and Empire Weavers. Other crates were unmarked.

At first, she found nothing. As she turned to leave, she caught the sound of faint sniffling and moaning. She honed in on the noise, discovering it was coming from a crate. Panicked, Ravenna searched for something to open the lid. Finding an iron claw sitting in the center of a pile of rope, she returned to the crate and pried open the lid. She shone the lantern light onto the tear-streaked face of a young girl with red hair and freckles. The girl's eyes opened wide, and she issued loud, frenzied whines.

"Shh…" Ravenna put her finger to her lips. "I'm going to help you, but you must be quiet. Understand?"

The girl nodded.

"You also need to help me find the others and stay with me. I'm afraid you'll be caught again if you wander off."

The girl nodded.

"Good girl." Ravenna helped her to stand and took the gag off her mouth.

The girl let loose a flurry of whispered words as Ravenna extracted her dagger and cut the rope from the girl's wrists. "Thank'ee, ma'am. Surely, the Good Lord sent'ee. I bless'ee for the rest of yer days. May those days be long and healthy on this earth." The ropes fell in pieces from her wrists. She rubbed her wrists and looked upward. "Thank'ee, Lord. Thank'ee. My name is Maggie. The scoundrels put me in the box last. I tried to watch and remember where the other girls are stored." She wiped her eyes. "There were eight of us."

As they worked on the next crate. Ravenna said, "I'm looking for a specific girl, my niece. Her name is Georgiana. Blonde hair, blue eyes. Have you seen her?"

"I didn't know the names of any of the other girls, and a few of them fit that description. We've been bound, gagged, and filled with laudanum the whole time. The only time we weren't gagged was to eat. If we dared say a word, we were beaten."

"I understand. Let's uncrate the other girls before we're discovered."

The two set about working to free the other girls. Some of the crates were filled with guns, swords, and cannonballs instead of girls.

Working with speed and focus, they freed more girls who jumped in to help untie their hands. Soon, six girls were released from their bonds. Ravenna's heart teetered. None of them were Georgiana.

As they lifted the lid on the last crate and helped the girl to stand, an unfamiliar man's voice rose behind them.

"What do ye think yer doin', lassies?" He sucked his yellowed teeth.

"Keep working," she whispered to Maggie. "Hand me a sword from the crate behind you."

Ravenna spun around, hiding her dagger in her skirts. The balding man was half-dressed, wearing only his shirt, pantaloons, and boots. He had a long brown beard, squinty eyes, and a sun-weathered face. He trained a pistol on them as he leaned on the stairs of the hold.

"I think I'm setting these girls free." Behind her back, she slipped her dagger into its sheath in her fan. "And I think you're going to let me do it."

He laughed, his pot belly jiggling. "Ye've got a wee bit of spirit. I like it. But ye won't be the first filly I've broken."

"Who are you?" Not that she cared. She was biding her time.

He stepped down into the hold. "I'm the captain of *The Milton.*"

"Take this," Maggie whispered behind her, pressing the hilt of a sword into her back. Ravenna clutched the hilt. She stepped back and to the side, gaining a stable fighting stance as she whipped the sword around to the *en garde* position.

He smirked, his eyes cold and reptilian as he lifted his pistol. "I think I'm going to have another hure to sell in France. Though yer a bit long in the tooth and bruised, you might be worth a coin or two."

Ravenna said a silent prayer that the lessons she'd learned from Mr. Norris would serve her well. Her mind raced to pick the best strategy. She inhaled and released a cleansing breath. She said, "Girls...scream!" As the girls screamed, Ravenna launched herself forward, spinning to the side and forward to create a moving target. As she stopped, she swept her blade downward to slice the captain's hand.

He cried out, dropped the pistol, and grabbed his hand. "Ye bloody hure! I'll tie ye to the mast and let the crows eat yer flesh."

Ravenna kicked his pistol out of the way as he launched himself at her. She sliced at him again, cutting him across the gut, but he grabbed her wrist and twisted, forcing her to drop her weapon. Wild-eyed, he grabbed her around the throat. The girls screamed in earnest now and huddled against each other in their panic. Ravenna clawed at his face, aiming for his eyes.

Braedon eased down the hold ladder and placed his pistol to the captain's balding head. "Release her now, or I'll dig a ditch through your skull."

The captain raised his hands in the air.

"Back away from her. Now."

The captain stepped backward.

"Now climb the ladder."

Donovan stood on the deck with a pistol aimed at the captain. "And don't even think about trying to fight or escape."

The captain climbed to the deck.

By the time Ravenna, Braedon, and the girls reached the deck, Donovan and Chadwick had the captain tied up.

The first signs of dawn flecked the horizon, and the seagulls and crows cried and circled above them.

Ravenna threw herself into Braedon's arms and cried. "Georgiana isn't here."

He held her close, kissing her head. "I'm sorry, my little raven. But you saved all these other girls, and I know they and their families will be forever grateful for your courage." He handed her a handkerchief. "We'll find Georgiana. I swear my life on it. I won't rest until you find her."

Chadwick lingered nearby, dabbing his busted lip and watching his men lead the captain down the gangway. His shirt was stained with blood, and his clothes were dirty and rumpled.

Ravenna said to him, "Where will the girls go?"

Chadwick clasped his hands behind his back. "For now, they will find rest and food at a nearby church. Then, over the next few days, we will question them about the identities of their captors and such. Once we give clearance, the pastor will help the girls get back to their homes. Some are from Edinburgh, but a few are from England, Wales, even Ireland."

Braedon extended his hand. "Thank you, sir, for your help. You've saved many lives today."

Chadwick shook his hand. "I'll have you fight by my side any day, milord." Then he offered his hand to Ravenna.

Ravenna shook his hand. "Thank you, Mr. Chadwick."

"I'm sorry we didn't find your niece. We'll keep searching." He released her hand. "We're going to discover the identity of the men who escaped on horseback, too. They're responsible for this, and I'm certain they aren't going to stop kidnapping these young girls."

Chadwick, Yarford, and Donovan led the girls down the gangway and helped them into a cart. Maggie turned, her fire-red hair tousled in the breeze. She approached Ravenna and Braedon. "What's your name, ma'am?"

"Ravenna."

"Your name will be in my prayers every day for as long as I draw breath. Thank you, ma'am."

"You're welcome, Maggie."

The girl turned to leave.

Ravenna caught up to her. "Maggie, one moment. I have a question."

She turned and lifted her chin.

"Did you know who captured you?"

"Josiah Emmett. He claimed he loved me and lured me to a place where we could be alone. Before I know it, I'm snatched up and put into a carriage."

Blast his eyes. That wicked scoundrel. "Where did they take you?"

"I don't know. They blindfolded me for much of the trip, and they forced me to drink laudanum. When I woke up, I was in a dark, stony room, almost like a dungeon. I remember it was loud. There were many people nearby."

Ravenna couldn't think of any building with that description. "How did you meet Josiah Emmett?"

"My mother asked to take some food to my father at the mill where he worked. Josiah was there."

"When was this?"

"A couple of days ago."

So the scoundrel was still luring and kidnapping girls! "Where does your father work?"

"The Empire Mill."

That was one of the names on the crates.

"Who owns the Empire Mill?"

"I don't know. My father had only been working there a couple of weeks."

"Where is the mill located?"

"Near Calton Hill." Maggie looked out across the dockyard. "They're loading up the girls. I should go."

"Yes. Mr. Chadwick will keep you safe. He'll have more questions for you, I'm sure. Thank you, Maggie. You're a brave girl."

A dimple formed in her cheek. "I'll be praying for ye, ma'am. And for yer niece. I pray ye find her." She turned and ran down the gangway, her red hair whipping in the breeze.

These men needed to be stopped. The Unity was at the center of all of this. And Ravenna was going to do everything in her power to stop them.

Chapter Twenty-Two

Ravenna managed a few hours of sleep before rallying to resume her search for Georgiana. She ran through information and events as Charlotte buttoned Ravenna's dress and fixed her hair.

Ravenna asked her, "Have you spoken to Aurélie this morning? Do you know if my brother has returned yet?"

"I did see her when I took breakfast to her and helped her dress. Mr. Connelly hasn't returned yet."

"Has she heard from him?"

"I don't think so, milady. She's quite upset this morning."

Ravenna's muscles tightened. He hadn't been home since yesterday morning, nor had anyone heard from him. *This was not good.*

Niall had gone out to meet Muir, but she didn't know why. Whatever his reasons, no good could come of it. Surely, Niall wasn't foolish enough to get involved in an assassination plot. In last night's rescue, she had confirmed Larson and The Unity were involved in the flesh trade. Rotherden was working with Muir, but for what reason, she wasn't certain. He certainly wouldn't be the first nobleman in history to try to topple a throne. Further, disgruntled weavers and other workers were implicated in the freedom fight and the plot against the throne as well. At the center of it all was this mysterious Muir man and The Unity.

Further, there were three men last night involved in kidnapping the girls who had escaped. Were one of them Muir? And one of them had a tight, nasally voice that had haunted her all night. The voice seemed familiar. Additionally, when she was down in *The Milton's* hold, several of the boxes were labeled Gutherie & Sons or Empire Weavers. Was it possible those businesses might know something about the missing girls? Or were their crates being used for nefarious purposes without the business's knowledge?

Charlotte brushed out Ravenna's hair with long, quick strokes. "I'd like to come with you this morning, if you'll have me. I need to find fabric to remake your torn dress." She fashioned Ravenna's hair into a single, thick braid.

"You're always a welcome addition—especially if Braedon and I get separated."

Charlotte pinned the braid into a chignon. "We can't let that vile Mr. Larson find you alone again."

"Indeed." Ravenna gathered her spencer, a bonnet, reticule, and black lace fan. "Have a light breakfast sent up, please. Whatever is easy."

Charlotte left the room.

Ravenna paced, running through her goals. While searching for Georgiana, she hoped to also speak with Aven Brown. She was curious about Callum and Mable, the couple who had helped rescue her from Larson's attack. Aven might know about potential uprisings—or rebellions against the king. Perhaps she knew something about the kidnapped girls or The Unity, too. After all, she had known something about Josiah Emmett. Perhaps she knew something about Rotherden and others. Maybe there was some connection to what was going on with Georgiana. She rolled the toad stone Aven had given her in her hand and dropped it into her reticule along with a vial of chamomile liniment.

As she stepped out of her room, she saw Lord Donovan coming out of his. He dropped a glove and bent to retrieve it. This triggered her memory. Last night at the docks, he had bent over to pick up something off the ground. "Good morning, Lord Donovan."

He paused. "Good morning, Lady Birchfield. I trust you've had some rest?"

"I confess, I haven't had much." She ran her bonnet through her hands. "I won't keep you. You appear to be going out."

"I am. I'm going to speak with Mr. Chadwick."

"Last night in the skirmish at the docks, when the three men jumped on their horses and escaped, I recall you picking up something off the ground. I'm curious, what did you find?"

"Oh, yes. I'd nearly forgotten about it. I'm glad you reminded me. I'm going to take this to Mr. Chadwick." He entered his bedchamber, rifled through a coat pocket, and extracted a gold pocketwatch.

"May I see it?"

"Certainly." He handed her the watch.

She turned it over in her hand, inspecting it. It was a simple gold watch. On the back was an etching of foliage around the edge, surrounding a set of initials. *A.S.* "Interesting." She handed the watch back to him. "Thank you."

They descended the stairs together to meet Charlotte and Braedon. Donovan left the house as Ravenna paused to put on her gloves. "Let's go. There is much to do." They started for the door, but the butler stopped them.

"One moment, please, milady. I was given a letter for you this morning and was told to deliver it straight into your hands."

"For me?" she said, confused. "Who could be writing to me? Who delivered it?"

The old man shrugged. "Some boy. He wasn't in livery. Looked like a street urchin."

She accepted the letter and flipped it over to open it. Her fingers froze over the black seal.

"Ravenna?" Braedon stepped forward. "What's the matter? You've gone quite pale."

"A black seal." She showed it to him. "The Unity." With shaking fingers, she opened the letter.

Jack and Jill went up the hill
Searching for their niece.
Jack fell down and broke his crown
And Jill will come tumbling after....

She handed the letter to Braedon. "It's a warning. I think they have Niall.

Maybe they've even hurt him. He's 'Jack.' That's why he hasn't come home."

"Then you must be Jill," Braedon said.

Ravenna nodded. "They're coming for me, and they know where I'm staying. The letter was delivered here."

"How?" Braedon frowned. "How could they possibly know?"

Ravenna thought. "Rotherden. He was here last night. He was with the assassination plotters at the Blue Boar. He's clearly connected to The Unity. There can be no doubt after this."

"I'll be having dinner with him tonight. Perhaps I can find out some information."

"Maybe they kept Mr. Connelly alive to get information from him," Charlotte added.

"How will we ever find him? I can't even find my niece." She put her hands to her temples beneath her bonnet. "What am I going to do?"

Braedon held her upper arms. "Look at me. We're going to proceed as planned today. We will do our best to find them both. That's all we can do."

She nodded. "You're right. We should go."

The August morning possessed a touch of humidity as the trio trudged down the hill along a little dirt path. A light breeze blew around them as butterflies flitted over purple thistle blooms. The landscape rolled with hills and pastures as far as the eye could see on one side, and on the other, in the distance, was the Port of Leith full of ships. The plaintive cry of bagpipes drifted down from the castle. It was a beautiful morning, and, for the briefest moment of selfishness, Ravenna resented that she couldn't enjoy this wild and beautiful country more.

Several hundred feet down the hill, a stone ruin emerged. The three paused, looking up at the structure consisting of one partial wall with glassless arched windows flanking the arched doorway, and above the door was a broken stone buttress supporting a bit of wall with another arched window. Across from this structure stood two partial stone columns, one shorter than the other.

"It was once St. Anthony's chapel," Charlotte said.

Ravenna said, "St. Anthony. The saint of lost things…" *How appropriate.*

Though she had been raised Protestant, her Italian mother had been Catholic. So Ravenna was aware of the saints and held a certain respect for them.

Charlotte continued, "I remember playing up here when I was a little girl. It's several hundred years old. I don't know when it fell into ruin, but it was a long time ago, to be sure. I think it was abandoned after the Reformation when the Protestants took over Scotland."

"That was nearly three hundred years ago," Braedon said. "How strange to be here in the modern world, face to face with something this old. I wonder what stories these old walls hold."

Ravenna stared up at the broken wall, trying to imagine what the building might've looked like, all stone, with sun pouring through stained glass windows, the echo of voices singing or praying. "It's breathtaking. How many people were married here? Or christened here? How many people prayed here or held funerals here? So much history." Touching the stone, she bowed her head, saying a silent prayer for Georgiana and Niall, praying her lost things would be found safe, alive, and unharmed.

They progressed down the hill and, as they neared the bottom, the scents of the city—fresh bread, fish, oil, dung, and coal smoke—assaulted her senses. Morning mist still clung to the street, slicking the cobblestones.

Ravenna said, "I would like to start with New Town since Niall was going there yesterday. Maybe someone there will recall seeing him."

They turned down Princes Street moving in the direction of Edinburgh Castle. New stores, rowhouses, and tenements lined the right side of the street. On the left side, an earthen mound path cut through Nor Loch, connecting Old Town and New Town. In the distance on a hill rose St. Giles' tall bell tower in the confusion of buildings along the narrow, winding, and hilly streets of Old Town. One side of the loch had been drained dry, and the other side nearer the castle, was only half full. On the bank of the loch stood a scaffold, crawling with workers like ants. A cacophony of hammering and shouting filled the air as pedestrians, vendors, laborers, and carriages flooded the streets.

Charlotte looked around in wonder. "It's changed so drastically since I've been here. I remember when this was an open field and the Nor Loch was full. I wonder why they drained it?" She shielded her eyes against the sun and stared at the loch. A few children scrambled and played in the dry side. On the other side, black and white swans floated on the water, ducking their heads and flapping their wings. "I'm sad to see it go," she added, turning to look at the other side of the street. "Ah, a linen-drapers. I need to stop here. They have better fabrics than the shop in Old Town. I'll be only a few minutes."

Charlotte ducked inside the shop while Ravenna and Braedon crossed the street to scan the landscape, discussing the stark contrast between Old Town and New Town. A mere strip of earth linked the past and present. In only a few hundred feet, she could step back into another time.

Braedon said, "I searched here some last night." He glanced over his shoulder. "Today we might try shops and houses."

"However, I don't want to spend too much of the day here. I still believe Georgiana is in Old Town, and I'm eager to continue my search for her. After all, I believe she's far more vulnerable than Niall. She's practically a child still. Barely out of her apron strings." And Georgiana's disappearance wasn't her fault. Whereas her brother Niall may have made choices to put him in his current predicament.

"I agree."

A black swan floated over to where an old tree stump and some brush had lodged against the muddy, rocky shoreline. The swan pecked at something with a splash of white, shook its head and tail, honked, then pecked again, catching her attention.

Curious, Ravenna stepped closer to the shore, shielding her eyes from the sun. "What is that?"

Braedon followed. "I can't tell. It looks like…discarded clothing."

Uneasiness prickled under her skin, and her scalp tingled. Something was wrong. "I want to get a closer look," Ravenna said.

"Here…" Braedon offered his hand. "Hold on. We don't need you falling into the water."

They picked along the edge of the embankment until they found a spot for solid footing and began their precarious descent. Near the brush, a white shirt buoyed in the water. But the clothing was not empty. A pale hand rested on the muddy bank.

She stopped and turned, nearly losing her balance. Braedon caught her. "It's a body," she said.

"Are you sure?"

"Yes! See the hand. It's a man. What if it's Niall?" She jerked her hand from Braedon's, lifted her skirts, and descended to the water. She splashed along the waterline, the mud sucking against her boots as she ran. She approached the body, drawing in a hard breath at the sight of his dark, wet hair. The man wore only his pantaloons and shirt, blooming with blood spots

Ravenna's heart thrummed, rushing blood into her ears. She knelt in the mud and lifted his face. "Niall!" Her screams for help sounded muffled to her own ears, her words lodged in a closing throat.

The hammering, the shouting, and the carriages stopped. The world went entirely silent. She slid her knees under his head. Leeches, slick and muscular, stuck to his skin. She ripped them off, launching them into the water, calling her brother's name over and over.

Braedon scrambled toward her, shouting, but the words scattered like chaff in the whirlwind in her mind. Braedon's face and his intense blue eyes stared down at her. He was talking, but she didn't understand his words as his hands worked to get hold of Niall. Then, above the rim of the Nor Loch, appeared the forms of other men, fear and concern etching their sun-weathered faces.

Men hustled toward them over the rocks and mud. One man helped Ravenna to her feet while the other men formed a line to assist Braedon in inching Niall's body up the chain of men to the ground above.

Ravenna, completely mindless of decorum or propriety, clambered up the side of the bank like a wild animal, crawling over to Niall. He lay limp as a willow branch, his bony and bruised chest exposed in the open neckline of his shirt. Red and purple marks the shape of a rope snaked around his neck. He was pale but not blue or gray, so there was hope.

"Niall," Ravenna slapped his face. "Niall! Wake up. Please wake up." She jerked her gloves off with her teeth and pushed her shaking fingers against his neck. A faint heartbeat. *Thank Heaven!* "Smelling salts!" She stood on her knees and looked around. "Does someone have smelling salts?"

A lady ran to her, digging in her reticule. "Here, lassie."

Ravenna opened the bottle and stuck it under his nose. His eyes fluttered, and he coughed. His eyes opened for a moment, then rolled shut again as he groaned, coughing and squirming on the ground.

"Thank heaven you're alive." She laughed through her tears.

Niall opened his eyes, squinting up at her.

Ravenna gripped the sides of his face. "It was The Unity, wasn't it?"

He nodded, his eyes widened, fearful. He attempted to speak, but his voice came out wheezy and unintelligible. He pointed at his throat.

"They ambushed you?"

He nodded again.

"Now will you please go back to Iverloch and sit with your wife and unborn child?"

Tears flooded his eyes. He nodded again, broke into sobs, and rolled to hug her. "I'm sorry," he wheezed.

"Sh-sh-sh," Ravenna wiped the mud from his face. "I'm sorry. I didn't mean to upset you. I just want my family safe. You'll be well now. You're safe." She placed a kiss on his mud-smeared forehead. "Can you stand?"

He shifted and pushed himself to sit, then shook his head. Braedon knelt on the other side of Niall. Ravenna and Braedon worked together to help him stand.

Niall stood limp, then slipped to his knees again.

Ravenna struggled to hold up her brother. "He cannot walk to Iverloch."

Charlotte ran from the store, carrying a bundle wrapped in brown paper. "How can I help?"

Braedon turned to the men who lingered nearby. "Can I rent someone's cart to carry this man to Iverloch Hall?"

A man stepped forward. "I have a cart."

Charlotte stepped up. "I'll escort him to Iverloch."

"Thank you, Charlotte. You're very good," Ravenna said.

Braedon made the arrangements with the cart driver, then assisted Niall and Charlotte into the back of the cart.

Ravenna and Braedon waved as the cart carried Charlotte and Niall across the Earthen Mound toward Old Town. Ravenna's stomach twisted into tight knots, and she said a silent prayer that they would arrive safely—and without incident—to Iverloch Hall.

Chapter Twenty-Three

Ravenna and Braedon ignored the stares, guffaws, and remarks over their mud-covered clothes as they wound through the narrow streets of Old Town toward Candlemaker's Row. Ravenna wanted a word with Aven Brown to see if the woman knew anything. Especially since she witnessed Aven's husband meeting with people to plot the king's assassination.

As they neared Aven Brown's house, several men lined each side of the street. They leaned against the buildings or sat on stools or crates, malcontent, scornful, men. Why weren't they at work? Tension filled the air. Something wasn't right. The hair on the back of Ravenna's neck stood at attention as the men eyed her and Braedon with suspicion.

Ravenna slipped her arm through Braedon's, pulling closer to him.

"What's wrong, my little raven?"

"Do you not feel it? The discontent in the air?"

"I do. Just keep walking. Don't look at them."

They increased their pace and found Aven's house. Ravenna knocked.

Answering the door, Aven's eyes grew into large moons as she took in the sight before her. She burst into laughter, shaking her entire body. "Ach, aren't ye a wee bit dreich? You're not fit to be seen by a pig farmer. Begging your pardon."

Ravenna looked down at her mud-covered dress. She was running out of dresses. Any more adventures and she'd be traveling back to London in her chemise and stockings. "Yes. We've had a bit of a tumble today."

"Come in, come in." Aven stepped aside, still chuckling. "What brings ye out today? And what happened to ye?" She tried to suppress her laughter, little snorts breaking through as she closed the door. "I'll put on a pot of tea. I think ye need it sorely."

"Please, don't trouble yourself," Ravenna said. "We can't stay long. I'm still looking for my niece. First…" Ravenna dug into her reticule and extracted the vial of chamomile liniment. "I wanted to bring this to your husband for his wounds." It was a ruse. She knew Samuel Brown was well enough to be out of bed. "It's the least I could do after you helped me."

"Ach." Aven accepted the bottle. "I thank ye for this, though I think ye need it more than he does. Ye must be feeling spry since you're out having adventures." Aven sat, her legs spread wide under her dress, planting her fist onto one leg and the other arm leaning on the table.

"I am well, though I look worse for wear." Ravenna smiled, her gaze wandering. "I notice your husband isn't here. How is he? Do you think this liniment will help him?"

"Ehrm…Aye…" She averted her eyes and pretended to swipe something off the table. Her voice trembled a bit. "Ehrm, I'm sure it will. He is feeling better, thank'ee for thinking of him. He's become restless from being stuck inside for so long, so he went out for a walk."

"I see." Ravenna paused, sitting at the table. "I have a matter of some delicacy to discuss with you…"

Aven glanced up at Braedon and then down at her hands.

"Do you or your husband know of a Lord Rotherden?" Ravenna folded her gloved hands on the table.

She snorted. "Why would the likes of me know anything of a lord?"

"Rotherden is about his size…" Ravenna pointed to Braedon. "Round face, thick brows. Looks a bit boyish."

Aven shook her head. "Don't know him." That was at least a partial lie. Though it was possible Rotherden was using a fake name. Maybe they knew him without realizing it.

Ravenna continued. "Do you know if your husband knows a man named Mr. Larson? A man with white hair and a limp?"

Aven frowned, digging through the archives of her memory. "Can't say we do."

"What about a man named Muir? " She described him.

"Not sure…." Aven narrowed her eyes. "Why're ye asking all these questions?"

"I think you're headed for great trouble. Please listen to me. After my attack, where did you take me? Whose house was I in?"

"Friends of mine. I happened to be visiting."

"What were their names?" Braedon asked.

Aven studied her fingernails. "Uh…Mr. and Mrs. Smith."

Aven was lying, but she didn't challenge Aven for fear she would stop talking. "Do your friends also spend time in the company of Mr. Larson or Lord Rotherden? Like your husband does?"

Aven scowled. Her voice shook. "I done told ye—"

A knock sounded on the door. With a soft grunt, Aven pushed herself to stand and jerked open the door.

Ravenna turned in her seat and craned her neck to peek around Aven's body. A woman on the other side of the door spoke in a low, hurried voice. Ravenna stood to see the so-called Mrs. Smith. The woman Aven had called Mable on the day Ravenna had been attacked. The woman froze.

"Wait," Ravenna said. "Please, come in. I'd like to speak to you, too."

Aven stood back and opened the door wider. "Come in, Mable."

The woman crossed the threshold and sat like a stone with her hands clasped tight together in her lap.

"First, I'd like to thank you for helping me in my hour of need."

Mable stood, rigid. "I did my duty."

Ravenna sighed. "I'll not delay. I think you both, and your husbands, are not only working with dangerous men, but you're in great peril."

Both women jerked their heads around to stare at her.

"What do you mean?" Aven said. "H-how are we in danger?"

"I don't know all the particulars, but I've pieced some things together. First, I believe you're engaged in activities that could get you in grave trouble. I also believe you're working with people who aren't just disgruntled workers. They are, in fact, political dissidents with an aim to separate from the crown."

Aven and Mable glanced at each other.

"When I was in your house, Mrs. Smith, if that is indeed your name, I noticed a large object covered with a cloth and some paper peeking from beneath the cloth. Also, your husband had ink-stained fingers. I believe he's running a printing press."

Mable shrugged a shoulder. "He's helping the workers to get their proper wages."

"That may be. Perhaps he's innocent. But I believe he's involved with people who are working against The Crown. Perhaps they're using your husband's mission as a cover."

"You're mistaken," Mable jumped out of her seat. "My husband and I are helping the workers."

"Aven," said. "I saw your husband and other men colluding over a map, which I believe was of Kew Palace. I have every reason to believe they are involved in a plot to assassinate the king."

Aven's mouth formed an O as she shook her head.

"I found a pamphlet. When one of the men dropped it on the floor, I retrieved it. The pamphlet spoke of removing the king from the throne by any means necessary. That is treasonous and seditious speech. A crime that carries a death sentence."

Mable and Aven looked at each other again. "My husband doesn't write such pamphlets."

"It's likely your husbands are involved in more than they're telling you. Or, your group has been infiltrated by traitors to The Crown who are using you as a shield. I think you may be sheltering political dissidents like the Irish Unity without knowing it. The Unity is dangerous. They want not only freedom for Ireland but to destroy England and topple the Crown."

"Impossible!" Mable gasped. She spoke to Aven in hectic Gaelic. Ravenna couldn't understand the language, but her hissing tone made her message clear enough.

Aven said, "Don't worry, Mable. If she wanted to turn us over to the law, she would've done it already."

Mable said something else.

Aven waved her away. "Auch! You're suspicious of everyone. She's not a spy."

Ravenna grew warm. Though Ravenna wasn't acting as a spy at the moment, she had been a spy at one time. "I'm not spying. I have no interest in what is going on in your town. I care only about finding my niece and returning home as soon as possible. I simply wanted to help by warning you. Especially after seeing your husband with plotters against the king."

"You needn't worry about warning us." Aven resumed her seat. "We're careful. And as for the Rotherden and Larson fellows, I've told ye I wouldn't know who they are or what they're up to."

Ravenna scratched her scar. "In fact, I think you do have something to worry about. Lord Iverloch and other officials know a rebellion is fomenting, and they are looking for the leaders now. I suspect they know more than they're saying."

Mable leapt to her feet. "I have to warn Callum. We have to get the printer out of the house." She rushed out, slamming the door.

Aven jumped up. "I need to find Samuel."

"Wait…" Ravenna stood. "Are you sure you don't know where Larson is? He likely has my niece or knows where she's being held."

"Oh, hang, Larson!" Aven swiped her hands through the air. "I know nothing about him. We have our men to save!" She jerked open her door. "Now go! Go! Before I regret ever meeting ye." She nudged them out of her house and slammed the door.

Ravenna stood, staring at the door. "I wish there was some way to help."

Braedon looked up and down the street. "You can't solve all the world's problems, Ravenna."

He was right. Besides, to assist Aven and her cohorts would mean entangling herself in a nest of dissidents and rebels. It was a risk she wasn't willing to take. She needed to focus on her family.

Braedon touched the small of her back. "We need to find Georgiana."

They turned toward Cowgate, stopping where it intersected with Blair Street. The mid-afternoon sun washed the buildings in deep gold. As they neared the South Bridge, Ravenna caught a glimpse of a young woman with flaxen hair in a blue dress like the one she'd given her niece. The girl was with a man, but Ravenna couldn't discern from his back if the man was Josiah Emmett or not.

But the girl looked a great deal like Georgiana. Was it her? She shouted, "Georgiana!"

The girl turned.

That must be her. "Georgiana!" She shouted again.

"Auntie!" Georgiana pulled at the man holding her, but he jerked her around, holding her fast.

Ravenna pointed at Georgiana. "That's her! The girl in the blue dress and blonde hair!"

But a crowd of men chased by soldiers rushed down the street as the girl's male cohort pulled her forward into the people and carriages crowding the Cowgate.

"Georgiana!" Ravenna shouted again. She dashed ahead, but her sore body, the smoky air, and side stitches diminished her ability to get enough air to run. She slowed her pace to a jog. Braedon ran ahead of her until he was impeded by a farmer's cart. Then he stopped.

Ravenna caught up to him. "What's the matter?" Ravenna panted, pushing her fingers into the stabbing pain in her side. "Where's Georgiana?" She searched the people crowded in the street. A short distance ahead, the arch of South Bridge Street crossed over Cowgate. She gripped his arm. "I know it was her. It had to be. We are so close, Braedon."

"She's gone." He slapped the side of the cart. "How? I wasn't that far behind them. Where did they go?" He opened his arms wide. "I don't understand."

Ravenna stood, hands on hips, regaining her breath. "How is it possible?" She walked toward the stone arch and stood underneath it. As she turned to look at Braedon, a young man exited from a door behind an arched support wall embedded in the bridge vault. *In the wall.*

"Braedon..." She moved to the door, crossing the street, narrowly escaping an oncoming carriage.

Braedon caught up to her as she opened the door and stepped inside. A thick stench of fish, urine, body sweat, and burning fat assaulted her senses.

She pulled her handkerchief from her spencer sleeve and pushed it against her nose. An echo of chatter and laughter swirled around them. Ravenna pressed forward toward the faint glow of light at the end of a narrow stone path with Braedon behind her. Stone walls and ceilings rose up around them. The ceilings dripped water from their cracks.

The path opened into a larger space with several tiny rooms about the size of the silver pantry at Birchfield Manor. Or perhaps these were once buildings that had been built over. "What sort of fright is this?" Ravenna whispered.

Each room was stuffed with the bodies of poor, wretched, and ragged people, from the elderly to infants. Many sat, drunk or drinking, gambling or smoking. Others worked at some craft from whittling wood, to dipping rush candles, to sewing by dim candlelight or cobbling shoes.

"My God…" Ravenna whispered. "Do these people truly live here?"

"It would seem so," Braedon said. "Unfortunately."

People sitting outside their rooms stretched out their hands, begging for food or money. Ravenna stopped, reaching for her reticule.

Braedon grabbed her hand and whispered, "Give them nothing. If you do, it'll be like blood in the water to sharks. We'll be set upon and likely not leave this place alive."

"They're desperate."

"I understand. I wish I could help them, too, but this is not the way. I assure you, while there are desperate people here, there are cutthroats and thieves of every stripe, too. It's the most logical place for them to hide from justice."

"I understand." She removed her reticule from her wrist and tucked the small purse into her bodice. Something spoke to her, an intuition. "She's here, Braedon. I *know* it. I feel it in my bones." She removed her fan from her wrist and held it, ready to release the blade. She examined the filth around her, kicking the rats away from her feet. "The thought of Georgiana living in this…*hell* is too much to be borne." The desperation to find her niece now tightened around her throat. "Georgiana!" she shouted, her voice echoing.

She continued to push forward, searching the dirty and haggard faces of extreme poverty. *What was happening to Georgiana down here?*

"Georgiana!" she called again.

A toothless woman, clearly mad, mocked her in a squeaky voice. "Georgie-Georgie- Georgie-ana!" Then laughed maniacally. She stood from her stool, hunched, dirty, wild-eyed, with tangled hair. Waving her arms, she hobbled toward Ravenna and shoved her. "Georgie-Georgie-Georgie-ana!"

Ravenna put her finger to the medallion on her fan, ready to release the blade. She didn't want to hurt this lunatic woman, but she would, if necessary.

A man now approached. "Are you looking for Georgiana? I know where she is. I'll tell you for a shilling." Malice glinted in his eyes. "She's in a room back here."

Braedon put himself between Ravenna and these other people, nudging Ravenna back toward the exit. "Go. We need to leave here. Now." He pulled his pistol from under his great coat and held it, pointed downward, but ready. He backed out as Ravenna turned to exit the tunnel.

They spilled into the fading sunlight. The stench of the underground city clung to Ravenna's clothes and coated her nostrils. It was all she could smell. "I don't know what I'm going to do or how I'm going to find Georgiana. How far do those tunnels go?" Her emotions blazed like a bonfire, erupting into tears. "We could search there for days. What am I going to do? I can't leave her here."

Braedon touched her cheek. "Don't worry. We will find a solution."

The watchman on the street announced the time.

"We must go. I need to dress for Rotherden's dinner party. See if I can discover anything else about our mysterious lordling."

"I want to return underground. I want to find my niece."

"Please, Ravenna, we will come back in the morning."

"But if they know we're here and that we're looking for her, they might not stay."

"I think they'll stay. I believe there is some other business keeping them here. Otherwise, they would've left already." He took a few steps, turned, and extended his hand, his eyes pleading with her to trust him.

She looked back at the door to the underground dwelling. Then back at him. He hadn't let her down yet. So far, he'd kept every promise he'd made to her—however provoking and irritating he could be sometimes. *This once. I need to not be let down. Please don't let me down, Braedon.* She stepped forward and put her hand in his.

Chapter Twenty-Four

A s soon as Ravenna returned to Iverloch Hall, she ran to see Niall. Aurélie and Charlotte sat around him. Niall had been washed and bandaged and was lying in bed.

"How is he?" Ravenna whispered.

Charlotte stood, putting her book in the chair. "Lord Iverloch was kind enough to call his personal surgeon, Mr. Campbell, who assures us Niall will recover. He needs plenty of rest."

"I understand. Has he had anything to eat since his return?"

"Some broth and strong tea," Aurélie said. "He's been asleep this whole time."

"The sleep will do him good. Let him sleep as long as he wants." Ravenna examined Aurélie's face. The swelling had reduced, but dark circles weighed her eyes. "You also rest as much as the baby will let you. Has the baby been active today?"

"Oh yes." A glow took over Aurélie's demeanor as she rubbed her rounded stomach. "The babe has been kicking and turning like a mule." She laughed.

"That's good." Ravenna's smile broke. If she were being honest, her happiness for Aurélie was undercut with an edge of envy and jealousy. She'd always wanted children of her own. A large family to replace the one she'd lost, to fill her home with vibrant life—music, dance, giggles, games, sticky kisses, inquisitiveness, and the exuberance only children could bring to a home. But Philip hadn't been interested. He'd already raised his boys with his late wife, and he was far more concerned about his career. Every time she broached the matter, he changed the subject or deflected with a meaningless response along the lines of 'We'll discuss the matter later.' But later never came.

Ravenna swallowed her emotion. "Hart, may I speak with you in the hall for a moment?"

"Certainly."

They stepped into the hall. The sunlight from the window at the end of the hall splashed across the floor.

"I need your help," Ravenna whispered. "I need you to procure the ugliest, dirtiest, most ragged clothes you can find."

Charlotte studied her, puzzled.

Ravenna continued. "Braedon and I discovered an underground city in Cowgate today. I think Georgiana is being kept there."

"An underground city?" Charlotte's brows shot up. "I'd heard about such a thing when I was a child, but I thought it was just a fairy tale my parents told us kids to make us behave."

"It's not actually a city. It's more like a filthy labyrinth beneath Edinburgh to house the most miserable creatures to exist."

"Dreadful." Charlotte frowned, thinking. Then her mouth dropped open. "You mean to go back there."

Ravenna nodded. "I do. Tonight."

"At night? That would not be wise."

"It's a risk I'm willing to take. If my niece is there, I cannot leave her in that hell one more day. I have to get her out."

"What about Lord Braedon? Is he going with you?"

"He's going to Lord Rotherden's this evening to see what he can discover about him."

"I should think Lord Braedon will not approve of this."

"Then it's a good thing he's not my husband and doesn't know about this, isn't it?" Ravenna snipped.

Charlotte wrung her hands. "What about Mr. Chadwick? Perhaps he will help you? He came here today, looking for you and Braedon. He wanted to ask you questions and to speak with Mr Connelly, but he was indisposed. Mr. Chadwick said he would come back tomorrow."

Interesting. Why did Mr. Chadwick need to speak to Niall? "Did he say anything else? Leave a message for any of us?"

"No."

"I know you mean well, Charlotte, and I appreciate the suggestion, but I must proceed carefully with Chadwick. I don't want him involved more than necessary with this family and our problems. I know you understand my reasons."

"Yes, of course. I understand." She paused, lifted her chin, and rolled back her shoulders. "In that case, I shall go with you, milady."

"I can't have you putting yourself in danger for me and my family."

"I have before. Because I consider you and your family to be *my* family too. I have no one else."

"But—"

"I cannot, will not, let you go alone, milady. I must insist and risk your displeasure."

Ravenna paused, searching Charlotte's pained features. *Good, steady, Charlotte.* She hated the thought of putting Charlotte in danger, too. She'd been so loyal through the years without fail, without complaint. Ravenna resigned with a sigh. "Very well. I don't want to put you in danger, but I'd be lying to say your help isn't welcome. I confess, the underground city is a frightening place."

Charlotte smiled.

"Do you still have the pistol I gave you a few weeks ago?"

"I do."

"Good. Bring that. I'll have my fan. We'll leave at midnight."

"I'll be ready." Charlotte dipped a curtsey and sped away to complete her tasks.

Ravenna returned to her bedchamber to wash off the mud, change her clothes, and take a small repast of pears, buttered bread, and wine. She needed rest, but the excitement and hope of finding her niece made any real rest impossible. All she could think of was returning to that underground maze, laying plans for how she would find Georgiana and get them all out safely. Braedon would be angry when he found out she went alone to find

Georgiana, but Ravenna was willing to endure his anger. She sipped her wine, the full body and complex notes of vanilla, black currant, oak, and a touch of spice unfurling delicate, warm tendrils through her body.

But there was more going on than just her niece missing. Ravenna herself had been attacked. Niall also. The Unity was responsible for Ravenna's attack and, it was likely, they were behind Niall's attack too. But why was the Irish Unity here in Edinburgh? Were they working with someone? Muir and his cohorts, perhaps? Samuel Brown? The weavers' discontent must be related to The Unity.

The Unity itself had begun as a movement of angry workers and farmers. However, there was also the matter of the king's assassination. Was The Unity connected to that as well? What did the king have to do with the weavers' issue? Her instincts told her that The Unity had infiltrated the weavers' group and were not only agitating them to create chaos in the kingdom, but also using them as a shield so The Unity could carry out their mission in the shadows while the weavers bore the punishment.

One issue at a time. Find Georgiana first. Then she could think about Muir, Samuel Brown, The Unity, and the worker-rebels. She drained her glass and stood, her muscles and legs aching from all the walking and running she'd been doing recently.

As she poured another glass of wine and selected a few pear slices, Braedon tripped into her mind, and a deep, penetrating fear overcame her. What if she were killed in her mission or severely wounded? What if she didn't come back? What if she never saw Braedon again? She couldn't leave this world without telling him her feelings. She looked at the door. Yet, the thought of crossing the hall and knocking on his door paralyzed her. No. That was impossible. Something held her back. A letter. She'd write him a letter.

She pulled her writing kit and paper from her portmanteau and sat down at a nearby table.

My Dearest Braedon,

How I've longed to call you mine. Yet fear has reigned me in. I know I hold my feelings close. At this moment, when I'm about to embark on a dangerous mission, I'm sorry I've kept you at arm's length. I'm sorry, too, that I didn't tell you of my mission. I didn't want to worry you or sway you from your work. I couldn't wait until tomorrow for you to come with me. My niece, the bit that's left of my family, needs me, and I cannot rest when I know where she is, but not helping her.

At any rate...I'm writing to tell you what you've wanted to hear these last months: I do love you. More than I have words to express. It cuts to think of you loving another. You are the first thought in my mind every morning and the last in my mind before I drift to sleep. And, if I die tonight, you will be my last thought on earth. You. Only you. Though I have feared you would break my heart, you are the risk I'm willing to take. After all this time, I can confess: You are the man I want to spend the rest of my life having adventures with.

Ever your little Raven....

She folded the letter and slipped it in her dressing gown pocket as Charlotte entered the room with a bundle of clothing.

Charlotte shut the door. "I have your dinner dress." She held it up, and the black and puce dress fell open. "It's the one you asked me to refashion." The dress consisted of puce muslin sewn into slits on the side, front, and back, and into the bodice and sleeves. "It's probably too simple, I know..."

"It's lovely. Thank you. I'll wear it tonight."

Charlotte beamed with pride. "Dinner will be served soon." Charlotte helped Ravenna put on the black and puce dress. "I also brought the other clothes you requested."

Ravenna looked at herself in the mirror. Though the dress had only a bit of color mixed with the black, it was a delight to wear color again. She smiled at her reflection as Charlotte buttoned the back of the dress. "I can't describe how much joy it gives me to see myself in even a splash of color." She ran her hands over the muslin skirt. "You finished it so quickly."

"It was a simple design. Lady Adair and Aurélie helped. We had nothing else to do all day while we watched over Mr. Connelly." Charlotte peeked over Ravenna's shoulder, smiling at her in the mirror. "I was happy to do it.

It's time for you to enjoy brighter days, no?"

"Indeed." Ravenna affixed her jet earrings as a soft knock sounded on her door.

Charlotte answered the door. "It's Lord Braedon, ma'am."

As Charlotte slipped out of the room with an armful of dirty clothes, Braedon stepped in, raking his eyes over Ravenna with admiration. "You look lovely this evening."

Her heart ached for him, to touch him, hold him, tell him everything she'd written in her letter. But her pride, her fear, stitched her mouth shut. "I am on my way to dinner."

"I wish I was dining here instead of at Rotherden's."

She gazed at him, taking in his freshly bathed skin and hair, the shaved jaw, delighting in the sweet, musky embrace of his cologne.

He hesitated. Then stepped forward. "There is something I wanted to give you."

She batted her eyes and tipped her head.

Braedon held out a small parcel wrapped in a lace handkerchief embroidered with his initials. She unfolded the corners of the fabric to reveal a small gold brooch locket in the shape of a heart encircled in tiny pearls. Inside the clear locket cover was hair braided and coiled. Upon closer inspection, the hair was his chestnut color and her own black color.

"It's lovely. Is this our hair bound together?"

"It is."

She touched the braid at the base of her head. "How did you get my hair?"

"A little bird helped me."

Ravenna thought. Then smiled. "Was she perhaps a little brown sparrow named Miss Charlotte Hart?"

He chuckled. "Yes. Though I will attest that she is less a sparrow and more a magpie since she managed to procure a lock of your hair without you knowing it."

Ravenna laughed aloud. "Yes. I think you're right."

"That laugh," he said. "And that smile." He touched her cheek. "I want to spend the rest of my days living in that warm light."

She ran her fingers over the brooch. "Thank you for the gift."

"Will you wear it now?"

"Yes. Of course."

"Please. Allow me." He took the brooch from her and, stepping closer, pinned the brooch at the base of her bodice. "This is a token of my promise to you. Just as these locks of hair are entwined and bound together, so too shall we be one day."

He was so close. She ran her gaze over his face, the lines of his jaw and brow, the little scar there above his eye. She inhaled his scent. His task finished, he stepped back, admiring his work.

She touched the glass heart. "Thank you," she whispered, her throat tight with emotion and desire. What if this were the last time she ever saw him? She wanted to tell him everything she'd written in the letter, spill it out over him like cool, refreshing water. But she couldn't say the words. They lodged in her chest like a stone. Instead, she pressed against him and pulled his mouth down to hers. He met her kiss with equal passion, hungry, consuming, his hands roaming over her body, pulling her tighter against him.

Suddenly, he broke the kiss and stepped away from her. "No. Not yet. Soon…" He smoothed his hair and adjusted his cravat. He stepped toward the door. "I should leave. You're in danger at the moment. And, I have some spying to do." He winked at her and opened the door.

"Braedon…" She ran to him.

He stopped.

Still, her words would not come. She longed to throw herself into his arms, let his embrace drain away her anxiety and cares. She stared up into his face, searching his eyes for her future, hoping for a kiss. Yet there, deep in those frosted blue pools, she saw it, for the first time—everything she hoped for and needed.

He said, "Good evening, my little raven. My love."

Chapter Twenty-Five

Dinner was uneventful, and the obligatory after-dinner conversation seemed to last forever. Ravenna watched the clock, eager to be about her business, though it was entertaining enough to listen to Lady Iverloch tell delightful stories of her childhood in Scotland.

"A time long gone, but never forgotten," Lady Iverloch sighed. "A time I hope we can reclaim."

Ravenna folded her hands in her lap. "It's impossible to go back to the way things were. How would you even begin to do such a thing?"

A slow smile spread over Lady Iverloch's lips. "We go back by holding on to our past and our traditions instead of adopting the ways of others."

"Others? You mean England? The Scottish government joined with the English government about fifty years ago. Long before you were born."

"Though I hadn't been born when Scotland was subsumed, I would love to reclaim what my family lost. You're Irish. You must understand what I mean."

"I am Irish, but my family were Loyalists."

Lady Iverloch sucked in a breath as though she'd been burned. "Oh. I see." She glanced around. Then forced a smile. "Pardon me. There is something I forgot to tell my husband." She stood, curtsied, and left Ravenna sitting alone. Ravenna excused herself on the grounds of a headache and returned to her bedchamber to wait for midnight.

When half past eleven rolled around, Ravenna dressed in her ragged clothes of worn and stained pants, too short and too wide, which she tied into place with a bit of twine. She pulled a stained and yellowed linen shirt over her head, which stank of old oil and mold. Over this, she donned a wool coat, too big with rips at the elbows. She tied the shirt collar closed with a black cravat, then knotted her hair on top of her head, pinning it tight against her skull and covering it with the hat. Slipping her fan onto her wrist, she tucked into her coat sleeve, the medallion near her wrist, ready to spring at her touch. She also dropped the note she'd written to Braedon inside her coat pocket.

By the time she'd finished dressing, Charlotte knocked on her door. She was dressed nearly identically to Ravenna. "Are you ready?" She held two lanterns.

"And you brought lanterns. Aren't you a clever creature? Clever enough to snip a lock of my hair without my knowledge, too, as I recently discovered."

"Only the smallest piece." Charlotte chuckled as she lit the lanterns. "Ordinarily, I would never dream of snipping your hair without your permission. But…" She shrugged, turning the flame low. "For a love token from a man like Lord Braedon…he is hardly a man I could say no to."

"The brooch is lovely. I'm glad, in this instance, for your little deception."

They stepped into the hall. "One moment." Ravenna stopped at Braedon's bedchamber. Her heartbeat increased with fear and anticipation as she slipped the note beneath his door.

They sneaked down the stairs, across the moonlight-dappled foyer, and stepped into the night. The warm air embraced them with a three-quarters moon peek-a-booing through thin clouds. Once they reached the bottom of the hill, they turned left, passing through nighttime revelers, vendors, and carriages toward the South Bridge tunnel. There seemed to be an agitated energy with more people than Ravenna had expected on the streets.

They approached a group of drunks and prostitutes leaning against the wall, talking and laughing. Ravenna hated the nightlife common in cities. She had endured this same seedy environment in the streets of London as she walked home or to a friend's house after her work at the theater. Or when she searched for her sister. The streets, especially at night, were unpredictable, dirty, and often dangerous.

Ravenna whispered to Charlotte, "Act tired and downtrodden. They're less likely to bother us."

"It wouldn't be an act." Charlotte snorted.

The prostitutes tried to get their attention, calling out to them, shaking their chests, lifting their skirts to reveal their legs.

Ravenna tugged Charlotte's sleeve as they picked up their pace.

When they reached the tunnel, Ravenna glanced around to ensure a prostitute, pimp, or footpad hadn't followed to rob them. "It's there at the end of the tunnel."

"What a frightening place," Charlotte whispered.

Shadows emerged from the tunnel, bedraggled, ragged souls who seemed agitated.

Ravenna and Charlotte kept their heads down, hanging close to the wall, doing their best to avoid attention and rats. They slipped into the shadowy tunnel and opened the door.

Darkness, the stench of rancid fat and fish, and the sounds of dripping water and skittering rats engulfed them. They eased down the path toward the faint glowing light at the other end. Voices, laughter, coughing, and groaning echoed against the walls, rolling toward them in waves like the cries from the bowels of hell in Dante's *Inferno.*

Finally, they entered a larger area with small rooms like caves or the structure of a wasp's nest, lining each side of the worn cobbled path. Blankets or cloths hung over some of the holes that served as doorways. Others stood uncovered, lending no privacy to whomever resided within. This place was both incredible and disturbing. Ravenna pulled her hat low over her face, peeking into each room. Each cramped space was about four feet by six feet, no larger than a jail cell.

One room held a family that included six children. Another room housed at least two families with infants and elderly crammed inside. A room of gangly, ragged men. One with bedraggled women. Another with forlorn parents and their mad daughter, screaming and talking to herself in the corner, clawing at the wall. Two men stepped out of a cell, pushing close to Ravenna and Charlotte, reeking of gin, and looking down on them as if trying to decide something.

The men seemed to change their minds when Ravenna and Charlotte skittered away like the rats. They turned the corner to another set of rooms and followed the path downward.

"My Lord," Charlotte whispered. "How large is this place?"

"I have no idea," Ravenna struggled to breathe through the smoke and stench.

Each room they passed was as broken and destitute as the one before it.

A gaunt skeleton of a man crouched in a doorway, muttering to himself. When he noticed them, he stood and raged at them. Ravenna put her hand inside her sleeve, her finger hovering near the medallion to release the blade in her fan. This man was deranged and couldn't help himself, but she would do what was necessary to protect herself and Charlotte. They sped away, and he returned to his crouching position in his doorway.

They pressed on, lifting their lights to peek in the holes serving as windows and doors. They had traveled at least a quarter of a mile when the path opened up into a larger room on the right; it was a tavern of sorts where men sat talking, gambling, and drinking. A copper still stood in the corner. A bootlegger's paradise.

To the right was another room, the smallest of them all. There, a girl sat, doubled up, her head resting against her knees. She had blonde hair. Ravenna stood in the doorway and whispered, "Georgiana?"

The girl looked up, confused, her face pale and bruised, dark circles under her eyes.

Oh, thank God! Joy burst inside Ravenna like the sun from behind a cloud. Every prayer, every hope was in this instant fulfilled. Georgiana was alive and relatively safe, but the poor, dear girl had clearly been through great trials. Ravenna wanted to embrace her, get her into a hot bath, nourish her with a heaping plate of food and clean clothes, and hold her tight. These maternal feelings gave rise to a deep, abiding anger as well. She wanted to destroy the men who had done this to her niece, her family. But she couldn't think of them now. The most important thing, in this moment, was getting Georgiana out of his den of human misery.

Ravenna tucked away her emotions and said to Charlotte, "Keep lookout."

She eased into the tiny room and knelt beside her niece.

Georgiana shrank.

The reaction cut Ravenna. She touched her shoulder. "It's me, Ravenna. Your auntie." Ravenna removed her hat and struggled to maintain her composure against the rank odor emitting from Georgiana. She clearly hadn't bathed in days.

Georgiana scrutinized Ravenna's face until the light of recognition shone in her eyes. "Auntie!" She squeaked, throwing herself against Ravenna, hugging her neck and sobbing. "I was certain I'd never see you again."

"We'll talk later. We need to leave now. Let's go." Ravenna helped her stand and nudged her out the door. "Make haste." Ravenna pulled Georgiana along.

They ran down the path, Ravenna leading the way with Georgiana and Charlotte following close behind. The further they proceeded, the higher Ravenna's hopes soared. Only a few hundred feet left to go, and they would be free.

Until two men stepped into their path. Larson and Emmett. Larson's beady eyes glimmered with malice, and Emmett's thin mouth twisted into a snarl.

Emmett grabbed for Georgiana. "Where do you think you're going, girl?"

Ravenna reached inside her coat sleeve, twisted the medallion on her fan, and drew the blade with a flick of her wrist. She sliced at Emmett, catching his hand. "Leave her alone!"

He whipped his hand back, holding it as blood trickled from between his fingers. "You foul strumpet!"

Larson laughed, closing in. "You never stop, do you, Ravenna?"

Charlotte moved around to stand with Ravenna, her pistol drawn, guarding Georgiana.

Larson ran his eyes over her. "And who is this slip o'woman? With her little pistol? You have only one shot, miss. I hope you have good aim."

"I'm close enough."

"Yes, but are you bold enough, lassie?"

Charlotte's eyes narrowed. "One way to find out."

Emmett lunged at Charlotte. As he attempted to wrest the weapon from her, the pistol fired, a loud bang ringing out with a puff of smoke. The sharp scent of gunpowder flooded the air, the shot failed to hit anyone. Emmett flung Charlotte against the wall and moved toward Georgiana.

"Charlotte!" Ravenna screamed, jumping between Georgiana and Emmett, swiping with her blade, wishing it was longer. "You'll not take her from me this time." He jumped, tucked, and dodged her every riposte.

People stood in their doorways, gaping at the scene.

Larson grabbed Ravenna from behind and swung her around.

She kicked the air and screamed, "Get off of me, you blasted devil!"

At the same time, Georgiana launched herself like a cat onto Larson's back, pulling his hair. He lurched and staggered.

Larson threw Ravenna down. The force of her body hitting the stone ground blasted the air from her lungs, and she dropped her blade, struggling to catch air like a fish out of water. Helpless, Ravenna could only watch as Emmett pried Georgiana off of Larson and dragged her by the hair toward where Charlotte lay.

Just as Ravenna's breath returned, Larson collected himself and fell on top of her, a gleam of wicked delight in his beady eyes. She tried to claw, kick, and bite as he snaked his bony, pale hands around her neck. Pressure built up in her eyes and face. Her breath cut off in her lungs as she slipped toward the dark pools of his eyes.

"I would ship you along with your niece, but you're clearly more trouble than you're worth."

Ravenna reached for her blade, a rock, anything she could use as a weapon. Her fingertips brushed against her blade. She stretched just an inch more. *There!* She grasped the handle.

Larson must've seen the triumph in her demeanor because he shifted away from her as she swiped her knife at him, slicing only his sleeve. Ravenna sat up, coughing, and scrambled away from Larson, who lifted to his knees and flung himself toward her again. The scar on her face itched. The scar *he* had put there. As he came down, she jammed her blade into the soft area above his hip. He froze and looked down, stunned.

"Stay away from me and my family," she wheezed. She rolled away from him and pushed herself to stand. Holding her blood-covered blade, she looked down on him, unsure if the wound was enough to kill him. If she was lucky, he'd bleed out in some dark alley and never haunt her again.

A man's voice called out in the distance. "Ravenna! Ravenna!"

Braedon. "We're here!" Relief washed through her as she pushed Charlotte and Georgiana toward the voice, through the jostling and growing crowd. "Go." She turned, watching Emmett and the crowd. *Where was Larson?* She searched the faces.

"Where is Larson? Where did he go?" She asked Emmett.

He smirked and shrugged. "Seems he flew away."

How? She'd been distracted for only a moment.

"Ravenna!" Braedon shouted again, his voice closer.

"Here!" She backed away from Emmett, training her blade on him.

"Make way!" Braedon pushed through the gathering people, separating them like wheat from chaff. Behind him followed Donovan and Chadwick, all with pistols drawn. All dressed down in only their shirts with pantaloons and boots under their great coats.

"Braedon!" Ravenna cried.

The three women pushed through the wall of people. Ravenna guided Georgiana to stand between herself and Braedon, determined to protect the prize she'd fought so hard to win.

Chadwick stepped forward. "What's going on here?"

Ravenna pointed at Emmett. "That man is Mr. Josiah Emmett. He is one of the traitors you're seeking. The other, Mr. Larson, has absconded. He's wounded, however. I can't imagine he'll get far."

Mr. Chadwick moved toward Emmett. "Wonderful news."

Emmett ran, but Chadwick, far more agile and faster than Ravenna had reckoned, gave chase. He knocked Emmett to the ground and whacked him with the butt of his pistol. "Enough! You're under arrest by orders of George III, King of England, for treasonous acts." Chadwick called out, "Lord Donovan. Help me get him up."

The men tucked their pistols and helped Emmett stand.

"Hold him tight," Chadwick said.

Donovan held Emmett's wrists as the fugitive struggled, kicked, and screamed. Chadwick pulled a set of iron manacles from the pocket of his great coat, locking them onto Emmett's wrists.

Emmett broke down in tears. "No! Nonononono…"

"That'll be enough, sir," Chadwick said. "You knew the risks when you began your treason against The Crown. You're not sorry for the crimes. Only sorry you've been caught." He turned to Donovan. "Will you assist me in getting this man to the jail in Edinburgh Castle?"

Donovan took one of Emmett's arms. "Gladly. I'm eager to report the details to the Prime Minister."

Braedon turned to the women and motioned down the hall. "Ladies, let's get you back to Iverloch Hall."

Emmett dragged his feet, still crying and struggling against the arrest.

Chadwick slapped him across the back of the head. "Enough! You were a man when you committed treason and kidnapped this poor girl, so you'll walk like a man to the justice you deserve."

Emmett hung his head, gasping through his tears. Then he pulled his legs beneath him and stood, staggering down the path.

Braedon wrapped his arm around Ravenna as she held on to Georgiana, and they all rushed out of the underground city, Charlotte leading the way.

When they reached outside, Georgiana spun and threw herself into Ravenna's arms. "Thank you for rescuing me. Thank you. He forced me to leave with him. I didn't want to. I didn't want to."

Ravenna hugged her, smoothing her hair and cooing at her. "Sh-sh-sh. I know. You're safe now. We have you."

Georgiana thanked Braedon for the proffered handkerchief and blew her nose.

"Come now, love," Ravenna spoke in soothing tones. "Let's get you back to Iverloch Hall."

Georgiana nodded, her face puffy with her crying and bruised from mistreatment. Ravenna led her niece down the street toward Lawnmarket. Ravenna asked Braedon, "How did you, Donovan, and Chadwick know where to find us? I thought you were at Rotherden's?"

"I was. When I returned to Iverloch Hall, I found your note. I knew immediately what you were up to. I roused Donovan and Chadwick, and we came to find you."

He looked down at her, his eyes full of unspoken, tender sentiment.

She squeezed his hand. "Thank you."

They turned onto Lawnmarket, the cobblestone road sloping down into the valley toward Holyrood Palace. Georgiana's usual bubbly, chatty demeanor had dulled into a quiet, dazed bearing as she shuffled down the street, occasionally dabbing her eyes and sniffling.

In the distance, bagpipes and drums rose up. Ravenna frowned at Braedon. "Bagpipes? At this hour? That can't be good."

"It sounds like someone is going to war." Braedon searched the street.

As they neared the bottom of the hill where Holyrood Palace stood, a roar of voices rose up. Ravenna and her party turned to see a wave of screaming men and women pushing toward them, holding torches. Like a tidal wave, they crashed over Ravenna, Georgiana, Braedon, and Charlotte, jostling them, shoving them aside. Braedon pushed Ravenna and Georgiana against the wall of a shop as Charlotte became separated and carried away in the crowd.

Ravenna watched her head bob among the people and then suddenly drop out of sight.

"Charlotte!" Ravenna ran toward the crowd, springing up on her tiptoes to find her.

Braedon shouted, "Ravenna!"

"No!" Georgiana screamed.

The force of the crowd carried Ravenna forward as she shoved through the sweaty and stinking bodies. She turned and pushed against the current, calling out for Charlotte, the din of the drums and the pipes drowning out her voice, as she searched through the horde. Several yards away, Ravenna spotted Charlotte, struggling to push herself to stand against the onslaught.

Ravenna swam against the current toward Charlotte. Reaching her, Ravenna grabbed her friend and pulled her forward. The women clung to each other, as elbows and shoulders pushed and banged against them. Pipes and drums beat the inside of Ravenna's skull like hammers. Ravenna searched for Braedon and Georgiana while also moving forward and to the right to pull free of the rushing throng.

Braedon ran alongside the pack, shouting and waving, "Ravenna!"

Georgiana tripped along behind him, her face etched with fear.

"Hold tight." Ravenna pulled on Charlotte, who clasped Ravenna's arm with both hands. Her focus on Braedon, Ravenna wove, like riding an ocean wave, back and forth and forward toward Braedon as the crowd carried them past Holyrood, approaching Calton Hill.

Ravenna and Charlotte popped out of the right side several yards away from Braedon and Georgiana. They all ran toward each other, meeting near the graveyard as the mob pushed forward to the weaver's mill at the base of Calton Hill. Within minutes, the sound of crashing glass echoed, and shouts rang out. Ravenna stood at a distance, watching rioters throw torches into the mill.

Several stragglers passed them, running to join in the riotous revelry.

Ravenna recognized a short, dumpy woman. "Aven!" She ran to her. "What are you doing? You aren't going to be involved in this, are you?"

"Aye," Aven said, her eyes intense with fury, glowed in the light of the torch she carried. "My husband is up front, and I'm going to join him. We're fighting for our rights and our wages. Something you lot wouldn't understand." She raked her eyes over Ravenna and Braedon.

"You're going to get in great trouble. They will hang you for this. The mill owner is protected by the government."

Aven looked down her nose with hard eyes. "We're going to die anyway. At least we'll die standing up instead of starving out."

Ravenna touched her arm. "Please. Save yourselves. Please, go home."

Aven jerked away. "And leave my people to fight alone? I'd be better off dead than to slink away a coward."

Ravenna watched, helpless, as Aven ran toward the mob. Fire now engulfed the mill. The mob sang an indiscernible song.

Braedon held her by the shoulder. "Let it go, Ravenna. You tried. They must play the cards the Fates deal to them now."

A horn sounded to their left. Over the hill poured a few red coats on horseback, followed by a dozen soldiers carrying bayonets and rifles. One of the officers turned his white horse and shouted orders to the soldiers who jogged in unison toward the burning mill. Soldiers and protestors clashed. Screams of people and horses ripped across the night, and shots rang out.

In an instant, Ravenna was swept back five years to Ireland. To the cries of her friends and family, shouts of soldiers, fires and smoke, and the scent of burning flesh. The squeals of pigs and horses, and the brutalized women screaming in pain in the streets. To the panic that tore through Wexford on that dark night when her world was forever changed…. She grew limp and fell to her knees, tears pooling in her eyes. Braedon helped her to stand as fire writhed against the shadows as smoke poured over the city.

The lead officer pulled out a paper and shouted "Hear ye, hear ye, by Royal proclamation 'Our sovereign lord the King chargeth and commandeth all persons, being assembled, immediately to disperse themselves, and peaceably to depart to their habitations, or to their lawful business, upon the pains contained in the act made in the first year of King George, for preventing tumults and riotous assemblies. God save the King!' You have now been read the Riot Act as required by law. You will disperse immediately or suffer the penalty of death!"

Aven, Sam, and several others picked up a stone and pulled their arms back, aimed at the lead officer.

Ravenna screamed, "Aven, no!"

Her voice was lost to the din all around. The workers launched their stones at the officers.

The lead officer lifted his sword. "Ready!"

The soldiers took their stance in a row in front of the horses.

"Aim!" The lead officer lowered his sword.

The soldiers aimed their rifles.

"Fire!"

The boom of the rifle-fire echoed in the valley. Smoke and the scent of gunpowder filled the air.

Georgiana cried out and covered her ears as the rioters scattered. A few men flew backwards, having been shot. The soldiers engaged the rioters, and the fight ensued. Several of the soldiers ran toward Samuel, Aven, and their friends. They tried to run, but the soldiers cracked them in the head or the back with the butt of their weapons. The officers wrestled other workers to the ground and bound their hands in shackles or ropes while most of the rioters broke and ran into the darkness.

"No!" Ravenna lunged forward as Braedon caught her about the waist. "No!" She broke into sobs.

Suddenly airborne, Ravenna was cradled tight against Braedon's chest and staring up at the stars blinking silently in the sky. Tears trailed down the sides of her face, and the memories of her parents and village floated before her as the smoke from the burning mill rolled in to blot out the stars.

Chapter Twenty-Six

When they had reached a safe distance from the disorder, Braedon set Ravenna on her feet.

Charlotte took her hand. "Let's go inside. A bath would be nice, wouldn't it?"

Ravenna nodded, still numb, still tethered to a distant and violent memory. The smoke of the burning mill scratched her throat.

"Come," Braedon whispered, placing his hand to the small of her back, guiding her up the hill toward Iverloch Hall with Charlotte and Georgiana following behind.

When they entered the house, Braedon ordered pitchers of water for the women and himself and a small repast of whatever food and wine was available, with apologies for the request at such a late hour. A footman and a scullery maid scrambled to fulfill the task.

They all climbed the stairs. As they parted, Ravenna hugged Charlotte. "Thank you, Charlotte. I will be eternally grateful for you and your courage tonight."

"Glad to do it, milady. You're all the people I have."

"You are as much my family as any born to me."

They wished each other goodnight and separated.

As Charlotte continued to her room, a shadow moved at the end of the hall, exiting Lady Iverloch's room. Ravenna, Georgiana, and Braedon stopped.

The shadow approached, finally revealing itself to be Lady Iverloch dressed to go out. "Lady Birchfield, good evening." She ran her eyes over Ravenna. "Forgive me, but why are you dressed in such a fashion?"

"Good evening." Ravenna bobbed a quick curtsey in greeting. Pain shot up her back, and her legs threatened to give way again. Exhaustion hollowed her out, and she yearned for a wash and a cozy bed. "I've been out, roaming, looking for my niece."

"Why are you wearing men's clothing?"

Ravenna looked down at her dirty pants and coat. "I thought I might travel unmolested in this disguise."

The scullery and footman rushed by with bathing supplies and food.

Lady Iverloch, her brows arched. "You seem to have run into some trouble."

"Quite." She ran her eyes over the lady in her cloak. "I notice you, too, are dressed to go out. Though it's quite late. Even the theater is closed at this hour."

She dithered. "Yes. Fresh air settles my mind whenever I can't sleep. After a short walk in the courtyard, I sleep like a babe."

Ravenna fought the smile creeping onto her lips. After witnessing Lady Iverloch and Lord Rotherden in the gardens recently, she knew exactly why a walk outside helped the lady to sleep. *Silver-tongued jade.* "Yes. Outdoor exercise can be quite…invigorating." The scent of jasmine perfume wafted from the lady.

Lady Iverloch turned her attention to Georgiana. "You must be the niece who has caused such a ruffle?"

Ravenna made the necessary introductions as Georgiana performed an unbalanced curtsey. "Nice to meet you, milady. I apologize we aren't meeting under better circumstances."

Lady Iverloch nodded her head, her emerald earrings glinting. "I'm glad you are safe. Welcome to Iverloch Hall. I'm sure you are all quite eager to return home now."

Georgiana said, "Yes, ma'am. I'm rather desperate to be home."

"And so you shall be soon enough. There is nothing so blessed and wonderful as one's home."

"Yes, milady." Georgiana said to Ravenna, "May I go to our bedchamber?"

Ravenna said to Lady Iverloch, "I think I'll join my niece. I'm sure you understand we are both quite tired. Good evening, Lady Iverloch. Enjoy your walk."

"Good evening…" Lady Iverloch floated down the stairs.

Georgiana whispered. "I don't think she's telling the truth. Who wears emerald earrings to walk in the garden at night?"

"Clever, girl. I noticed that too."

"What do you suppose she's really up to?"

Ravenna narrowed her eyes. "I'm not sure. But I do want to find out."

As soon as Ravenna closed the door to her bedchamber, she embraced Georgiana. "I'm so happy we found you." Ravenna hugged tighter, wishing she could hold her niece forever. "I will never let you go again. I will do a much better job of protecting you."

"It's not your fault…" Georgiana mumbled through her tears and sniffles. "It's all my fault. I was so foolish to trust him."

Ravenna pulled away and wiped Georgiana's tears. "No, no, darling. Nothing is your

fault. He is entirely to blame." She pulled a screen around the tub. "Come wash. You'll feel much better."

After Georgiana bathed, she sat at the table by the window, wolfing down bread, cheese, and wine as though she hadn't eaten in days.

Ravenna knelt in the small bath basin, her mind running over Aven and Samuel. She couldn't close out of her mind the image of the Red Coats aiming and shooting their guns, the voice of the commanding officer, and the arrest of the Browns. She scrubbed her skin with soap and rinsed it with rose water. She couldn't get the stench of gunpowder and fire out of her nose, hair, and skin.

When her bath was over, she wrapped up in a dressing gown and poured herself a glass of wine. She stood by Georgiana, putting her arm around the girl's shoulder. "Do you want to talk about it?"

Before Georgiana could answer, a soft knock sounded on Ravenna's door. She opened the door. "Braedon…"

He said, "I'm glad you're awake still. There is something I would like to discuss with you. May I come in?"

"Certainly. Wine?"

"Yes, please."

She motioned to a couple of chairs near the dark fireplace and moved to pour the wine.

Braedon sat. "When I was at Rotherden's this evening, I came by this letter." He handed it to her.

She smiled, handing him a glass of wine. "How exactly did you come by it?"

"Let's say Rotherden does a poor job of hiding important information." A faint smile played on his lips.

"As long as you didn't procure the letter the same way he did."

"What do you mean?"

She shared what she had witnessed the night Lady Iverloch gave the letter to Rotherden.

He pretended to think. "I had no idea such letter delivery options were available, or I might've availed myself of it."

She lifted a brow at him as he laughed. She opened the letter.

Dearest—

Tell your friends our new life begins on the 5th of November, a historic time. Our other friends will be in the location we discussed, at the determined time. As that particular clock strikes, we will begin the merriment at home, and not stop until the new dawn rises or we dance ourselves to death!

Ravenna frowned. "What a strange letter." If this were to fall into anyone else's hands, they would likely pass it off as a vague letter between two friends discussing a happy time. But she knew better. She'd seen too much of late to think this was anything other than a coded letter between rebels, dissenters, or spies. "What do you think this means?"

Braedon said, "I think, based on things we've witnessed, this letter is saying the plot to kill the king will go forward on November 5th. The historic day of the failed gunpowder plot in 1605, when rebels had attempted to blow up the English parliament."

"The letter says *As that clock strikes....* Which clock? There was no mention of a clock, but the word *that* indicated something specific. A clock striking, striking..." She sipped her wine, thinking. "Perhaps the clock strike indicates the assassin striking his target?" She paused, catching a faint floral scent. She placed the paper under her nose. Jasmine.

"What is it?"

"Jasmine. Smells like Lady Iverloch's perfume." She held the paper under his nose.

He nodded, swirling his wine. "Do you think she's involved?"

Ravenna hesitated. "Likely. It's not out of the realm of possibility." She leaned on the arm of her chair and counted with her fingers. "This might be the letter he claimed from her last night during their tryst. First, she's quite devoted to Scotland and cares nothing for the country's loyalty to The Crown. Second, she and Rotherden are lovers. Third, Rotherden is working with political dissidents."

"So Rotherden and Lady Iverloch are working together to kill the king and free Scotland." Braedon sat back, stretched out his legs.

"They must be. With her connections to the nobility and his connections to the government, it would have been simple for them to get a map of Kew Palace, learn the king's schedule, and place an assassin. Someone like Samuel Brown wouldn't have been able to achieve that."

He sipped his wine. "True. I wonder to what extent Lord Iverloch is involved?"

Ravenna bit the inside of her lip. "It's difficult to say. I have detected nothing from him that would indicate a divided loyalty." She returned to the letter. "*We will begin the merriment at home and dance...*

"Home being Scotland?"

"Likely. Assuming they are discussing Scotland..." She studied the letter. "Whatever the merriment is, it won't stop until the *new dawn,* or they *dance to death.* There's something dark and threatening there. Dawn could mean a new day, but could also mean a new life, a new way of life."

"And they'll dance themselves to death in celebration?" He sat back in the chair, balancing the wine glass against his thigh. "That doesn't make sense."

"Dancing could also mean swordplay, right? They'll dance, meaning fight, to death."

"So perhaps this means the *new day* means a new kingdom, a new ruler. Therefore, at the time King George is assassinated, the rebels will strike in Scotland or Ireland? Or both?"

"It would be the perfect time for a rebellion—to strike when England is on its knees at the fall of its leader."

Georgiana said, "It will be both."

"How do you know?" Ravenna shifted to look at her.

She turned in her chair. "They talked about it. I didn't hear all the particulars, but I heard enough. They were exchanging girls to France for munitions and also getting investors to purchase munitions. They were then going to ship those munitions here and to Ireland."

"Did you happen to hear about who the investors are?" Braedon asked.

"One who owns Empire Weaving. I can't remember his name, but I saw him."

Ravenna said to Braedon, "Empire Weavers was one of the company crates I saw on the ship." She turned back to Georgiana. "The man you saw, what did he look like?"

"Tall, skinny. Blonde hair. Big teeth."

"Thank you, Georgiana." Ravenna faced Braedon. "That sounds a great deal like Mr. Sinclair, does it not? Matches his description, and he owns a mill."

He nodded. "It does. Do you know which mill he owns?"

"I do not, but we should find out."

"I've kept you ladies awake too long." He stood. "I'm sure you're both exhausted."

"Tomorrow, I'll procure a sample of Lady Iverloch's handwriting so we can compare it to

this."

"Then we'll give it to Chadwick." Braedon pulled her into the hall with him and closed the door. He touched her cheek. "Are you well after tonight's skirmish? I know you had a fondness for Mr. and Mrs. Brown, and you have an unpleasant history with the soldiers."

She looked down at his hand. "I can't stop thinking about them. Surely there is a way to help them."

"I don't think so. But we can discuss it with Chadwick. Perhaps we can beg for leniency for them?"

"Perhaps."

He kissed her forehead. "Try not to think about it. Try to think of better things."

"Like what?"

"Like you have saved many girls from torment. You saved your niece. And…" His fingers traveled to her neck, slipping under the neck of her dressing gown. "You might ruminate on my growing fondness for you. Or the pleasure of a kiss from one who adores you." He kissed her tenderly, sending thrills under the surface of her skin. "Sleep well, my love."

Ravenna returned to the bedchamber, light and warm, and climbed into bed. She yawned. "Braedon is right. I am exhausted." She had scores of questions about what had happened to Georgiana, but they could talk about it later. She squeezed her eyes shut, trying to think of anything except the Browns and the evening's riot.

Georgiana crawled into bed beside Ravenna and blew out the candle. "I will help you get a copy of Lady Iverloch's handwriting." She settled into the pillows and under the counterpane.

"I cannot allow you to get involved. You've been through a horrible experience. I want you to be safe and protected now. If you were caught…." She shook her head against the pillow. "No. I cannot allow it."

"I want to help you."

"Georgiana…"

"Auntie, I must do this. Those men took me, held me against my will. And other girls, too. They did horrible things to us. I want to contribute somehow to bringing to justice anyone who is involved. I've learned what evil looks like, and I won't be helpless again."

Chapter Twenty-Seven

The next morning, Ravenna and Georgiana took breakfast in their bedchamber. They sat at the table by the window in their dressing gowns, enjoying scones, cream, jam, cold ham, and tea.

Ravenna had questions about Georgiana's abduction. She wanted to talk about it, but didn't want to upset her niece. She thought about her approach as she smeared a dollop of cream on her scone. "So…" Gathering her thoughts, she glanced outside at the crows slicing the gray skies. "I would like to know what happened? Did you ever meet Mr. Larson before Emmett kidnapped you?"

Georgiana stirred sugar into her tea. "I did see him hanging around the outside of the garden one day, and he spoke with me, but I told you of that instance. You warned me to stay away from him, and I obeyed you. I never saw him again until Emmett kidnapped me. I had no idea Larson was the same man outside the garden."

Ravenna chewed her food. "Did you have any indication of Mr. Emmett's intentions?"

"At first, I thought I loved Mr. Emmett and that he loved me."

"Did he say he loved you?"

"He did. He said he'd grown very fond of me in the days we'd been working together. He pulled me close and kissed me, most unexpectedly. I pulled away and ran to my bedchamber, but he pursued me."

"When was this?"

"The day of the kidnapping."

Georgiana blushed, looking down at her plate of ham and bread. "He came into my bedchamber and spoke to me tenderly. He said he wanted to run away and elope."

"I was flattered, but scared. I asked him why we couldn't marry the proper way, with the reading of the banns, in a church, and with a wedding breakfast. With friends and family present."

"What did he say?"

She blinked, cutting her ham. "Now, when I think of it, he never really answered my question. Professed he was so in love he couldn't wait, but…" Her bottom lip quivered, and her voice grew watery. "It's quite clear to me now he never…." She put her hands over her face and sat back in her chair. "I was such a fool."

"Oh, darling…" Ravenna's heart twisted in her chest. She rushed to Georgiana's side and put her arm around her. "No. He abused your trust and your heart, my love. None of this is your fault. Not even a little."

Georgiana sniffled and nodded. When she had regained her composure, she said, "After I told him to leave, because I needed time to think, I caught him in your bedchamber, going through your wardrobe."

Ravenna returned to her seat. "Looking for my jewels, no doubt."

"Yes." Georgiana nodded and blew her nose. "When I caught him, I tried to run to tell Mr. Banks to have Mr. Emmett ejected from the house. But Emmett caught me and held me at knifepoint. He made me write the letter and then took me down the servant's stairs."

Ravenna held her hand. "I'm so sorry, poppet. You must have been terrified."

Georgiana nodded. "I was. He took me to an old building in Smithfield, and I was put in a cart with other girls. They made us lie down and put an oilcloth and straw over us."

"We found the girls when they were loaded on the ship. I had hoped you would be among them. Why weren't you?"

"I had the good fortune to be sick with an influenza. To protect their investment, they kept me separate, informing me I would be included on the next shipment."

Ravenna reached across the table and put her hand over Georgiana's. "I'm so thankful we found you in time. I'm sorry it took so long to find you." Ravenna's throat tightened around her words. "We tried. We looked for you every day."

"I know. I'm so thankful you found me when you did. That's why I want to do everything I can to help you catch whoever is behind this."

Ravenna beamed. "My brave girl. Very like your mother."

Georgiana smiled over the rim of her teacup. "Or you." She sipped her tea. "How are we going to procure a sample of Lady Iverloch's handwriting?"

"I will need to think about it. First, we must dress and visit your uncle Niall and his wife, Aurélie. They have come from America, and I'm sure they're eager to meet you."

After breakfast, Ravenna and Georgiana stepped across the hall to Niall and Aurélie's room. Aurélie was in a dressing gown, sitting up in bed with a lace bandeau around her dark curls, reading. Niall stood at the window, dressed in all but his coat, a bandage wrapped around his head.

"Should you be out of bed?" Ravenna asked.

He turned stiffly. "Aye. I'm right as the rain. What good will it do to lie up in the bed if I'm drawing breath?"

Ravenna scratched her scar. "I'm happy to see you up and about. I've been worried about you. Though I hope you will not strain and give yourself time to heal."

"Aye, Aurélie has already—" His gaze fell on Georgiana. "Helen...I mean, you must be...Georgiana?"

Georgiana nodded. "Yes."

He walked toward her, arms open. "I'm your Uncle Niall." They hugged. He pulled away and looked her over. "What a pretty thing you are. The very spit of your mother." He kissed her forehead. He laughed through tears. "I haven't seen you since you were a young lass."

Aurélie slid out of bed and tottered toward them as Niall turned to her. "I'd like you to meet my wife, Aurélie."

Georgiana bobbed a curtsey. "A pleasure to meet you, ma'am."

Aurélie laughed, her dark eyes brilliant. "Lord, child, no. I'm your auntie." She embraced her.

When they separated, Georgiana looked at her with interest. "You're from America?"

"I am, child."

"You have an accent. Like French."

Aurélie laughed. "I'm a Creole, child. A little French, a little African, and a little Chitimacha Indian."

Georgiana's eyes widened. "Are you going back to America? I would love to visit there someday."

"Not any time soon. We are staying here for a while. Though I'm sure we'll visit again eventually. You're always welcome to visit, though the decision will be your Aunt Ravenna's."

Ravenna added, "Or your mother's, if we find her soon."

Niall's smile faltered. "What are the chances of finding Helen, do you think?"

Ravenna shrugged. "It's difficult to say. London is a very big place, full of more people than I could count. I've been looking for her for six years and haven't found her yet."

Shame twisted his features. He turned and motioned for Ravenna to join him across the room. When they had reached the corner, he ran his hand through his long, dark hair. "I want to thank you. For…everything. I know what a trouble I've been to you. To Aurélie." He shook his head and looked down. "Things have been…complicated."

Ravenna crossed her arms and tipped her head. "What do you mean?"

He ignored the question. "All I could think about last night was how awful it would be to leave Aurélie to raise our child alone. Where would she go? What would she do? How would my child fare without a father?"

Ravenna clenched her jaw, the words *I told you so* like barbs in her mouth. His epiphany was the very thing she'd been trying to tell him. "I understand you would love to see Ireland free and self-sufficient, too. I'm sure you'll find a way to do it without much bloodshed."

He hemmed. "Aye. But it's not my problem to solve anymore."

Her eyes grew wide. "What do you mean?"

"I'm laying down my sword. I can't fight a losing cause only to sacrifice my family. I've sacrificed too much already. I will do my best to help the poor and the working people, but I can't put my life and the lives of my family at risk for groups like The Unity, who have no concern or respect for our lives or our sacrifices."

"I'm so glad you've come to your senses."

He laughed. "I suppose it had to be knocked into me." He pointed to the wound wrapping on his head. "But I had seen Larson and Emmett and was on my way to report them to Mr. Chadwick when I was set upon in New Town."

"You should know Mr. Emmett was arrested last night."

He gazed at her with concern. "What about Mr. Larson?"

"He escaped. For now. But I can't imagine he will be free for long."

"Is that so?" His eyes darted, and he turned to look out the window, shaking his head and rubbing his face. "Oh, Lord help us," he whispered.

"Do you think Mr. Emmett will say anything about you?"

"I doubt it. We don't know each other." He blew out a breath. "I'm far more concerned about Larson. He will come for us."

"I'm far more concerned about him being caught alive. Aren't you?"

He searched her face, puzzled.

"If he's caught alive, he will talk about you. About me. He will implicate us in his treasonous acts. Then imagine what will happen to us. Do you think The Crown will care that the only reason I participated in espionage was to save you? You, who was in fact working with the rebels for a time."

"I'm so sorry, Ravenna. I never wanted you involved in any of this."

"But there's something else I want to know. Why were you at the docks? And why have you been hanging about with Mr. Muir?"

He licked his lips. "I wish I could tell you. I can't say anything yet. I need more time." He rubbed his face.

What did that mean? Why wouldn't he tell her about his activities and why he was spending time with Mr. Muir?

Aurélie said, "Niall? Are you unwell?"

Niall put on a bright demeanor, approaching her. "I'm well. Only a little sore. And tired. I think I need some broth and tea. Perhaps a nap." He wrapped an arm around her and hugged her against his side while staring at Ravenna. Through his eyes, he silently communicated to Ravenna: *If anything happens to me, take care of my wife and child.*

Ravenna nodded.

Chapter Twenty-Eight

Ravenna turned to Georgiana, "Your auntie and uncle need rest. Come, there is something I would like to discuss with you." When they stepped into the hall, Ravenna whispered, "We're going to get a sample of Lady Iverloch's writing. Come with me."

Ravenna stopped a maid in the hall carrying an armful of sheets. "Pardon me, can you tell me if Lady Iverloch is in her bedchamber?"

The maid said, "She's nae in her room, milady. She's in the kitchens preparing the menus with the housemistress, ma'am."

"Thank you."

The maid curtsied with a smile and rushed away with her bundle.

Once the maid disappeared down the servants' stairs, Ravenna and Georgiana ran on tiptoes down the hall to Lady Iverloch's room. She stooped to peek in the keyhole, in case the maid had been wrong.

She whispered to Georgiana. "Stay here and watch. Don't let anyone in the room."

"What if Lady Iverloch comes?"

"Distract her. Ask her if she would help you with something in the library or the garden."

Ravenna slipped inside the bedchamber. It smelled of jasmine perfume, like the letter Braedon had found in Rotherden's home. The red trim around the white bedclothes matched the red velvet curtains. Red floral and plush ivory chairs and a red velvet sofa sat on an ivory carpet in front of a dark fireplace. A large medieval tapestry depicting a unicorn trampling a lion hung on the wall. A meaningful political image from the 12th century. The unicorn symbolized Scotland since King William I "The Lion," and the lion symbolized England since Richard I "The Lionheart" when the Plantagenets were in power.

In this tapestry's message, the unicorn would defeat the lion, meaning Scotland would be victorious in its fight for freedom against England. Or at least, that was once the hope until England prevailed and subsumed Scotland under one crown in 1707. The common belief was that the unification had been peaceful. However, as Ravenna had recently learned, that wasn't true. There were pockets of rebels who continued to resist and fight for freedom. Interesting that this tapestry hung in Lady Iverloch's room. She had spoken before of her love for Scotland. Her lover, Rotherden, was working against the Crown. Lady Iverloch was becoming more and more a person of interest.

Ravenna searched the room: The jewelry on the vanity with her collections of cosmetic containers and perfume bottles. The remains of a half-eaten breakfast sat on a table by the window. Discarded clothes lay in a heap at the end of the bed. The maids hadn't been here to clean yet, but they soon would be. She needed to hurry.

Ravenna ran to the writing desk by the other window. She opened the bottom desk drawers first, but found only blank paper and letters from other people. Then she opened the small door on the top of the desk by the inkstand. Inside was tucked a letter to "R." She flipped the paper. There was a red seal on the back—a saltire with a thistle flower in the middle over what appeared to be a dead or sleeping lion. She looked at the seal stamp on the inkstand; it had simply an R and I with ivy surrounding it.

Inside the small cabinet where she found the letter was the other seal with the saltire and thistle. She found a third seal stamp: a wild mountain cat with words across the top: *TOUCH NOT A CATT BOT A TARGE.*

Ravenna rolled back to her Irish Gaelic roots, to words dusty from lack of use. Though Irish and Scottish Gaelic were different, there were some similarities. A *targe* was a shield. *Touch not a catt* was easy enough. Through context, she was able to translate the phrase to mean *Touch not a catt without a shield.* This was a family or clan motto. Perhaps Charlotte would know which one. But the meaning was clear enough: cats were intelligent, predatory, sly, and unpredictable animals, so it was best not to touch one without a good defense. *Interesting.*

This did not look good for Lady Iverloch to have three different seals, two of which appeared quite political and contrary to the English Crown. These politically charged seals, the letter, and the tapestry painted a most interesting picture of Lady Iverloch. Ravenna needed to speak with Chadwick to see if he had any suspicions toward the Iverlochs.

She opened the letter and skimmed it. It only incriminated her fidelity as a wife. But it was a perfect sample of the lady's writing. She slipped the two stamps into her bodice along with the letter, sampling the lady's writing. Ravenna turned to leave, her eye catching the edge of a doorframe peeking out from behind the tapestry. She pushed back the cloth and tried the door. It opened to a round stairwell with stairs going up one side. *Very interesting.* Did these stairs lead to the Widow's Peak Lord Iverloch had discussed in the painting he'd shown her?

She stepped inside. There were two doors. She opened the other. It led to the hallway. She looked up at the twist of stairs spiraling upward at least another story. Ravenna climbed the steep stone stairs. Upon reaching the top, she opened the door to the left, revealing a narrow promenade that stretched across the length of the tiled roof. This was the spot Lord Iverloch indicated in the picture the first night she'd spoken with him: The Widow's Peak. She stepped onto the stone promenade, the wind whipping her hair and dress, strong enough to nearly knock her over. She stood at the balustrade that reached to her hips, looking out across the villages and rolling hills washed in purple heather to the right, and the Port of Leith and Holyrood Palace to the left.

She imagined an unknown woman, long ago, watching her husband or son sail or march away to war. That long-ago lady came here every day, searching, waiting for his return. When he didn't return, or when she'd received news of his death, or when an invading army battered at the doors of the hall, the woman, desperate and driven to madness, climbed over the rail and dove to her death to evade a life of desolation or torture. Such was the legend of Lady Montrose that Lord Iverloch had shared.

Inside, thrills rippled through her as the wind seemed to plunge inside her, filling her, and lifting her like the hot air balloon she'd seen exhibited at Vauxhall once. She peeked over the edge of the balustrade at the jagged cliffside and rocks below that bordered a small loch. Fear shot through her, forcing her back from the edge against the wall of the house. This was the most amazing and terrifying thing she'd ever seen. She didn't want to stay, but didn't want to leave either.

After another scan of the landscape, Ravenna returned to the stairwell and took the door to the left, entering the hallway. This door, too, was behind a tapestry. She'd seen the tapestry a dozen times on her way to her bedchamber, but had never paid any attention to it.

Georgiana frowned, confused. She looked at the bedchamber door, then at Ravenna. "How…?"

"It's a door to the Widow's Peak tower and to Lady Iverloch's room."

Braedon exited his bedchamber. "Don't you look like that cat who ate the cream? What are you up to, my little raven?"

"Only exploring the mysteries of this old house." Still roused from her experience on the promenade, she was eager to share it with him and him alone. She turned to "Georgiana, I have the items I need. Thank you for helping me. Please go back to our bedchamber or ask the butler to show you the library."

"I'd love to see the library." Georgiana curtsied and ran downstairs.

When Georgiana had disappeared, Ravenna flashed a coquettish smile and grabbed Braedon's hand. "You must see this."

He lifted a brow. "I'm intrigued." He followed her up the stairs to the promenade.

"Isn't it amazing?" She watched him enjoy the scenery.

"It is, indeed." He soaked in the vista before his gaze finally settled on her. "Though, I daresay, seeing your pleasure brings me the greatest delight. You're more beautiful now than ever."

"This is the Widow's Peak Lord Iverloch told me about."

"How did you come to find this?"

Ravenna flashed a grin. "I have something else to show you." She reached inside her bodice to extract the letter and stamps.

His eyebrows shot up. "Of all the times I imagined I might see your charms, I never imagined this."

She laughed. "Stop it, you rogue." She showed him the items she'd extracted from Lady Iverloch's bedchamber and explained everything.

"Aren't you a crafty little raven?" He examined the seals.

"Once we confirm the writing is indeed hers, we should give these items to Mr. Chadwick, too." She returned the stamps and letter to her bodice for safekeeping, Braedon watching with interest.

He took her hand. "My dearest Ravenna, I've had something on my mind for a few months, and this time, this place, is the perfect opportunity to bring to fruition the long-held desires of my heart." He reached into the fob pocket of his waistcoat. "I was going to do this tonight, under the full moon in the garden, but I can't think of a better opportunity or location than this moment, this place." He knelt before her and held up a ring with a large oval sapphire in the center, encircled with diamonds.

"What are you doing?" Ravenna asked.

He ignored the question. "This ring has been worn by seven generations of women in my family, including my own mother. I have fervently loved and admired you since I first laid eyes on you. Will you make me the happiest of men? Will you honor me by wearing this ring and being my wife?"

If she were being honest, she couldn't imagine her life without him. As she searched his blue eyes, she saw a future with him she'd never seen with her late husband, Philip. She couldn't imagine waking up every day and Braedon not being there, lying next to her, sharing her life. She wanted not only him but a future with him as his wife and the mother of his children. She wanted a family with him, wanted to share all her joys and trials with him.

She smiled, happy tears in her eyes. "Yes. I want nothing more than to be yours forever, Braedon." She paused. "As long as you'll stop provoking me."

"Provoking you is the only reason I want to marry you." The corners of his eyes crinkled as he slipped the ring on her finger and kissed her hand.

She giggled, pulling him to stand, and threw her arms around him. They kissed, hungry for each other, as the wind whirled around them, encircling them in a celebration dance.

They separated, pressing their foreheads together. He cupped her face in her hands. "You are the most beautiful, amazing woman I've ever known, Ravenna. And I can't wait to spend the rest of our lives together."

Chapter Twenty-Nine

Joy like sunbeams carried Ravenna down the stairs. "I can't wait to tell everyone."

They stepped into the hallway, holding hands.

He turned her hands over and bent to kiss her palms. "Can you at least wait until I can join you?"

"Where are you going?"

"I have a bit of business in town. Let's tell everyone tonight at dinner.

"I will try to wait." She looked at the ring, watching it spark. "I have a question, though."

"What's that?" He tucked a tendril of her hair behind her ear.

"What would possess you to bring the ring with you to Scotland?"

He smiled. "I have carried this ring with me every single day since my return from Italy. And every day, I've tucked it into my fob pocket and attached it to the latch so I wouldn't lose it. I've simply been waiting for the perfect time."

She flashed a teasing smile. "How did you know I'd say yes?"

He laughed. "I didn't know. It was quite a gamble. But I suppose I have a taste for adventure." He lowered his lips to hers for a kiss. He added in a quiet voice, "I don't know about you, but I think I'm most looking forward to the honeymoon."

She giggled and nudged him playfully. "You silver-tongued rogue."

He kissed her neck. His soft lips and warm breath sent tingles through her. He said, "I'm off to my business. I'll see you at supper."

His fingers slipped from hers, and she watched him jog down the stairs, thinking about the honeymoon. She, too, was looking forward to it. She clapped her hands over her smile and turned toward her bedchamber, wondering how she was going to keep the happy news quiet until supper.

Charlotte was in Ravenna's bedchamber, putting clean clothes in the wardrobe, and Georgiana was stretched across the bed with a book.

"Charlotte," Ravenna said. "You're just the person I would like to speak with." She extracted the letter and stamps from her bodice and dumped them on the bed beside Georgiana. "I found this stamp in Lady Iverloch's room. Do you know who this crest belongs to?"

Charlotte studied it, then looked at the floor, searching the recesses of her memory for the information. While she thought, Ravenna retrieved the purloined letter from her medicine chest to compare it to the one she had stolen from Lady Iverloch's bedchamber.

At last, Charlotte said, "McBain. Clan McBain. Of course! It makes sense now. Clan McBain fought with the Jacobites at Culloden near Inverness, which is the land of their family seat. It was the last stand of the Scottish Jacobites to keep the throne in the hands of the Stuarts and out of the hands of the English Hanoverians. But, of course, it divided the country as some clans sided with the English and others allied with the Jacobites."

"Like in Ireland."

"Yes."

Ravenna looked at the letters, comparing the writing. "Look here, Charlotte." She laid the letters side by side. "I think the same hand wrote this."

"Lady Iverloch?" Georgiana stretched her neck to see the letters.

"Yes." Ravenna nodded. "She's from Clan McBain."

Charlotte placed the stamps on the bed. "It's possible her clan never forgave the conquest of the Jacobites. Perhaps her clan wanted more than a Stuart king."

Ravenna toyed with the ring Braedon had given her. "In other words, they wanted Scottish independence, so they colluded with others who wanted to assassinate the king."

Charlotte sat on the bed. "Two factions working for different things, but toward the same end."

"Yes." Ravenna crossed her arms. "One wants to kill the king. One wants Scottish independence. But if they work together, they can destabilize England through the king's assassination—"

"Then strike with a well-funded, well-armed rebellion. And based on recent happenings, it's likely the Scottish rebels are working with the Irish rebels." Charlotte frowned. "It's likely they're both working with the French, too."

"No doubt. Napoleon is likely looking for a weakness in our nation to exploit. In fact, he could be behind all of it, pulling all the strings using the Irish and the Scottish as puppets to sew division in the kingdom and topple the kingdom from within."

"And the girls were going to be shipped and sold in France," Georgiana added, sitting up. "I even heard Emmett and Larson talking about connections in France."

"Exactly," Ravenna said. "We must find a way to stop her. I'm going to speak with Chadwick today."

Ravenna and Charlotte waited in the dining area of the Black Horse Inn. The room was crowded with travelers, and the air smelled of cabbage and sausage.

Mr. Chadwick descended the stairs in a snug blue suit and boots polished to a mirrored shine. He bowed. "Ladies." He draped his great coat over the back of his chair and set his hat on the table. "You catch me on my way out."

"We won't take much of your time, Mr. Chadwick." Ravenna opened her reticule to unload its contents. She placed the two letters on the table alongside the two stamps she procured from Lady Iverloch's room.

He studied the items, then sat. "What am I looking at?"

Ravenna explained. "This is a letter Lord Braedon collected from Lord Rotherden's house. And these stamps I obtained from Lady Iverloch's room."

"Why am I not surprised to learn you and Lord Braedon are a couple of footpads?"

"Insult me all you like, sir. But there is a purpose to this. This letter details, in coded language, when you can expect the attack on the king. It is written in the same hand as this love letter Lady Iverloch had written to Lord Rotherden, but never sent."

He cocked a brow as he looked over the letters. "Interesting…" He took up one of the stamps. "And what are these?"

"These are stamps of a political nature."

Charlotte interjected to explain Lady Iverloch's connection to Clan McBain. "Her family were Jacobins and fought against England in the Battle of Culloden. Lady Iverloch seems unwilling to lay down her sword, however."

Ravenna added, "Lady Iverloch is not loyal to the English Crown, and neither is Lord Rotherden. I believe they are behind the plot to kill the king in order to create chaos and weaken England. What I can't know is if it's of their own accord or if they are puppets of Napoleon. Either way, once the king is dead, they mean to ignite a Scottish revolution for independence. At the same time, I think the Irish Unity will begin a revolution in Ireland, and France will begin an invasion. Three attacks at the same time while England fights Napoleon abroad. It's not likely England would survive it."

He nodded, working his mouth in thought. "Seems we have quite a dire situation on our hands, Lady Birchfield. Other information I've received seems to support what you're saying." He stood and donned his great coat and hat. "Thank you for bringing this to my attention." Gathering the letters and stamps, he dropped them into his pocket. "Good day, ladies. I have some business to attend to."

"If I can be of service…" Ravenna stood.

His dark eyes penetrated her. "Milady, if your help is required, I shall let you know." He straightened his coat. "It's best for you to keep your distance."

"I understand. Have the kidnapped girls been returned to their homes?"

"They have."

"I'm glad to hear it. Do you know if other girls have been captured?"

"I don't know. Though I have reason to believe they may be looking to capture more girls to make up for the ones they've lost."

"Mr. Chadwick. One last question. Have you found Mr. Larson?"

"We're still searching for him."

"I see." She wrung her hands.

He glanced at her hands. "Don't worry, Lady Birchfield. I'm sure we'll find him soon."

"Mr. Chadwick. I have another question, please. The other night at the mill riot, there were two people arrested: Samuel and Aven Brown. Is there anything that can be done to help them? Or to compel leniency?"

"Why should you wish to? Are you sympathetic to the rioters?"

"The mill keeps cutting wages. The workers are suffering. I can't deny having some sympathy for them."

"They made poor choices, milady. There are ways to fight for one's beliefs and causes without violence."

"Granted. I don't condone the violence. From either side. But surely something can be done to help the Browns?"

"Who are these people to you? How do you know them?"

"They're strangers, really. But Mrs. Brown was especially kind to me when I was searching for Georgiana. And she saved me from Larson's attack."

"They have committed crimes, Lady Birchfield."

"I understand, but perhaps they can get a reduced sentence?"

He looked down, and his shoulders slumped. He sighed. "It's not likely they can be helped, milady." Sadness weighed his voice. "I understand your concern for them, and your compassion is admirable. The officers followed the law. They read The Riot Act and informed the mob of their duty to depart. They were informed that failure to comply would result in death. Instead, the rioters threw rocks. An act of aggression against The Crown. They chose to ignore the law. They will be dealt with accordingly."

"What does that mean? A trial? A prison sentence?"

"Death. They're going to be hanged today at noon in Grassmarket along with several other rioters who were arrested."

She and Charlotte exchanged a panicked glance. "What time is it now?" Ravenna asked.

He opened his pocket watch. "Quarter of noon." Returning the watch to its pocket, he said with sadness. "I'm sorry, Lady Birchfield. There's nothing to be done now. They made their choices, and those choices have consequences."

She nodded. "I understand." When they left the inn, Ravenna said to Charlotte. "I'm going to Grassmarket."

They climbed the hill to Grassmarket at the base of Edinburgh Castle. The space was bordered with tenement housing, rental rooms, business, vendors, and a livestock pen for animals being sold to market. Vendors shouted their food and drink specials. Musicians sang about the brave workers who burned down the mill. Hundreds of people gathered their voices rising to a dull roar, adding to the cacophony around them. Were there not a scaffold at the center of the crowd, Ravenna might've thought they stumbled on a circus exhibition or a parade.

The Browns, their friends Mable and Callum, and a few others were already on the scaffold, the nooses around their necks. Some of them were somber, some crying, some defiant and angry. Aven stood defiant. No doubt she thought of her mother, who also stood defiant when she was tried and executed for witchcraft. In this moment, Aven probably believed she had made her mother proud.

The executioner pulled black sacks over their heads. The officiant announced all their names and their crimes. Then he shouted. "Let this be an example to anyone who would ignore and disregard the law and the commands of The Crown. Long live the King!"

Ravenna trembled. "I can't watch this." She spun around and headed back down the hill with Charlotte on her heels in time to hear the scaffold's bottom drop.

Chapter Thirty

Ravenna dragged her way up the hill to Iverloch Hall, sadness weighing her steps, the sound of the scaffold trap door dropping echoing in her mind.

Charlotte said, "Even if we weren't here, milady, the Browns would've suffered the same fate. They were involved in criminal activities."

"I know. It's difficult. The complexity of humans. How they can be kind on the one hand and criminal and brutal on the other. All within the same human."

"That's true." Charlotte picked petals off a flower. "I know you feel badly for them, but you helped uncover the plot to assassinate the king. That should help you feel better."

"It should, but it doesn't. I wish Aven and Samuel hadn't been put in such a position that they felt it was necessary to attack the mill. They shouldn't have died for it. Especially when they were being used to hide worse criminals without their knowledge."

"All of it is an ugly business, milady. But if they had gone home when you asked them to, they might still be alive today. They chose to stay and fight. They chose their fate."

Charlotte was right, of course, but the truth was difficult to accept.

Upon her return to Iverloch Hall, Ravenna found a small package on her bed; it was a brown paper parcel tied with twine and a bundle of heather, bog moss, and thistle in the knot.

"What's that?" Georgiana entered the room with her book.

"I don't know." Ravenna opened the paper to reveal a simple, but luscious red, silk dress, the color of poppy flowers. The front was pleated with a red satin ribbon trim, which repeated on the short, puffed sleeves and the hemline. A red satin ribbon tied just under the short bodice.

Ravenna pulled it out of the paper and held it up. A small train pooled at her feet.

Georgiana gasped. "It's beautiful."

"Indeed, it is."

Georgiana picked up a slip of paper. "It says *Ever yours, B.*" She beamed and said in a sing-song voice. "It's from Lord Braedon." She giggled behind her hands. "I'm so happy for you. He's so handsome and charming."

Ravenna spread the red dress on the bed and ran her hands over the smooth silk. Joy like a field of poppies in the sun lit up inside her, dispelling for a moment her worries and cares. Her mourning was over, along with all those unhappy black dresses. She didn't love her late husband any less, but it was time to embrace life and love.

"I'm wearing this dress tonight."

A knock sounded at the door, and Lady Catherine entered in a pale blue dress with a red sash under her bosom. It was a strange color combination, and Catherine rarely wore such vibrant colors. "Good afternoon, darlings. I have been sent on a special errand."

"How mysterious," Ravenna said.

"I've been asked to tell you to put on your red dress and accompany me for a walk." Catherine grinned like the cat who'd eaten the cream.

"Why?"

"It's meant to be a surprise. I need you to trust me, my friend."

"This is very strange," Ravenna laughed. "But I'll play along."

"Make haste. I'll help you."

"Should I change my dress?" Georgiana said.

Catherine patted her cheek. "You're lovely in your white muslin. Stay as you are."

When Ravenna had changed, she said, "I'll get my spencer and bonnet."

Catherine stayed her. "Don't bother with them. Come along."

"I don't know what's happening, but it seems exciting." Georgiana clapped her hands together in glee.

Catherine opened the door and waved them into the hallway, where Aurélie and Charlotte stood with bundles of wildflowers.

"What is this?" Ravenna said.

"You'll see soon enough. Take these." She handed a bouquet of flowers to Ravenna and Georgiana.

Ravenna accepted the bundle of purple heather and thistle, surrounded with wildflowers of shades in pink, white, and yellow. "How lovely." She sniffed the flowers, her own excitement growing.

The women exited Iverloch Hall and trailed down the hill. The wind ruffled their skirts and hair, and the scent of the earth rose up around them in a sweet perfume. Butterflies kited around the heather and thistle as the song of the castle bagpipes lilted over the city. Ravenna hung close to Aurélie to ensure her safe descent.

They rounded the corner where the ruins of St. Anthony's chapel stood, to find all the men of their party: Yarford, Donovan, Niall, and Braedon.

Ravenna stopped. "What is this? What is happening?"

Charlotte smiled at her. "Milady, Lord Braedon, swept up in the charms of Scotland, asked me to perform our traditional handfasting ceremony to seal your engagement. And he wanted us all to be a part of it."

Handfasting was an ancient Celtic marriage tradition. It wasn't a legally binding marriage in these modern days, and the bonds could be broken with greater ease than a legal marriage, but some people continued the practice in more remote areas. Ravenna's own grandparents had been handfasted.

"How lovely." Georgiana squirmed in glee.

Ravenna beamed, placing her hand in Braedon's offered hand. She whispered, "You'll do anything to get to our honeymoon sooner, won't you?"

Laughter filled his eyes. "I promise you, on my honor as a gentleman, I shall wait until after our official wedding."

"That's a few months from now. What if *I* don't want to wait?"

He feigned offense. "Lady Birchfield, you shock my tender sensibilities."

Laughing, she linked her arm with his so she could press closer to him as he led her to stand inside a circle of flowers on the ground.

He leaned to whisper in her ear. "You are so beautiful, you take my breath away."

She hid her blushing smile in her flowers.

Charlotte held out her hand. "I'll need the representatives to provide the three ribbons or ropes, please."

Braedon removed his coat and hat and handed them to Donovan. The wind tossed his hair, kissed with red tints in the sun. He then removed his cravat, as did Niall, and Catherine removed her red sash. They all handed the items to Charlotte.

Charlotte stepped toward Ravenna and Braedon, the linens and ribbon draped on her arm. "I need your right hands." Charlotte placed the two hands together as Ravenna and Braedon gazed at each other. "Don't let go," Charlotte said.

"Never," Braedon said.

Charlotte draped Braedon's cravat on his hand. "Lord Braedon, this represents you and your family through the generations." Then she positioned Niall's cravat on Ravenna's hand. "Lady Birchfield, this represents you and your family through the generations."

Ravenna's eyes filled with tears, wishing her family were all together, alive, and here to bear witness to this moment. She could just see her dear Papa shake hands with Braedon and pat him on the back. They were men cut from the same cloth. Gentlemen with a love of sport and outdoors pursuits, both charming, mischievous, and full of spirit.

In the center of these cloths, Charlotte lay the red ribbon. "This represents your new life together, where today you will be bound to begin your own family to last for generations." She began wrapping the pieces as she spoke. "This handfasting is a symbol of the binding commitment William, Lord Braedon and Ravenna, Lady Birchfield, make to each other, a promise to stand by each other through all joy and hardship, and to love and cherish one another for all of their days." With the knot complete, Charlotte shifted the knot to rest on top of their hands. "As your hands are bound together by this cord, so too, shall your lives be bound as one. May you forever be one, sharing in all things, in love and loyalty for all time to come. May the road rise to meet you. May the wind be always at your back. Now you may speak your vows if you wish." She stepped aside.

Braedon cleared his throat. "My dearest Ravenna, I promise from this day to our last to love, honor, cherish, protect, and provide for you and our family. To be your champion and your bold knight in times of darkness and in times of light. I will be your shelter and your safe harbor. I will be your true companion in adventure, turmoil, and in peace. I will never stray from your side until death parts us. This I vow to you, to these witnesses, and to our God above." With his free hand, he wiped the tears from her face.

Ravenna swallowed her emotion. "My dearest Braedon, I promise from this day to our last to love, honor, and cherish you. To provide a warm hearth and be your greatest confidante. I promise to be your shelter and safe harbor. I promise to bring you warm joy, like the sun, and to flow with you on the waters of our lives together, though they carry us over rocks and through storms or peaceful valleys. I will never stray from your side until death parts us. This I vow to you, to these witnesses, and to our God above."

Charlotte said, "Now you may withdraw your hands and create the knot to bind your promises."

Ravenna and Braedon separated their hands and pulled on their side of the cloths to form a knot. They kissed as the men clapped and the women showered them with wildflowers.

The party walked back to Iverloch Hall as Niall broke out in a traditional Irish song, "Just Give Me Your Hand."

Ravenna and Braedon held hands, walking up the hill with Georgiana in front, holding the wedding knot between her two hands like a delicate bird.

Braedon said, "I'm sorry we won't have a wedding feast. Though I have arranged for us to have a ginger cake and shrub drinks on our arrival."

"I couldn't ask for more," Ravenna said. "We will have a wedding feast when we marry and every day after, if you wish."

When they entered Iverloch Hall, they were led to the drawing room where they were served a slice of ginger cake, fruits, and shrubs, a refreshing liqueur made of rum, sugar, and citrus.

Lord and Lady Iverloch entered the drawing room.

"I understand we have a handfasting to celebrate," Lord Iverloch said. "Congratulations! He lifted a glass of shrub. *"Slàinte Mhath!"*

Everyone followed with *Slàinte Mhath!*

Lord Iverloch set down his glass. "In honor of the couple, we have purchased tickets to the assembly rooms this evening. I would like to invite you all to come with us to dance and celebrate. The Comte d'Artois and his lady are rumored to be there this evening as well."

Ravenna beamed at Braedon. This would be the most perfect day of her life if the shadow of treason, rebellion, and death didn't hang over their heads.

Chapter Thirty-One

Ravenna floated down the staircase in her red dress, her dark hair piled on her head, specked with white primroses, loose ringlets framing her face. She wore both the brooch and the ring Braedon had given her. Georgiana jogged down the stairs ahead of her in a green satin dress.

Braedon stood at the bottom of the stairs, surrounded by their other friends and family. He watched Ravenna, a look of mischief and admiration in his eyes as a smile teased his lips.

When she reached him, he took her hand and kissed it. He leaned close to her ear. "You look like a rose in a moonlit garden."

Her cheeks grew hot. "Thank you for the dress. I don't know how you managed it, or the ceremony today. You're all surprises."

"Your lady's maid has worked tirelessly on our behalf. You should probably give her a rise in salary." He slipped his arm around her waist. "Perhaps now you will favor me with a dance? I've been waiting for a long time."

He was referencing months ago when, at a ball, he had asked her to dance, though she was still in mourning, wearing her widow's weeds.

She grinned at him. "I think I can promise you all the dancing you desire." In this moment, wearing this delightful red dress he'd given her, he had answered one of the secret desires of her heart: to cast off her mourning attire, wear bold colors again, and return to life as she once knew it. He was offering her the gift of life and love. A future.

The assembly rooms were located in New Town in George Street. The building was of light sandstone, built in the Neo-Classical style with a columned portico, tall windows, and arched entryways. Torches lit the exterior, and a crowd of people filed into the three arched doorways. Ravenna and Georgiana flanked Braedon as they entered the grand pale green ballroom. Bright, quick notes of a Scottish reel and three massive, sparkling crystal chandeliers greeted them.

Georgiana bounced in place to the music. Niall approached her. "Would you like to dance?"

"I would love to." She gave him her hand, and they jumped into the dance while Aurélie and Ravenna watched them with pride.

"They are both excellent dancer." Aurélie tapped her fan in time with the music.

"Indeed, they are. My father was a good dancer. It must come from his side." Ravenna said.

Braedon turned to Ravenna. "Speaking of dance, I believe you owe me one." He held out his hand.

"Nothing would give me more pleasure." She took his hand, and he led her to the floor, where they hopped and spun and skipped on the current of the energetic music. It had been over a year since Ravenna had danced; it was complete freedom, like flying, as though she'd sprouted wings and soared on the wind over the hills and valleys of Edinburgh.

After a few dances, Ravenna stopped. "I'm quite thirsty now. I wonder where the refreshments are."

Braedon led her off the floor to a chair along the wall. "I'll get a drink for us."

"Thank you." She sat and fanned herself, watching Georgiana go down the dance line with Catherine.

As she enjoyed watching the dancing, admiring the various ladies' dresses, she caught, there in the corner, Niall shaking hands with Mr. Muir fellow, of all people. Niall had sworn he had left The Unity, that he was dedicating his life to his family instead of Ireland's fight. Yet, here he was socializing with Muir. If he were caught in such company…her heart dropped. Chadwick. He was approaching Niall and Muir. He stopped, looked around in a calculating manner as though he took the measure of every person in the room. He looked in Muir and Niall's direction, touched his ascot, tipped his head to the left, then walked away.

Ravenna looked in the direction Chadwick had indicated. Lady Iverloch stood near the window speaking with her husband, Lord Rotherden, and a few acquaintances. The candlelight sparked in the silver beading on her blue ball gown.

Where was Georgiana? Ravenna searched the room and found her niece in the far corner of the room, talking to none other than Mr. Sinclair!

Ravenna jumped up and pushed her way through the crush of people. She sidled up to Georgiana. "There you are. I came to see if you wanted to dance."

"I'm quite tired at the moment, Auntie." Georgiana fanned herself. "I was just speaking with Mr. Sinclair about his business. He owns a mill." She pinned Ravenna with a knowing look.

Ravenna picked up on the silent communication. "Oh, yes. I do recall you mentioning that at dinner the other night, Mr. Sinclair. Remind me what sort of mill do you own?"

Mr. Sinclair looked down at her with the bleary eyes of a man who had consumed too much drink. "A weaver's mill."

Ravenna knew the answer. She just wanted to hear his voice. His tight, nasally voice. The same voice she'd heard at the docks the night she'd helped to rescue the girls. "Oh, yes. Of course. I remember now. But I don't think you ever mentioned the name of your mill. Which one do you own?"

He snorted. "Well, now I own nothing but a pile of ashes. The mill I *once* owned was Empire Weavers, until those Scottish dogs burned it down."

Empire Weavers. The same company name was stamped on the boxes aboard *The Milton* when they had saved those kidnapped girls.

He continued. "However, I will have retribution. They were all rounded up and taken to jail, where they belong. Now they will receive the king's justice." He downed his champagne punch.

Georgiana's flaxen tendrils waved in the breeze of her fan. "Mr. Sinclair, what do you intend to do after such mistreatment?"

Sinclair handed off his glass to a footman. "I'm not certain. I will meet with investors, naturally. But I won't be able to do anything until I return from France."

Ravenna's brows shot up. "You're going to France? I thought it was too dangerous to travel while we're at war."

He looked down his large nose at her with dark reptilian eyes. A corner of his large mouth ticked upward. "I'm not concerned."

Ravenna opened her fan and batted her eyes coquettishly. "How brave. I've always wanted to go to France, but now with the war, I'm terrified. When do you leave?"

"Tonight."

"A night? Why wouldn't you wait until the morning?"

"I leave the particulars up to the captain, who is more knowledgeable about the tides and such than I am."

"Good evening," Lord Rotherden patted Sinclair's back. "I'm sorry to interrupt, ladies, but there is someone I would like you to meet, Mr. Sinclair. Ladies, please pardon us." The men bowed as Ravenna and Georgiana curtsied.

"You are not to be near those men again," Ravenna said, behind her fan.

Georgiana spoke in a low voice. "I know exactly who those men are, Auntie. I saw them in the underground city with Mr. Larson. But that deplorable wretch, Mr. Sinclair, didn't recognize me. I think he was too deep in his cups. And I'm clean and dressed nicely." She linked her arm with Ravenna's as they strolled through the room. "I was able to speak to him before Lord Rotherden arrived. I pretended to be one of Mr. Larson's *companions.* I said he had promised to see me before he left town. Sinclair said Mr. Larson was leaving town tonight. *For France.*" Georgiana cocked her brow. "Auntie, I'd say the chances are high that Larson is going to France aboard *The Milton* with Sinclair *tonight.*"

"I'd say you're right in that assessment."

"After all, it makes sense for all the conspirators to flee the country together to seek shelter with their patrons of rebellion."

"Indeed. Especially since they are likely aware they are being hunted by Mr. Chadwick and his men."

"We should look for him there aboard *The Milton*." She patted Georgiana's cheek. "What a clever and brave girl you are."

Georgiana's demeanor hardened. "Those men are going to pay for taking me from my home, terrifying me, abusing me, and attempting to sell me like livestock in another land. I want to see them brought to justice before I leave Edinburgh."

Braedon approached with two glasses. "There you are." He handed Ravenna a glass. "I'm sorry I didn't bring one for you, Miss Sullivan."

"Not to worry, Lord Braedon. I was just on my way to the refreshment room."

"Before you do that, Georgiana…" Ravenna craned her neck, searching the crowd. "We need to speak with Mr. Chadwick. Then you may get your refreshment."

"What's the matter?" Braedon sipped his drink.

"We have some information for him. There he is." She pulled Georgiana along as Ravenna pushed through the crowd with Braedon on her heels.

Chadwick stood alone by an open window, watching the people.

"Mr. Chadwick. I have some information."

"Not here. Meet me in the gallery in five minutes." He spun from them and disappeared into the crowd.

Ravenna, Georgiana, and Braedon climbed the stairs and traced the shadows of the gallery, away from the balustrade to avoid notice.

A voice spoke from the shadow in a windowed alcove.

"I'm here." Chadwick leaned against the wall, the moonlight slicing across his face.

Braedon chuckled. "Must we be so secretive?"

"Tonight? Yes. My men and I are here working. Some of the people we're watching know about you two and your actions here in Edinburgh. I can't let anyone see me talking to you. What information do you have?"

Ravenna said, "Mr. Sinclair owns the Empire Weaver's mill that was burned down the other night."

"Yes."

"His company was shipping crates to France. The same crates the girls were in when we rescued them," Ravenna said.

"That much, I already know."

"Did you also know that Mr. Sinclair is sailing to France tonight?" Georgiana asked.

He paused. "Interesting. I did not know that. Did he say what time?"

Georgiana shook her head. "Unfortunately, he didn't. Lord Rotherden interrupted our conversation before I could learn more."

Chadwick leaned on the window, looked up at the moon, then looked at his pocket watch. "The moon hasn't reached its meridian yet, so the tide isn't fully risen. It's eleven now. I would say within the next few hours, the tide should rise high enough for the ship to sail."

Ravenna said, "We have reason to believe Mr. Larson is on *The Milton*, that he, too, will be traveling to France with Mr. Sinclair."

"Is that so? We shall look into it. Thank you both. Do either of you have any other information?"

"No. But if I find any new information, I'll let you know." Ravenna said. He started to leave, and Ravenna stopped him. "Mr. Chadwick, I have a question. If Mr. Sinclair was working with The Unity and he was helping them transport the women, why would the Scottish rebels burn down his factory?"

Chadwick tucked his watch in his fob pocket. "From what I understand, there's some infighting between the groups, which often happens in these rebellions. My intelligence has reported that the Scots grow increasingly impatient. The Irish are moving too slowly, and more are invested in their own fight against The Crown. The Scottish workers want relief now. They are less interested in an independent Scotland and more concerned with fair wages and steady employment. Mr. Sinclair, it seems, complicated things when he reduced their wages for the third time in six months. Perhaps he thought his co-conspirators would protect him and his factory."

Braedon said, "So the common cause is fracturing."

"Yes." The moonlight glittered in Chadwick's dark eyes. "My only concern is if the traitors will be caught and if the cause will fall apart before the king is killed."

Chapter Thirty-Two

Ravenna, Georgiana, and Braedon leaned on the gallery balustrade, looking down on all the dancers as Chadwick slipped away like a mouse.

Niall stood on one side of the ballroom alongside his wife, watching the crowd. Across the room, Muir watched Niall. Lord Iverloch talked with Catherine and Yarford while his wife danced with Lord Rotherden.

Muir scratched his chin. Niall nodded and whispered to Aurélie; then he crossed the floor toward Rotherden. He spoke to Rotherden, who nodded and left Lady Iverloch. Niall and Rotherden stopped to speak to Sinclair, and all three men headed out of the ballroom. Chadwick, Muir, and three other men followed like dogs on the hunt.

"Something is happening," Ravenna said. "I want to ensure Niall is safe." She ran down the stairs with Braedon and Georgiana following. She cut through the people and out of the building where Chadwick, Muir, and their men were handcuffing Rotherden, who protested how he was nobility, a clerk to Lord Iverloch, and how Chadwick was making a grave mistake.

Rotherden seethed. "With all my connections, I will ruin your life, Chadwick."

Ravenna ran to her brother, "Niall! What's happening?"

Niall crossed his arms. "Justice."

Mr. Sinclair broke free of the men and dashed across the street. Niall gave chase, knocking him to the ground. They grappled in the street until Chadwick and Muir caught up and pulled them apart. Niall and Muir held Sinclair down, and Chadwick put shackles on him. They stood him up and dragged him, kicking and screaming, to a cart with armed Red Coats. They loaded up Lord Rotherden as well, who was now attempting to bargain his way to freedom.

Chadwick said to the driver. "Take them to the castle. We'll begin their transport to Newgate prison in London soon."

Niall dusted himself off and returned to Ravenna's side.

"That was quite brave of you," she said.

"Doing my duty."

Muir clapped Niall on the back. "Good job, mate."

"Happy to do it."

The men laughed and shook hands. Muir spoke to Chadwick, hopped on his horse, and raced away toward the Port of Leith. The other men who had helped in the arrest also mounted their horses and followed Muir.

Ravenna frowned in confusion. She said to Niall, "I thought Mr. Muir was a dissident."

"And that I was working with him, I suppose?" Niall cocked a brow at her. "I told you I

was here to set things right. I've been working as an agent with Chadwick and Muir to help bring down the dissidents."

"But you were talking about Irish freedom when you first arrived."

"Aye. I'm still torn on the issue. I love my homeland and always will. I want Ireland to be its own nation, free from England. And it was hard to stand and watch those poor Scottish workers get arrested when all they wanted was jobs and fair wages. I still have a heart for the workers and the poor. But The Unity and their way of doing things was wrong. And Mr. Muir gave me a path to bringing them down. I'd always felt guilty about the part I played in The Unity because of my naivete and impetuousness. We did more damage to Ireland and her cause than we helped. Larson never really cared about Irish freedom, not really. He was after revenge."

"What do you mean?"

"I met Larson some eight or nine years ago at the White Oak tavern. He was angry that the Englishman who owned his family's land had kicked them off the land because he wanted livestock instead of crops. Livestock brought in more money with less chance of the weather destroying the profits."

For a brief moment, Ravenna felt sorry for Larson. She understood his motives. But any and all sympathy flickered and died with a recollection of his actions.

"Why didn't you tell me you were working *with* Chadwick? Why did you argue with me about your beliefs?"

"Mr. Chadwick wanted my absolute discretion. I thought it was better and safer if you, Aurélie, and everyone else remained ignorant of the particulars."

"How did you meet Chadwick? How did you know him or who he was?"

"Through Muir. I met him in York. He picked up on my accent. Our conversation led to the Irish situation. He found out we were headed to Edinburgh and that Georgiana had been kidnapped. When he helped to get me released, he said I owed him some assistance. He said since I was Irish, he wanted my help to root out some dissidents."

Panic fluttered through Ravenna. She pulled him aside and whispered, "How do you know he hadn't been tracking *you*? Maybe he knows about your past and mine. Maybe you're his real target."

He shook his head. "No. I don't think so."

"How do you know? Muir is clearly a double agent of some sort. And what if Larson tells him about you and me when he's caught?"

Niall sighed. "I've done my best to heal the past, Ravenna. If I need to, I'll return to America." He walked away from her.

It was a difficult situation. If Larson managed to escape, Ravenna's family would never be safe. If he didn't escape, then she and Niall might be in more trouble than they could bear.

Ravenna approached the corner where Chadwick stood with Braedon. "What about Larson? And Lady Iverloch?"

"Rotherden!" A female voice cried behind them. Lady Iverloch stood in the doorway, tears in her eyes, her hand over her mouth.

Mr. Chadwick started toward her. "Lady Iverloch. I'd like to have a word with you."

She turned and ran.

Ravenna gave chase, but the crowd slowed her pursuit. Lord Iverloch stepped in her path. "Lady Birchfield, what is this about? Why are you chasing my wife?"

"I don't have time to explain, please—"

"I insist on knowing what has happened."

It was too late. Lady Iverloch was gone.

Ravenna asked bystanders. "Where did she go?"

They pointed down a hall.

She followed the hall. It was dark but for the pools of moonlight pouring from the windows lining the passage. A sweaty footman hurried from the end of the hall. There was no good reason for a footman to be in this hall when his job was in the ballroom.

Ravenna stopped him. "Pardon me, did you see a lady run this way?"

He bowed. His eyes did not meet hers, but looked slightly above her. "No, ma'am."

"Has anyone else been in this hall?"

"Not that I've seen, ma'am."

He was lying.

Ravenna looked up and down the empty hall. At one end of the hall was a tall mirror about six feet in height, flanked by two stone pedestals with fresh flowers in vases and a rug on the floor. Something was off. One of the pedestals was off-center compared to the other.

The footman said, "Pardon me, ma'am, but we are quite busy this evening." He bowed and walked away without waiting to be dismissed.

She didn't try to stop him. He wasn't going to be of any assistance anyway. She approached the mirror. The pedestal on the right had been moved. The dust ring on the floor and scattered flower petals indicated as much. The rug was wrinkled. A bit of silver winked at her in the moonlight. She inspected the spot and picked up a bead from the carpet. It was very like the beading on Lady Iverloch's dress.

Lady Iverloch had been here. Was it possible this mirror was a door to a secret passage? It wasn't unheard of. Many buildings had such passages to allow for a quick and safe departure in the event of an emergency. She felt along the right edge of the mirror frame until her hand hit on a latch. She pulled it down, and the mirror popped open. She drew the mirror open. It was a passage. She stepped inside, her slipper grinding on something like a rock. She picked it up. Another silver bead. Lady Iverloch was too far ahead to catch her now.

Braedon and Chadwick approached.

"What are you doing?" Braedon said. "Did you find Lady Iverloch?"

Ravenna shook her head. "She's escaped." She held up the bead. "Beads from her dress on the exterior of the mirror and the interior of this passage. I believe she escaped through here, and I think a footman helped her."

"I wonder where she's going?" Braedon stared into the dark passage.

"I don't know. Back to Iverloch Hall?"

"Or somewhere unknown to us," Braedon said.

Ravenna said, "I met a footman here in the hall. I believe he helped her to escape. Perhaps he knows where she went."

"Let's find him," Chadwick said.

They searched the ballroom, inspecting every footman in the assembly rooms.

"He's not here." Ravenna pushed her hair out of her face. "He must've left after I spoke with him in the hall."

"She could be anywhere." Braedon watched the dancers.

"Maybe she went to *The Milton* to escape with her compatriots," Ravenna said.

Chadwick interjected. "She'd be foolish to go to the ship. Some of my men are going there now to capture Larson. If she goes there, we are sure to catch her."

Everyone except Lord and Lady Iverloch returned to Iverloch Hall. Lady Iverloch was still on the run, and Lord Iverloch had stayed behind at the assembly rooms with Chadwick for questioning and to look for his wife.

On the way back to Iverloch Hall, Ravenna said to Braedon, "I'd like to leave first thing in the morning. I don't want to stay here any longer than necessary. I expect Lord Iverloch will be in a foul mood and want to be rid of us after tonight."

"I agree," Braedon said. "Though I will lament leaving this beautiful and wild country. It's the sort of place I could spend the rest of my days."

"Yes. I would've liked to have seen more of Scotland."

"Perhaps we can return for our honeymoon when people aren't trying to kill us."

Ravenna lifted a brow. "Then we'd best not come back to Edinburgh."

Chapter Thirty-Three

Ravenna and Georgiana, eager to return home, awoke early to pack and prepare for their travels back to England. They ate a quick breakfast of cold ham, bannock bread with butter, and tea.

When the footmen came to retrieve their luggage, Ravenna asked them, "Have Lord and Lady Iverloch returned home? I would like to thank them for their hospitality."

The blond one shook his head. "No, milady."

"Do you know where they are?"

"We haven't heard, milady."

"Have the carriages arrived?"

"Yes, milady. We should have everything ready for your departure within the hour."

When the time came to leave, Ravenna and Georgiana left their bedchamber.

Georgiana said, "Maybe we can have a few sightseeing tours on our way home?"

"Possibly," Ravenna said. "If they don't delay us too long."

"I'd like to see a bit of the country before we go home."

"We'll see." Ravenna put on her gloves

Braedon exited his room, whistling, his coat draped on his arm and his hat in hand. "Good morning, ladies." He bowed.

Ravenna warmed at the sight of him, her future husband. He kissed her cheek. "Good morning, my wife-to-be." He bowed to Georgiana. "Miss Georgiana." He offered his arm to Ravenna, and they all descended the stairs.

As they reached the bottom, Ravenna froze. Mr. Chadwick occupied a bench in the hall, his hat balanced on his knee. Dark circles and heavy bags weighed his eyes. Yet, his clothes and hair were as pristine as always.

"Mr. Chadwick? How long have you been here?" Ravenna approached him.

Mr. Chadwick stood and bowed. "Good morning, Lady Birchfield, Lord Braedon, Miss Sullivan. I haven't been here long, only a few moments."

"Why are you here?" Braedon said. "Is something the matter?"

"Nothing of a concerning nature. I wanted only to bring Lady Birchfield her family jewels. We have managed to retrieve them from Larson before he sold them for munitions."

"My jewels?"

Georgiana put her hands over her mouth. "Oh, thank heaven. I was afraid we'd lost them forever!"

He pulled a velvet bag out of his pocket and handed it to her.

Ravenna opened the bag and peered inside. "Thank you so very much!" She clutched the bag to her heart. "And my family thanks you."

"I can't promise every piece is in there. He might've sold a piece or two, but we recovered what we could."

She dumped them on a small hallway table. She touched every piece. The earrings, necklace, bracelet, ring. "They're all here. I can't believe it." She returned them all to the pouch.

"I trust you've arrested Larson, then?" Braedon clasped his hands behind his back.

"When we left the assembly rooms last night, my men followed Mr. Larson and cornered him on *The Milton*. They managed to capture and arrest him. As they transported him to Edinburgh Castle, he apparently had some poison on him. He ingested it either before arrest or during transport. Either way, he died before my men, or I could question him."

Tears sprang to Georgiana's eyes. She threw herself into Ravenna's arms, sobbing. A shock of relief washed over Ravenna as she comforted her niece. "Sh-sh-sh. All is well. You won't have to worry about that wicked man ever again." She gave the girl her handkerchief and spoke in soft tones, "Please give us some privacy."

Georgiana nodded. She curtsied to Mr. Chadwick. "Thank you, sir. I'll be able to sleep at night again." She said to Ravenna. "I'll walk in the garden until it's time to leave." She exited the house.

Ravenna blinked at him, her mind a swirl of thoughts and emotions. At last, she and her family were safe. They no longer had to worry about Mr. Larson or about him revealing any information about Niall or herself. "I'm both happy and sorry for this outcome. I'm glad my family and I will be safe. But I worry there are others lurking in the shadows."

He nodded. "A valid concern. We will continue to ferret them out. I believe, ultimately, the group will fall apart. They are already starting to fracture."

"What makes you say so?" Braedon asked.

Mr. Chadwick smiled. "First, whenever a leader dies, his followers are thrown off balance. They don't know who to follow. A few try to take over, but others rise to challenge them, and the infighting begins. But…" A mischievous glimmer entered his eyes. "My agents have their methods to speed the process along."

"What do you mean?" Ravenna said.

"With the help of Mr. Muir, my agents are being planted in The Unity and other groups for the sole purpose of provoking fractiousness and causing a spiral toward chaos and eventual dissolution. A few words in one or two ears are enough to cause mistrust and eventual collapse." His eyes followed footmen carrying luggage down the stairs.

Ravenna listened, astonished. "I thought Mr. Muir was simply one of your Bow Street Runners."

"Mr. Muir is far more than that. He's one of my…*provocateurs*. He pretends to side with the dissidents to expose them. He was instrumental in exposing the assassination plot against the king. Your brother, too, was a great asset. He keeps secrets well. Perhaps I can use his services again."

Had Mr. Chadwick discovered something about Niall's past? Or her own? She wanted to ask, but was afraid to. Her questions might alert him to things she'd rather keep secret.

The corner of Chadwick's mouth ticked upward. "I see you have questions, milady. Your brother approached me, on the advice of Mr. Muir, and offered his services. When I asked him why, he said he wanted to serve the king his family had always been loyal to."

Niall had surprised her and had played his part well. She never knew he had such acting talents. Was this a way of both making money and ensuring her family's safety by being close to the people who would spy on them? "Thank you, sir, for letting me know about Mr. Larson. My family and I are ever grateful to you."

"You're quite welcome. I must confess, I had another reason for coming here today. I've not yet located Lady Iverloch and was hoping to speak with her. Have you seen her?"

Ravenna and Braedon exchanged a glance and shook their heads.

"No," Ravenna said. "I haven't seen her since last night. I assumed you caught her."

He shook his head. "No. We have Lord Iverloch in a cell at Edinburgh Castle. We've been questioning him. He doesn't know where she is. He claims to know nothing about the plot to assassinate the king or his wife's political ambitions. If we find no evidence against him, we'll release him soon."

"Surely she can't stay away from Iverloch Hall for long," Ravenna said. "She will need money and resources."

"She could have friends helping to shelter her." Chadwick put on his hat and looked up at the gallery. "I wish I could search her room."

"Why can't you?" Ravenna asked.

"I'm waiting for the magistrate to give me a warrant for permission to search and seize any necessary property for us to use as evidence in the trial." He sighed, "Well, I'll do the search another day." He forced a quick smile. "I don't want to detain you longer. I see you're packing to travel. I assume you're returning home to England?"

"We are. And eager to be on the road," Braedon offered his hand.

Chadwick shook his hand. "I understand you two are engaged to be married. Congratulations. I hope you have a blessed union."

The kindness shocked Ravenna. "How did you know about our engagement?"

A sly smile crossed Chadwick's mouth. He winked. *"Bon Voyage."*

Soon after Mr. Chadwick left, the rest of the travelers descended the stairs in happy chatter.

Catherine beamed. "Good morning, everyone. I'm not looking forward to being cramped in a carriage for a week, but I'm ready to be home." She cast an artful grin at Ravenna. "After all, we have a wedding to plan. Are we leaving now?"

"Soon," Yarford said. "Once the carriages are loaded, my love."

"I, however, will not be leaving with you all," Donovan said.

Ravenna and Catherine gaped at him.

"What do you mean you're not coming with us?" Catherine pouted. "You're staying here?"

"I am. For a while longer. I have some reports to gather concerning the foiled assassination plot, the burning of the mill, and other such seditious activities. I expect I'll be only a week or two behind the rest of you."

"You aren't staying on at Iverloch Hall, are you?" Ravenna said.

"No. I've rented rooms in Grassmarket near the castle. I don't want to be here when Lord Iverloch comes back from jail."

A footman entered the house and spoke to Braedon. "We have the luggage loaded, milord."

Ravenna said, "I want to look again in my bedchamber to ensure I haven't forgotten something. I'll be back in a moment." She ran up the stairs and checked her room. Georgiana had left a pair of stockings behind. *Of course.* She checked the other rooms, just in case. She came out of the last room, closing the door. The other end of the hall, where Lady Iverloch's bedchamber resided, beckoned to her. Her curiosity drew her forward.

Was there any evidence that she had packed things in advance to leave the country? Was there anything left behind to implicate her husband? Mr. Chadwick needed a warrant, but Ravenna didn't.

She ran on tiptoes down the hall to Lady Iverloch's bedchamber. She knocked on the door. When there was no answer, she stepped inside and closed the door. A ghost of jasmine perfume hung in the air. Ravenna opened the wardrobe first. No clothes seemed to be missing. She checked the vanity table. No cosmetics or jewelry were gone. Yet, she wasn't here. Interesting.

Ravenna checked the writing desk. A letter sat on the desk, sealed. She was about to break the seal and read the letter when the doorknob rattled. Probably a maid. Though she was leaving, she still didn't want to be caught snooping in Lady Iverloch's room. She tucked the letter in her bodice as she dashed across the room and closed herself in the stairwell leading to the Widow's Peak.

Ravenna looked up the spiral staircase, recalling the first moment she'd visited the promenade, the thrill and delight, the sense of freedom it had brought to her—almost like she was flying. She wanted to feel that way again—just one more time. She eased up the stairs and stepped onto the promenade as a gust of wind shoved against her.

The wind fluttered her dress and swirled around her. She stood at the balustrade, looking out at the purple-washed hills rising to kiss the clouds, the Port of Leith in the distance, and its busy harbor. Ravenna closed her eyes and pressed her face into the wind and the sun, wishing Braedon was here to experience Scotland's beauty with her one last time.

Further down, from the corner of her eye, she noticed a splash of red jutting from under the balustrade. She moved closer to inspect it. Red slippers. *Odd. Why would slippers be out here?* She leaned on the banister to look at the landscape below, at the jutting rocks and crags. At first, she couldn't believe what she was seeing. Blinking, she focused in on the splash of red velvet around white lace wrapping a limp body with limbs akimbo among the heather and thistle.

Lady Iverloch. Ravenna clapped her hand over her mouth. Was it an accident or…the legends Lord Iverloch had told her about the Widow's Peak rushed back to her. History and the present collided, the ghosts of all the women the Widow's Peak had claimed before rising up around her. What had been wild and beautiful moments ago transformed into something dark and Gothic as if pulled from the pages of Walpole's *The Castle of Otranto.* The Widow's Peak had claimed another soul.

She ran from the promenade and down the stairs, crashing into Braedon as she flew from behind the tapestry.

He caught her. "Ravenna? I've been looking for you. We're waiting for you at the carriages. What's the matter? Why are you so frantic?"

"She's dead, Braedon." Ravenna fought for breath.

"Who?" He frowned.

"Lady Iverloch. She's lying on the rocks below."

"Show me."

She shook her head. "I don't want to go back up there."

"Very well. I'll be back directly."

She removed the letter from her bodice and opened it

My Husband,

Please forgive me.

You know where I came from. You know the oppression my people have suffered. After the Clearances claimed my family lands and destroyed my people, I have carried a knot of thorny hatred in my heart for the English and for the Crown, which has only expanded with time. I have ached and hungered for an independent Scotland. I could no longer bear to see my beloved country beaten into submission. They have stripped so much from us. In a hundred years, will our country be at all recognizable? Will our ancient roots and traditions be nothing but ashes? I cannot bear the thought of it.

Rotherden offered me freedom. He hated the king, too. Hated all monarchies. Inspired by France and America, like me, he saw a new vision for a new Scotland—an independent Republic of Scotland.

You will hear rumors that I never loved you, though I did. In my way. I confess, unbeknownst to you, I saw in you an opportunity to get near the throne to cut its throat and watch it bleed. You treated me kindly and lovingly, which perhaps I didn't deserve for the way I used you. You were my shield so I could work in secret. For that, I appreciated you.

Yet, Rotherden offered me what you could not: freedom and hope. For Scotland. For me.

I cannot go on. Rotherden, the heart of my heart, the man I loved as much as my homeland has been taken from me. He has been arrested and will be executed—a vicious, violent death—for treason. And, if the English dogs have their way, I will not be far behind. But in this, I will prevail.

Rotherden's fate is sealed, and we will never meet again in this life, so I will join him in the next. At least there we will have the freedom we so desperately craved for Scotland.

Saor Alba

Fiona

Braedon came out of the stairwell and put his arm around her. "Are you well?"

She nodded. "Yes." She handed him the letter. "You should see this."

He read the letter and folded it. "My God. Iverloch will be crushed."

"Indeed. I don't know him well, but he seemed genuinely fond of his wife. In a matter of hours, his whole life has fallen apart. I can't help but feel sympathy for him. The letter at least seems to exonerate Iverloch."

"I agree. We should give this letter to Chadwick."

"Though she was a vicious woman, I hate leaving her on the rocks below. Perhaps we should send some staff to move her body indoors?"

"No. She should stay where she is. Chadwick would need to see that her death was intended. He and his men will need to study the death."

Ravenna sighed, rubbing her forehead. "I just want to go home."

They descended the stairs and alerted the butler about Lady Iverloch, asking him to send a messenger to Mr. Chadwick at the Black Horse Inn or the Edinburgh Castle.

Ravenna and Braedon exited the house to find Niall, Aurélie, and Georgiana in their carriage, Catherine and Yarford in theirs, and Charlotte waiting in the last carriage for Braedon and Ravenna.

Lord Donovan stood in the courtyard. "Seems I'm the only one here to bid you all farewell," he said to Ravenna and Braedon.

Braedon shook his hand. "I know we've had our differences, Donovan, but I'd happily have you at my side in any fight."

Donovan smiled. "I assure you the sentiment is mutual."

Ravenna said to Donovan, "When your business here is finished, you are welcome to come to Birchfield Manor to shoot as many grouse as you please. We'll have a room prepared for you."

"Gladly. I will do my best to end my business quickly."

"Mr. Chadwick should be arriving soon with his men." She handed him Lady Iverloch's last words. "Please ensure he receives this letter. We found Lady Iverloch."

His brow shot up. "Have you? That's excellent news!"

Ravenna shook her head. "Though she escaped last night, she apparently came back here at some point, unbeknownst to anyone. She wrote this letter, then leapt from the Widow's Peak, ending her life on the rocks below. You can access the Widow's Peak stairwell through the door behind the tapestry in the hall near her bedchamber. I don't know how her body can be retrieved. It's a dangerous climb to be sure."

The light drained from his face. "I see."

"I'm sorry to leave you to oversee this horrible event—"

He waved his hand. "Think nothing of it, Lady Birchfield. Chadwick and I will tend to it. You've done everything you can do, and you achieved what you came here for. Miss Sullivan is safe."

Chapter Thirty-Four

After seven days of travel, the exhausted party descended on Birchfield Manor, a grand English baroque-style home of buff stone and two wings surrounded by neatly trimmed shrubs. A grand reflecting pool stretched for several yards in front of the home. Ravenna melted in relief to finally be back home. She squeezed Braedon's hand and bounced in her seat. "We are here."

Georgiana looked out the window. "What a beautiful house." Her brow wrinkled. "Do you think Harrison will be happy to see me?"

"I think he will." Ravenna patted her knee.

"I treated him so poorly…" Georgiana toyed with the strings of her reticule.

"I think you'll find Harrison quite forgiving. He's always had a special fondness for you."

"I didn't appreciate him before, his kindness, generosity, and easy manner. But all those days when I was in the company of Emmett and living in that underground city, I found myself thinking of Harrison quite often and wishing I could see him again."

The carriages came to a stop in front of the house. Harrison stood on the steps to greet the travelers. The sun fired his chestnut hair, long and mussed on top. Handsome in his olive linen coat and tan pantaloons, he looked every bit the lord of the manor.

He greeted Ravenna first, kissing her cheeks. "Welcome home, Amma. I'm so happy you're here."

Her stomach knotted. Harrison didn't know about her engagement or the pending nuptials. How would he take the news that she was considering marriage so soon after her mourning ended?

"It's good to be home and so good to see you. May you and I have a private conversation after we're all settled?"

He looked at her, puzzled. "Certainly."

Ravenna motioned to Braedon. "You know Lord Braedon?"

"I do." They shook hands.

Harrison shook hands with all the men as they stepped down from their carriages. "My friends and I suspended the activities of the Glorious Twelfth to wait for your arrival. "As soon as you're all rested, there will be plenty of shooting and fishing and picnicking to be had."

When Georgiana stepped down from the carriage, Harrison stiffened and flushed. He bowed. "Miss Georgiana." His eyes searched her face. "I'm very happy to see you."

She smiled sheepishly. "I'm happy to see you as well. I've thought often of you."

His surprise flashed over his features. "You are? You have?"

Georgiana took his hands, tears welling in her eyes. "I owe you many apologies."

"Not at all. I..." He glanced around at his family and friends. "I hope we can find some time to talk soon. Our gardens are quite lovely."

"Yes." She glowed. "There's so much to tell you. Perhaps we can take a turn in the gardens this afternoon?"

"I would like that very much."

Ravenna smiled to herself, hope warming her heart. She'd had many reservations about anything blooming between Harrison and Georgiana. All the feelings had seemed to be on Harrison's side while Georgiana had been content to flirt and play. Yet, Georgiana's recent experience had sobered her. For the first time since the girl had reentered Ravenna's life, she noticed a sense of attraction and sincerity on Georgiana's part toward Harrison that hadn't been there before.

Harrison spoke to the group. "Please, everyone, welcome. Come in. I'll have everyone shown to their rooms and get you some refreshment." He stood aside and motioned to the open front door.

After a quick wash and changing her traveling clothes for a comfortable pink muslin dress, Ravenna descended the stairs to find Harrison in his study.

"May I have a word?"

He set down his pen, surprised, and stood. "Of course. I see you're no longer in your weeds." He lifted a brow, a knowing smile brushing his lips. "I presume it has something to do with what you wanted to discuss with me? Lord Braedon, perhaps?"

She blushed, wringing her hands. "Yes, in fact. But there's more I would like you to know."

He sat on the edge of his desk, anticipation marking his features. "So?"

She steeled herself. "I love you. And I loved my life with your father, your brother Thomas, and you." She blew out a breath. "I wanted you to know that while I was in Scotland, Lord Braedon and I became engaged and we had a handfasting ceremony to seal the engagement." His jaw fell slack, and his eyes grew wide. "Braedon will go to his home parish tomorrow to speak with his vicar to begin the reading of the banns. And I'll speak with our vicar tomorrow as well. We hope for your blessing."

He sat for a moment, taking in the information, then rubbed the back of his head. "This is amazing news, Amma." He jumped from his desk and hugged her. "I am so very happy for you both." He kissed her cheek. "Of course, you have my blessing."

"Truly? I was so worried you might not accept me getting married so soon after your father's death."

"It's been a year. And you're young yet. Of course, you should marry. When is the happy day? Will it be in our village church? Or in London? Or here at Birchfield Manor, and we'll have an enormous breakfast feast, invite the entire village."

He was more excited than Ravenna. She laughed through happy tears. "I don't know. I haven't thought of the particulars yet, but I'm so very relieved and glad you approve. We would marry anyway, of course, but it's better to know you won't be upset with us."

"I want only your happiness. Though, I admit, I'll be sad to see you leave

Birchfield Manor. Especially since we just finished the repairs on the cottage for you. Perhaps you should see his grounds at Rushingwood before you agree to marry him. He may be a pauper peer."

They laughed.

She said, "I know this is all so unexpected, but I hope, if all goes well, you will have plenty of company here soon enough."

"What do you mean?"

"Maybe you won't be a bachelor much longer."

He looked down at the floor. "Do you think Georgiana would marry me? Do you think she could love me?"

"I think she could. In time. She's been through a terrible ordeal, so she will need patience, time, and understanding."

He frowned. "What happened to her?"

Ravenna motioned to the sofa. "Join me over here." They sat on the sofa under the window, and she explained what Georgiana had endured.

When she had finished, he gritted his teeth. "Thank you for telling me, Amma. I had no idea. Your letter mentioned she'd been kidnapped, but I didn't know the rest. I will do everything in my power to be her comfort and protection from now on. If she will have me."

She cast a sly side glance at him. "I think your chances are very good."

The next day, everyone gathered on the grounds of Birchfield Manor for a picnic. Braedon, Yarford, Niall, along with Harrison's friends took turns shooting targets. Ravenna, Aurélie, Catherine, and Charlotte sat on blankets, nibbling on fruit and pastries. Though it was unusual for a lady's maid to sit down with an employer and her friends, Ravenna had insisted. Harrison and Georgiana stood under a pear tree where he plucked a pear from the bough and handed it to her. She blushed, gave him a coquettish smile, and cupped the pear in her hands as they strolled along the garden wall, walking quite close together.

Catherine leaned in and said to Ravenna, "I think Georgiana and Harrison will not be long behind you for their wedding vows."

Ravenna watched the young couple, smoothing her white muslin dress. "It's possible. I hope so. They would be good for each other, I think." She chuckled. "They both need stability, which the responsibility of running the estate, marriage, and a family will bring."

Aurélie ate a strawberry. She glowed in her white dress and white bandeau, sheltered under her parasol.

Ravenna said, "How long will you and Niall stay at Birchfield? I hope you will stay on until after the baby is born at least."

"At least. I'm not able to travel anymore."

"That's a relief. I hope you will stay forever, if you like," Ravenna said. "In fact, when Braedon and I relocate to Rushingwood after our wedding, you and Niall will be welcome there for as long as you'd like. I'd love to have my niece or nephew around for a proper spoiling from their auntie."

Aurélie grinned. "I would like that very much."

"If you stay, what are your plans, Mrs. Connelly?" Charlotte asked.

"Niall will get work somewhere. He talks about opening a shop. Wherever we settle, I would like to open a school and teach children in the village."

Ravenna sipped her tea. "I do like the idea of teaching the poorer children to read, write, and cipher. And there are no schools within five miles of here. I will help you get it established." She selected a small tart. "I might even help you teach."

Catherine popped a grape in her mouth. "*You* teach in a school? Braedon will have you so busy in the nursery, you won't have time to teach anyone else's children."

The women laughed.

A footman came toward the party with a man and a woman in tow. The man wore the flat black hat of a clergyman.

Ravenna squinted, shielding her eyes from the sun. As the pair came nearer, she realized the man was Reverend Howarth, the director of The Spitalfields House for Penitent Prostitutes, the charity Ravenna had supported and worked with for years.

"It's Reverend Howarth. There must be an emergency for him to make the trip from London. Excuse me for a moment." She pushed herself to stand and jogged toward them.

"Lady Birchfield," Reverend Howarth puffed and panted. He removed his hat, wiping the sweat on his brow with a handkerchief. He bowed and returned his hat to his head. "It's a pleasure to see you again. I'm glad to see you are well. I stopped by Gordon House, but learned you came here. I couldn't delay. I came directly with great news." He turned to the lady in pale blue and a straw bonnet standing beside him.

Ravenna gazed at the woman with blue eyes and blonde hair who looked like an older, thinner Georgiana, but for her slightly hooked nose, like…like Papa's. Her heart plummeted into her stomach. "Helen?" she squeaked.

The woman smiled and nodded. "Ravenna?"

Tears sprang to Ravenna's eyes as she launched herself to hug her sister, the sister she had been searching for. "Helen." She broke into sobs. "I'm so happy to see you. I've looked for you all these years. Thank God in His Heaven you have come at last."

They held each other, crying. When they finally separated, Ravenna shook Reverend Haworth's hand. "You are a good, good friend, sir. I know I can speak on behalf of my family when I say we are eternally grateful for you." She held her sister's hand and said to them both, "Please, please come and picnic with us."

Reverend Haworth said, "I should probably return to London." He checked his watch.

"Nonsense," Ravenna said. "We have plenty of rooms here. Stay the night if you must. There are some matters I would discuss with you at any rate. Come."

He said, "Well…I do love a good picnic."

She pulled Helen toward the picnic area, with Reverend Haworth following behind. Ravenna shouted, "Niall, Georgiana! Helen has come home! She's home!"

Georgiana froze, her eyes wide. "Mama?" Her voice broke, and she ran toward Helen. "Mama!" She threw herself against her mother. They embraced, shaking with sobs. After all this time, mother and daughter who had been separated for years were once again united.

"You're so beautiful," Helen looked her daughter over. "I'm so sorry for everything. Truly. I tried to come back for you, but your aunt wouldn't let me see you."

"Don't talk of that now," Georgiana said. "I'm just so happy you're here." They hugged again, breaking only for Niall to hug and kiss his sister through tears of joy.

"After all this time," Niall's voice grew watery. "I haven't seen you these seven or eight years at least."

"It has been a long time." She dabbed her eyes.

Niall said, "Please forgive me for leaving you, Ravenna, and Georgiana at Aunt Brendae's. If I had it to do over again—"

"Don't fret over that now, love." Helen touched his cheek. "I don't want to spoil our happy reunion with talk of regret. All is forgiven now. I just want us to never be parted again." She pulled Niall, Georgiana, and Ravenna into a group hug.

Helen and Reverend Haworth joined Aurélie, Catherine, and Hart on a picnic cloth. The reunited family spent the rest of the afternoon in delighted conversation, recalling past sweet memories and becoming reacquainted.

When the sun sank low in the sky and the picnic drew to a close, Ravenna and Braedon walked arm in arm toward Birchfield Manor.

"You've had a great deal of excitement today," he said.

"I have. It's been absolute perfection."

He stopped and pulled her to him. "You're happy then?"

She ran her hands over his linen waistcoat. "I am excessively happy. We are home. My family is no longer in danger, and we're reunited. I have my wonderful friends. And, best of all, I have you." She pulled him closer. "Every one of my hopes and prayers have been answered."

He kissed her, tucking a hair behind her ear. "Perhaps we can make the family larger."

"As soon as possible, I hope."

He kissed her again, with longing. "If it will make you happy. Won't it be a great adventure? A pack of little Williams and Ravennas running around, all brilliant, beautiful, and half-wild."

She laughed. "That would make me happy above all things. My dearest, Lord Braedon, my champion, guardian of my heart and life. I'm ready for our next great adventure."

A Note from the Author

Dear Reader,

Welcome to the culmination of the Widows & Shadows series. I'm so happy you've followed Ravenna's adventures this far.

Widow's Peak, in many ways, was my favorite book to write because it allowed me to relive some cherished memories from a visit to Scotland in 2023. Though part of my heart has since remained in the Highlands, I really enjoyed Edinburgh, too. During my time there, I learned about two things that ignited my imagination for this story: Mary King's Close and the Underground City. Both of these locations reside beneath the streets of Edinburgh and once housed people. That's right, people lived *under* Edinburgh.

This is not especially unique. There are many other places in the world where people once lived underground in Turkey, Israel, Italy, England, United States, and Australia. Often these dwellings date back to ancient times where people intentionally built underground. In other situations, like Edinburgh, the new city covered over the old city. The Edinburgh Underground "City" had never been intended for habitation. But, according to *ForeverEdinburgh.org*, desperately poor and homeless people sought shelter in the Underground. It wasn't long before criminals moved in as well with brothels and illegal taverns. All these elements played on my mind, and I knew I had to include the Underground City in *Widow's Peak*.

I wish I could write more about these underground dwellings, but time and space are limited here. As with the other two *Widow* books, I've woven in threads of real history and taken liberties with these real people and events to create the fictional world in *Widow's Peak*.

One place that features prominently in the story is King Arthur's Seat in

Edinburgh, a hill cresting at over 800 feet high near Holyrood Palace at the base of the Royal Mile. In the book, a great house, Iverloch Hall, sits atop this hill. Also, on this hill are the ruins of St. Anthony's Chapel. In real life, to my knowledge, no house ever stood on top of King Arthur's seat, though there is some evidence a fort, traced back to 5000 B.C., once stood there. I took liberties with Iverloch Hall's placement because I needed it for the fictional legends surrounding the house and for other key elements in the story. The real part I included was the ruins of St. Anthony's Chapel. This is one of those instances where I will need to write a blog about the details of this mysterious site. However, it's enough to say here that it is a real place, and when I learned of it, I knew it had to play an important part in *Widow's Peak*.

Another place which has a connection to real history is the inn where Lord Braedon stays upon his arrival in Edinburgh: The Deacon's Docket. Though the name is my own creation, it is inspired by the real Deacon Brodie's Tavern in Edinburgh which sits on a street corner in Lawnmarket, not far from St. Giles' Cathedral. The tavern's interesting history will surely be another blog entry, but in short: in the 1700s, Deacon William Brodie was a respected cabinet maker and businessman. However, he enjoyed gambling and other vices, running up high debt. When he couldn't pay off his debt, he turned to a life of crime, recruited locksmiths and other helpers, and began robbing people's homes at night. With this wild history, I couldn't possibly pass up the chance of including this tavern in my story. And isn't it just the place a presumed rascal like Lord Braedon would stay?

Further, there are a couple of key people mentioned in the book who deserve a mention here: the Comte d'Artois, later known as King Charles X of France, owed his life to Scotland. Though he played a minor role in *Widow's Peak*, he was a real historical figure. The Comte was brother to Louis XVI, who, in 1793, was beheaded alongside his wife, Marie Antoinette, during the Reign of Terror preceding the French Revolution. The Comte managed to escape France to find safety in England and eventually ended up in Scotland.

The other historical figure I wanted to mention played a large part in shaping the legend of Iverloch Hall in the novel: Lord Montrose. Much of his history is described in the book. He was a Scottish nobleman, poet, soldier, and eventually the captain general of Scotland. He supported Charles I in the English Civil War (16420-1651). When Montrose was defeated in the Battle of Carbisdale, he escaped and sought shelter with Neil MacLeod of Assynt, whom he believed was an ally. However, MacLeod betrayed him and turned him over to the government. Eventually, Montrose was put on trial, found guilty, and suffered the fate of beheading and quartering. For those who don't know what quartering is, I'll spare you the graphic brutality and issue a Reader Beware Alert should you decide to look it up. Yet, with this death, Montrose's reputation changed from traitor or martyr, depending on your loyalties, to romantic hero and brilliant military strategist.

Finally, I wanted to mention a historical event alluded to in *Widow's Peak*, the Calton Riots. In the book, the weavers are out of work and upset. They are laid off, unpaid, disrespected by employers, and technology and mass immigration threatens their jobs. Further, the Irish and others, desperate for work, not only immigrate *en masse* into England and Scotland to compete for jobs, but charge cheaper prices for their weaving work. These situations tended to create great poverty and starvation, which often resulted in riots. Such events have occurred in history too many times to count.

The riots in the book are inspired by a real historical event called the Calton Weavers' Massacre or the Calton Weavers' Strike, which occurred in 1787. This event is important because it was the earliest such industrial dispute in Scottish history. Calton is a town just outside of Glasgow and the weavers there enjoyed great prosperity until technology and labor force competition lowered wages and depressed the economy. The workers grew angry and bitter and began to strike, set fires, and destroy machines to protest a twenty-five percent wage cut. Eventually, troops were called in to suppress the mobs. As tensions escalated, the troops fired on the rioters and six of the weavers were killed. The strike ring leader, James Granger, was tried in Edinburgh and found guilty of "forming illegal combinations." He was sentenced to be publicly whipped through the streets of the city then was banished from Scotland for seven years.

Though I didn't detail the whole of the event, I felt it was emblematic of the many issues present throughout Great Britain and Europe at the time. So, I shifted the Calton Weaver's Massacre to Calton Hill in Edinburgh, which, to my knowledge, was never a site for mills though it did host a quarry and farmland at one time; it was also used by washerwomen to dry their laundry. Later, it became a site for monuments. Nevertheless, I thought it would serve as a good place for the disgruntled weavers to riot. Though the workers' strike and riot are a backdrop event in *Widow's Peak*, it serves to add complexity and historical texture to the fictional environment.

Lastly, as mentioned in previous books, I would like to reiterate that The Irish Unity in this book is in no way related to actual Irish rebellion groups. Instead, I took real historical circumstances and events in Ireland and mixed them with an amalgamation of historical Irish groups to create The Irish Unity featured in the *Widows & Shadows* series. The political climate in Ireland has always been complex and dynamic. As with many political upheavals and movements, battle lines are often drawn through families and friend groups, fracturing relationships. I wanted to reflect this throughout the series, though the first two books focus on it more than the third. Further, as with most well-intentioned rebellions or revolutions, they are sometimes co-opted by groups with mixed or even sinister motives, which can muddy the waters and undermine even the best of causes. I sought to show that as well.

However, at the end of it all, this is a work of fiction merely inspired at times by real people and events—a bit of escape from our modern world, which has too many upheavals of its own.

I'll do my best to better unpack some of the history mentioned here on my blog at www.michellebennington.com. If you're interested, please do follow me there for blog posts, newsletters, and updates on new releases.

I hope you have enjoyed this series. I'm always working on something new, so keep a lookout for what's next!

Best wishes,
Michelle

About the Author

Born and raised in the beautiful Kentucky Commonwealth, award-winning author Michelle Bennington developed a passion for books early on that has progressed into a mild hoarding situation and an ever-growing to-read pile. When she's not creating contemporary or historical worlds full of mysteries, she can be found engaging in a wide array of arts and crafts, spending time with family and friends over tables of puzzles and games, traveling, and attending tours involving old homes, history, and ghosts.

AUTHOR WEBSITE:

www.michellebennington.com

SOCIAL MEDIA HANDLES:

Facebook: https://www.facebook.com/michelle.bennington.7

Instagram: https://www.instagram.com/michelle.bennington.author/

GoodReads: https://www.goodreads.com/author/show/22406377.Michelle_Bennington

BookBub: https://www.bookbub.com/profile/michelle-bennington

Also by Michelle Bennington

Widows & Shadows Series (Level Best Books/Historia):
Widow's Blush
Widow's Fire
Widow's Peak

Small Batch Series (Level Best Books):
Devil's Kiss
Mermaid Cove
Unbridled Spirits

Hazardous Hoarding Series (Turner Publishing / Keylight Books):
Dumpster Dying
Killer Cache